REVIEWS

"Tour Secrets 2 is even more entertaining than the first book. I was emotionally exhausted when I finished reading because I could visualize the words coming to life. I highly recommend Tour Secrets 2 by Winkk."

APOOO Bookclub

"Tour Secrets 2 is another successful novel by Winkk. She takes you on a journey in the entertainment business that will leave you thinking twice about the so-called glitz and glamour. I was impressed with the way Winkk gave so many different twists and turns and kept me wanting more. "

Urban Reviews

"The author Winkk never gave you a moment to breathe before something else was happening. I love the characters and the shock value in the book. Great job to the author for telling a story from a dancer point of view. Very interesting and a must read - page turner."

Worldwide Readers Bookclub

A NOVEL BY

W I N K Katme

PUBLISHING

Ailam Publishing LLC
P.O. Box 43413
Chicago, IL 60643
www.ailampublishing.com

ISBN 978-0-9837759-2-8
Library of Congress Control Number: 2011912094

First Ailam Publishing LLC trade paperback edition September 2011

Book Cover Concept by: Winkk and Graphix by Dzine

Book Cover Design by: Graphix by Dzine

Book Cover Photography by: Reginald Payton

Book Cover Model/Dancer: Regina Daniels

10 9 8 7 6 5 4 3 2 1

Manufactured in the United States of America

To order additional copies of this book contact:
Ailam Publishing LLC
ailampublishing@aol.com
P.O. Box 43413, Chicago, IL 60643
www.ailampublishing.com

Acknowledgements

I thank God for everything I've accomplished and I look for his directions as I follow my dreams. I'm so thankful for the people that are now in my life and happy that we will continue to grow together.

To Mom and Dad thank you for continuing to tell me "Don't stop and keep writing." You encouraged me to continue no matter what and I love you dearly for the support. Thanks for always being my biggest fans.

To my husband, thank you for allowing me to write and follow my dreams. I love you for taking this journey with me. To my daughter, you're the reason I strive so hard. I hope you learn from this experience and know that if you work hard you can accomplish your dreams. Dream big baby and don't let anyone take that away from you. I love you.

Marcia, Alven, Montoya, Anita, Ebony, Tamala: I love you guys dearly and I'm glad that you are here with me to experience my dreams. Thank you for supporting me and being my cheerleaders. I love you guys and I couldn't do it without my family.

Special thanks to: Stanley, Kathy, Katherine, Herman, Britney, Vida, Tracy, Antoinette, Regina, Self Pro Motion, Lorenzo, Blake Martin, Prototype, Koolaid, Nicole, Tony Binns, Rolling Out Magazine, Reginald Payton, Art Sims, Urban Reviews, John Smith, Choklit Jok Morning Jumpoff Show, Power 92 Radio, Merrlyn, , APOOO Bookclub, Carla Dean, 102.3FM, Raw TV, WVON, Teranz Boutique, blog talk shows, WCSU, Johariel Hair Salon, Ty Ku Liquors, Remy Martin, Vince Bass, Mary Datcher, my Facebook family, my Twitter family and Myspace family and all the talented dancers and entertainers. Thanks to all the readers for holding me down on this project and enjoying the words that poured from my mind.

Please forgive me if I'm forgetting anyone, but you know you are in my heart. I've already started writing my next novel, so get ready it's going to be juicy! ;0

Love ya,

TOUR SECRETS 2

by W I N K Katme

Music and Raven's passion has secured their position as dancers in the music industry. They realize how low-down and dirty the business can be – with sex, money and power ruling the people around them. They continue their dreams as they prepare to dance on tour with Que, a Platinum-selling recording artist. Unaware of his grueling rehearsals and his controlling and erratic personality, they are unsure if they can keep up with his tour.

As much as they want to simply enjoy their new-found fame, the two are constantly chased by scandals and haunted by the past – a murder they both witnessed. Now that they have received everything they dreamed of and more, they are not sure if they can handle their new successful life. They struggle to live their passion for dancing while keeping their secrets amidst the judgmental eyes of the music industry.

CHAPTER 1

"Make a right at the corner," I said, while enjoying the cozy ride of the Bentley.

The luxury vehicle was black with peanut butter-colored leather seats. It was shining like it had just been driven off a new dealership car lot. It had every amenity you could think of including a navigation system, adjustable back seats and a sound system that made you feel like you were sitting front row at a live concert. Receiving this star treatment made me reminisce back to my last tour.

The outfit I wore made me feel like I belonged behind the wheel of the Bentley. I had on four-inch leopard printed heels, black leggings and a white fitted shirt that hung just below my butt along with a short cropped black leather jacket. I wore my favorite diamond pear-shaped earrings, four silver diamond bracelets, a diamond ring and three long silver chains with a large diamond butterfly pendant.

I kept my look simple, yet expensive and stylish. My makeup and hair was perfect, and I looked like I was ready for a photo shoot as I carried my oversized Louis Vuitton purse and matching luggage. My diamonds sparkled enough to let you know they were real, and I complemented my look with soft smelling perfume.

My dancer salary was great, and I was happy I didn't have to take my clothes off to make this type of money. I was legit and earned my money respectfully as a professional dancer who traveled the world on tour with platinum-selling recording artists. I had made it and was moving forward with my dreams.

"Music!" Kia shouted loudly, interrupting my daydreaming.

"What," I yelled.

"Is Raven going to be ready?" Kia asked, annoyed.

"She should be waiting outside of her building," I told her.

Kia had been Que's personal assistant for over two years, and he groomed her into a mini version of him. She did exactly what he told her to do and with major attitude. She was a bitch with a capital 'B' and she was already pissing me off. She was driving us to Que's house to meet his dancers and crew, get our itinerary, and board the tour bus headed to Atlanta to start rehearsing for the tour.

Riding in Que's Bentley confirmed he was financially stable, and I knew we would be well taken care of. Raven and I would continue to travel first class like we did with Slyy. We were used to the best and being treated like celebrities. So, it would be hard for us to accept anything less.

Kia's hair was pulled back in a long ponytail and she had on Chanel prescription glasses. She looked very plain and was not like the usual stylish women Que kept around him. She wore a white crisp button-down shirt with several buttons left undone to display her bulging large C-cup breasts. Her diamond studs glistened in her ears and her blue jeans fitted her shapely figure perfectly.

Her makeup was very simple, but one's attention would be drawn to the expensive diamond chain and pendant around her neck. Her French manicure was flawless and she topped off her look with a large Gucci purse and matching shoes. She had an 'I-don't-play-attitude' and didn't say much to me on the way to Raven's house. By the looks of her style and personality, I didn't know what to expect from Que's tour.

When Kia and I pulled up in front of Raven's condo, she was not outside.

"Where's your girl?" Kia asked with an irritated tone.

"She's probably on her way. I'll give her a call," I said, then took out my cell phone and dialed Raven's number quickly.

"Que hates when people are late," Kia said, while looking at me through the rearview mirror.

"Raven hurry up," I said as soon as she answered.

"I'm on my way," Raven shouted.

"You know if we're late, Que is going to curse us out," I snapped.

"He's not going to say anything," Raven replied.

"You must have forgotten who we're working for. You know Que don't play," I said, reminding Raven about Que's personality.

"Girl, I'm going to work him like I did Slyy. I will have him eating out of the palm of my hand," Raven responded nonchalantly.

"Whatever. Just bring your ass out of the house," I demanded.

"Well, well, well! I see somebody has a new attitude!" Raven said, shocked.

"I hope you can handle it," I replied.

"You just remember I'm the bitch with the biggest attitude!" Raven snapped.

"Stop stalling and hurry up!"

"I'm coming," she said, then quickly hung up.

"She's on her way," I told Kia.

"If she's not here in five minutes, I'm going to leave her," Kia said casually peeking at me through the rearview mirror. Something about Kia told me that if Raven was not outside soon, she was going to put the car in drive, step on the gas and not look back.

I hadn't hung out with Raven in over a month because she was always out of town working on some modeling jobs. I was excited to see my best friend to catch up on things. Her schedule was so busy that it was hard for us just to talk on the telephone.

I closed my eyes, leaned my head back on the soft leather headrest and impatiently waited for Raven. I didn't like idle time because it made me think about my nightmares, and it seemed like my mind kept drifting off, remembering things I didn't want to remember. Immediately, I started thinking about my life a month ago.

I was still haunted by Slyy's death and prayed no one found out that Que murdered him while Raven and I were in the room to witness it. Still very uncomfortable and on edge, I couldn't seem to shake it off. Raven felt the same way I did and kept busy to keep her mind off of things. Que seemed to be doing fine and acted like nothing happened.

I had become depressed and felt sheltered, not wanting to go anywhere and staying in the house most of the time. The only thing that kept me sane was going to the gym occasionally and hanging out with my family.

I was always reminded of Slyy from the radio constantly playing his music or the media talking about his death on television repetitively. I felt like he was haunting me from his grave. I hated him for what he had done to me, but for some reason, I couldn't feel any satisfaction from his death because I was too afraid I might go to jail for being a witness to his murder.

Some days I felt like I didn't want to live, and other days I was strong and wanted to keep moving on with my life. Dancing on Que's tour would keep me busy and my mind off of things. I just wanted to feel normal again and for things to go back to the way they used to be.

My mom had been calling and bugging me every day, and I still didn't feel like talking to her. She had never called me this much and I'm not sure why she needed to talk to me, but it would have to wait until after Que's tour. I was in no mood for her "I told you so" speech.

Que assured me that going on tour with him would take my mind off of Slyy's murder. I hoped he was right. Although he was turning into a person I didn't know anymore, he was still my friend. At least Raven and I would be with a whole new crew and not have to deal with Slyy's entourage and the drama that came with them. Having a new crew, we didn't have to feel uncomfortable because none of them knew about our secret.

Que had to push his tour back in order to finish up some producing he was doing for another artist. He stayed busy, not wanting anything to remind him of the night he killed Slyy. He seemed to be totally focused on success and money, the two things that will get you in trouble.

It had been one month since Slyy's death. The news had died down about his murder, and Nadine was out on bail awaiting her trail. My conscience was still bothering me knowing she was accused for his death.

I heard Janice started filming another movie and had finally started moving on with her life. She was a strong woman and was handling Slyy's death by continuing to work, just like everyone else. The media was saying Janice was in court trying to fight for Slyy's estate, but since she wasn't married to him, his money or property didn't belong to her. However, she felt that since they had been together for so long, she was entitled to all his money.

After dealing with the dancers on Slyy's tour, being raped and beaten by Slyy, dealing with Raven snapping out on me, Slyy's assistant Garrett's attitude, and watching Slyy get murdered, my heart was hardened and cold. I now fell into a category that I didn't want to be in. I allowed someone to abuse me and I dealt with it because I wanted to dance on tour so badly.

I forgot who I was, and losing my soul, I let Slyy mistreat me. Now, I couldn't allow myself to be the same person and be eaten alive. I had seen a lot and experienced so much that now I didn't give a fuck. I just want to dance and get paid. Fuck the world! Fuck these dancers! Fuck everyone! Just pay me and get the hell out of my face.

I know I have some major issues going on inside. Slyy took something from me, and I didn't know how to get it back. Now, I was about to start a new tour fucked up in the head, which was a recipe for disaster.

Once Que's tour was over, I'm going to make an appointment to see a psychiatrist because I definitely needed help. I refused to continue to stay messed up in the head. I was not going to allow Slyy to continue ruining my life from the grave.

"Is someone going to help me with my bags?" Raven asked, opening the car door and awakening me from daydreaming.

"You're on your own," I told her.

"We're riding in a Bentley with no first-class service. Now that's ridiculous," Raven commented, obviously upset.

I wasn't about to help Raven with her bags. I had to put my bags in the trunk by myself and she needed to do the same. We had been spoiled from Slyy's tour, but we quickly realized this tour would be different.

Kia pushed a button, and the trunk door opened slowly. Raven looked at me and rolled her eyes. She was not used to handling her own bags. Kia never looked at Raven. Instead, she just stared straight ahead while Raven put her bags in the trunk and got in the backseat with a major attitude.

We were only allowed to bring two bags. Que insisted that if we brought more bags, they would be left behind. So, we packed the largest bags we could find and they were full to capacity.

"Wow! You look great, Raven," I told her as soon as she got in the car.

"Oh my God! I see we both got a makeover. Music, you look fabulous!" She said, surprised.

"Thanks. Look at your hair! We both dyed our hair blonde," I said, laughing.

"I can't believe you cut all your long, beautiful hair off!" Raven screamed.

"What happened to your short hair? You added weave," I yelled back.

"We totally switched our styles and we looked hot. I love your shoes," Raven added.

"I love your shoes, too," I said, commenting on her four-inch black patent leather heels. "I see we're both dressed to impress," I added, admiring Raven's black and white jumpsuit with her diamond accessories.

"Those bitches are going to be jealous," Raven said, laughing.

"Let's not start any mess," I replied, frowning.

"I'm not starting anything. I'm just telling the truth," Raven said, while touching up her makeup.

We both had very different hairstyles but the exact same color. Raven got rid of her short haircut and went for a long, straight Kim Kardashian weave. I cut all my hair off to a very short Halle Berry haircut. I needed a new look to go with my new attitude.

"You're always making us late," I said, hitting Raven in her arm.

"We're not late," she told me.

I took a deep breath and shook my head. Raven knew I hated when she wasn't on time. It was a bad habit she needed to change.

"What's up?" Raven said, speaking to Kia.

"Hello," Kia responded in the most professional voice.

"What is that about?" Raven asked, as she rolled her eyes at Kia.

"She doesn't talk much," I responded in a low tone. "So what's up, girl?" I said, while giving her a hug and kiss on the cheek trying to change the subject.

"Are you ready to do this again?" Raven asked me.

"Of course," I replied, eager to get started.

"I'm ready to dance!" Raven said, snapping her fingers.

"I just hope you don't pull that shit you pulled on Slyy's tour!"

"Music, I apologized to you for that. Let's not start on a bad note."

"I'm just letting you know that I'm not putting up with your mess."

"Damn, Music. What's with this tough attitude?"

"I'm just tired of people running all over me, and I'm not taking it anymore."

"Music, you know I got your back. I promise I won't hurt you again."

Raven was really feeling herself on Slyy's tour and wanted to be the head bitch in charge even if it meant stabbing me in the back, which she did. Somehow, she came to her senses and apologized to me, but I don't think I will ever trust her. I will always watch my back around her. I don't think I can ever forget that my best friend tried to get me fired from a job by badmouthing me.

"We're cool, right?" Raven asked.

I didn't say a word. For the first time, I really meant what I said. I was not taking any shit from anyone. Que and Raven said I needed to change my ways. Now they would see the new me.

"We're good," I said, knowing my trust with her was limited.

"I hope this tour is fun. I don't feel like going through any more drama," Raven whispered, not wanting Kia to hear us.

"If it's not cool, I'm leaving," I whispered back.

"You know we can't leave until the tour is over," Raven replied.

"I know."

"How quickly do you think I can work Que's pockets?" Raven asked, smiling.

"I don't know," I said, annoyed.

"I've been talking to Que ever since we've been home from Slyy's funeral. I really like him and can't wait to see him," Raven told me while blushing.

"A lot of women want Que, so you better have your A-game on."

"It will only take me a week to work my magic," Raven confidently replied, smiling devilishly.

"You think you got skills, huh?" I asked, teasing her.

"I can suck a dick better than any woman," Raven said proudly.

"Both of you guys are my friends, so I don't want to be in the middle of this," I whispered, making sure Kia didn't hear us.

"You won't be in the middle of anything. Just remember I'm your girl," Raven said.

"Don't come on this tour acting crazy," I warned her.

"Don't worry. Let's just have some fun."

"I'm thankful we're working again," I said, giving Raven a high five as my phone started to ring for what seemed like the umpteenth time.

"Damn! Answer your cell phone," she told me.

"No, it's just my mother," I said, annoyed as I hit the ignore button.

"Is she still trying to talk to you?" Raven asked.

"Yes, but I don't feel like talking to her right now. She's always so negative, and I don't need that right now."

"Your mother be tripping sometimes, but maybe she really has something to tell you. She has never kept calling you like this. Maybe something is wrong," Raven said.

"I'll call her when this tour is over. That way, I will have some peace," I replied, then took a deep breath.

We continued talking and playing in each other's hair for the long two-hour drive to Que's house. Not knowing what to expect, we were sure we could handle anything that was thrown at us.

With our new look and my new attitude, we were ready to take on the world. Every tour had some type of drama, and although we didn't know what drama would occur on Que's tour, we were ready to deal with it because we were much stronger.

CHAPTER 2

Two hours later, we were pulling up through the secured gates of Que's mansion and it was almost midnight. We drove along the long lighted driveway to the front door. I was mesmerized when I saw his incredible three-story house that looked like it was made of glass and it was glowing. There were tons of lights on the inside and outside of the house. The grass was so green that it didn't look real, and the landscaping was amazing.

The house was so gigantic I couldn't see where it ended. The large terrace on the second floor was overwhelming, and the house was too much to take in all at once. Towards the back of the house was a five-car garage where three tour buses, two black Escalades, a Mercedes Maybach, and a Hummer were parked.

Raven and I looked at each other and our mouths fell to the floor. We couldn't believe how lavish Que was living. Raven started smiling and rubbing her hands together because she knew she had hit the jackpot and had every intention of taking all of Que's money.

"Wow! Que didn't tell me he was living like this!" I said, shocked.

"This is why he doesn't want people to know his home address," Raven said.

"Why?" I asked.

"Because people will know just how much money he really has," Raven replied.

"The more money you have, the more problems you have," I said.

"Que has money!" Raven said excitedly, knowing she was going to get some of it.

"I wonder why he didn't tell me he was living this way," I said to myself, confused.

Kia stopped the car, opened the trunk, and got out quickly. Raven and I were still sitting in the car looking at the house. It was obvious the music industry had been very good to Que. His album was number one, and he was producing number one hits for many superstars. He also had a clothing line and was working on a couple of movies. He had his hands in everything as he kept busy and continued getting paid. I just didn't realize how much he was getting paid until now.

Raven and I thought Slyy was rich and treated us like stars, but after seeing Que's mansion and being picked up in his Bentley, we knew Que had Slyy beat. Before Slyy's death, the media tried to start a feud between the two of them, saying they were competing against each other.

Que didn't really like the fact that he had to share the spotlight, but decided to join forces with his biggest competition, and it paid off for him. Now Que was leading the pack, especially since Slyy was out of the picture.

"Music, we're about to get paid!" Raven said with excitement.

"Yes, we are!" I said, agreeing.

Kia made a call, and within a few seconds, the front door opened. Two large security guards stood in the doorway without moving. With huge muscles bulging out of their shirts, they looked like they were wrestlers from the WWF. They had stern looks on their faces, and you could tell they didn't play around. Raven and I waited for them to open the car door for us, but it never happened.

"These big-ass baboons are not going to open the car door for us?" Raven asked, annoyed.

"I guess not," I said, irritated.

They were not going to help us with our bags and we didn't understand why they were acting so rude. They really needed to be taught some manners, and I made a mental note to put this on my list of things to talk to Que about.

Raven and I finally got out and grabbed our luggage out of the trunk. We didn't even wait for them to help us carry them because we knew they wouldn't. Thank God for whoever invented wheels on luggage.

"Follow me," Kia told us.

"Oh, now the bitch can talk," Raven said, pissed off.

"Keep your eyes on the prize," I said, trying to calm her down.

As soon as we got our bags, a man came out of the house, got in the car, and drove it away quickly. We followed Kia and the two buff security guards through the front glass double doors.

The entrance to his house was all white, with beautiful marble floors and high cathedral ceilings. A large five-tier chandelier hung from the ceiling that looked like it had to cost millions of dollars. It was so vivid and beautiful, and also the first thing you noticed when you walked into his house.

There was a huge round table in the middle of the entrance that had a tall crystal vase with long-stemmed exotic looking flowers in it. On the left wall was a huge striking waterfall that looked like it was ten feet tall. The entrance smelled tropical like we had walked into a garden. The staircase was directly in front of us and made us adjust our eyes quickly because it was extraordinary. It was completely made of glass and twisted and turned until it reached the second floor.

We walked a few steps and the floor plan opened up wide to a posh, sunken, all-white room. The room had white uniquely-shaped furniture, a white grand piano with a glass vase holding burgundy exotic roses, and walls that had a few colorful architecture paintings on them that coordinated with the burgundy and white theme. It was so dramatic and appeared that no one ever went into this room.

As soon as Raven and I were getting overly excited by telling Kia to show us the rest of the house, she stopped us.

"Wait right here," Kia said.

"Can we sit down in the white room?" I asked.

"No. Que doesn't like people in this room unless they are invited by him," she replied, then walked away.

"We're supposed to just stand here and wait?" Raven asked, confused.

Kia never responded and continued walking away.

"I hope Que is not getting all Hollywood on us," I said.

"Girl, this is some bullshit. They could have at least given us a chair or offered us something to drink. What type of ghetto shit is this?" Raven said.

We stood in one place waiting for Kia to return. One security guard went with her and the other stayed with us. We didn't even try to talk to him because he seemed like he meant business and wasn't too friendly.

We waited for one hour. We were furious and our feet were hurting. By this time, we were both sitting on the floor annoyed and restless. When Kia finally returned, we looked up at her.

"Follow me," she instructed us.

We grabbed our bags and followed her. We were trying to be optimistic about the situation, but they were wearing our patience out. We followed Kia back out the front door and walked to another part of the house. We entered a large, bright room that was a beautiful shade of orange and had all of Que's number-one hit awards on the wall and his five Grammy's were displayed.

The room was filled with a large orange-colored pool table, a chess table, and every video game you could imagine from Ms. Pac Man to Centipede. There were even two lanes for bowling. It was obvious we had walked into his game room. The specialty rugs on the cherry hardwood floor had pictures of Que's album covers on them. It was truly unique and impressive. Either Que had taste or he hired an experienced interior designer.

Pictures of his family and friends were showcased all around the room. I was surprised to see he had a few pictures of me up on the wall. Raven pointed at the pictures of me and smiled. I felt special to have my pictures displayed because he had always been like a brother to me, and I was always the sister he never had.

We walked through the room and entered another room, which was a large rehearsal studio. There were four large, plush couches, chairs, ceiling-to-floor mirrors, and an amazing sound system. The room was large enough for his entire stage show to set up.

Six girls were doing a dance routine, and Que and his crew were sitting front row and center watching. The room smelled like a gym, and you could tell they had been rehearsing all day.

When Raven and I walked in, no one even noticed us. Still amazed, I continued to look around and couldn't wait to see the rest of the house.

"Have a seat and Que will be right with you," Kia said, then went and sat next to Que.

Que never even acknowledged us, and we suddenly felt uncomfortable and out of place.

"Finally we can sit down," Raven said, angry.

As soon as the dancers finished their high energy routine, Que stood up, put his hand over his head, and rubbed it hard out of frustration.

"I only hire the best dancers. I've given you plenty of time to get this routine together, and you're still fucking up!" Que shouted.

Not knowing what was going on, Raven and I looked stunned. The dancers appeared to be nervous as they listened to Que yelling at them.

"Tipp, you keep fucking up! Now get the fuck out of here!" Que shouted furiously.

You could hear people gasping because they couldn't believe he was firing her. We knew immediately who the dancer Tipp was because she started crying, but she never moved. Raven and I looked at each other and frowned, confused by the whole scene.

Even with no makeup, Tipp was a pretty, petite girl with a very light complexion. I didn't know if she was White, African American, Mexican, or some type of mixed race. She had a very innocent, unique look with brown-colored eyes, short brown hair, and perfectly shaped thick eyebrows. She looked like she was 5'6" and wore a size four.

"Whoever doesn't like it can get the fuck out. This is my motherfucking house, and I run this shit. Don't come in my house and fuck up my show. There are tons of people dying to be on my tour, so I don't need any of your asses," Que said, as he pranced around yelling and waving his hands in the air furiously.

"Please give me another chance. I know the choreography. I was just nervous. I can get the routine," Tipp pleaded.

"Shut the hell up. You don't know the choreography, because if you did, we wouldn't be having this conversation," Que shouted.

"I know the routine," Tipp said, as tears poured down her face.

"You know it?" Que asked sarcastically, laughing.

"I got it down," Tipp replied with confidence.

"Since you know the choreography, do it by yourself. The rest of you sit down and let her do it alone. You know it perfectly, right?" Que said, irritated.

"Yes," Tipp said.

"If you fuck up one move, I promise I will fire you!" Que said seriously.

This whole scene was making me truly uncomfortable. After watching her do the routine when we walked into the room, I knew she would mess up the choreography. I felt sorry for her. It brought back memories of Nicole messing up on Slyy's tour. There was no saving her.

The music played and Tipp started dancing. You could tell she was trying to be focused and get the routine perfect. She started off good, but having Que standing directly in front of her staring, started making her uncomfortable. She started feeling the pressure.

As soon as she messed up the first dance move, Que's eyebrow rose and he looked at her disgusted. He allowed her to keep dancing, but once she made the first mistake, it was downhill after that. He finally put his hand up, gesturing to stop the music.

"You just proved my point. You can't do the choreography without making a mistake. You're pitiful," Que said, appalled.

Tipp was too embarrassed to say anything. So, she stood there and took the verbal abuse from him.

"Get the fuck out of my house!" Que demanded.

"Please give me another chance," she pleaded.

"You're not going to fuck up my tour. I don't need this shit and I don't need you. Get out!" Que shouted.

"Please, Que. I don't want to leave the tour. I'll do anything to stay," she said as tears continuously rolled down her face.

"You'll do anything?" Que asked, slowly raising his eyebrow curiously.

"Yes," Tipp said slowly, not knowing why he was looking at her that way.

"Let me get this straight. You will do anything to stay on my tour?" Que asked, while looking at her intriguingly.

"I will do anything to stay. Please don't fire me!" Tipp said, continuing to beg.

"If you want to stay on my tour, you need to do exactly what I tell you to," Que said.

"Okay, I'll do it," Tipp said, still crying.

"Get on your knees and suck my dick," Que said seriously, looking directly at her.

"Huh?" Tipp responded with a confused look.

"Suck my dick if you want to dance on my tour!" Que demanded.

"In front of everyone?" She asked, puzzled.

It was obvious that Tipp and Que had slept together because she wasn't concerned about sucking his dick. She just didn't want to do it in front of everyone in the room. Raven and I, the two security guards, Kia, and about ten other people were all watching.

"If you want to dance, start sucking!" Que said, while standing with his arms crossed.

Not moving, Tipp started crying loudly. Que's body language told us that he was getting tired of waiting on her.

"Get out of my house! You're wasting my time!" He shouted.

"Please don't do this," Tipp begged.

"Can you guys escort her out of my house?" Que told his security.

"Okay, okay! Please stop! I'll do it," she said.

Tipp moved closer to Que, got on her knees, and started slowly unzipping his pants as tears flowed down her face. He stood with his arms crossed and looked unimpressed.

"Hurry up!" He yelled.

Tipp continued crying as she pulled his long, thick, enormous dick out and held it in her hands. She stared at it like she was contemplating what to do next. She looked up at Que hoping he would change his mind, but he didn't. He looked at her, closed his eyes, took a deep breath, and blew the air out vigorously.

"Get out of my house!" Que said, frustrated with her taking too long.

"Wait, please!" Tipp pleaded.

At that very moment, she had to decide if she wanted to dance on his tour badly enough or if she had more respect for herself. This is where she had to decide if she was going to lose herself and give in to the money and fame. She chose her dance career.

Tipp opened her mouth and inserted Que's large dick inside. She started sucking him very slowly. Once she started, she continued like no one was watching her. Raven and I looked at each other and couldn't believe what we were seeing.

No one else in the room seemed to be shocked by this display and didn't show any emotions. They all appeared too nervous to say or do anything.

"This is some crazy shit," I whispered to Raven.

"Damn, Que got a big dick," Raven said.

"It is big," I agreed, stunned by his size.

"I can do a lot with that," Raven said, smiling.

"Girl, get your mind out of the gutter," I said, poking her in the side.

"She ain't sucking his dick right," Raven commented, while studying Tipp's techniques.

"Raven, be quiet," I said, hitting her on the arm.

We continued watching the live porn show in utter shock. We couldn't believe what was going on right in front of our faces. I blinked my eyes a couple of times to make sure I was actually seeing it.

"Stop," Que said, clearly aggravated while pushing her head away.

The room was so quiet you could hear people breathing. I was afraid to make a sound and still flabbergasted from the whole two-minute episode.

Tipp got up off her knees, wiped her mouth, and looked down at the floor totally embarrassed. Seconds passed without anyone saying a word. It was so tense and uncomfortable in the room, I couldn't take it. Que kept looking at Tipp like he was thinking, and then he finally spoke.

"I want you to leave now!" Que said casually, while gesturing for her to leave the room.

"Why?" Tipp asked, surprised.

"You're fire!" Que said, while signaling for his security to put her out.

"I can't believe you're still firing me after what I did for you in front of everyone!" She yelled.

"That's what you get for being so desperate to dance. You're nothing but a nasty bitch!" He shouted back.

"Why are you doing this to me?" She yelled.

"You should have never degraded yourself like that," he replied.

"I can't believe this!"

"I can't believe you would suck my dick in front of everyone. I don't want a desperate dancer working on my tour," Que said, acting unconcerned about her feelings.

"I did it because I wanted to dance on tour with you," she said, growing irritated.

"Tipp, you know you were fucking up the choreography. So, sucking my dick wasn't going to help you," he told her.

"But I thought…" Tipp said before Que interrupted her.

"If you will suck my dick to dance, you would do it to someone else. Whose dick are you going to suck next?" Que asked sarcastically.

"You made me embarrass myself and you're still firing me? I hate you, Que!" Tipp yelled, kicking and screaming as security escorted her out the room.

"Only a nasty tramp would do what you did. You're a dirty bitch! Get out of my house!" He yelled.

"Que, please don't fire me. I want this job! I need this job! Please!" She pleaded.

"You need to get the fuck out!"

"Don't do this. Please!" Tipp said, as the door closed behind her.

I grabbed my forehead and massaged it. I couldn't believe Que would pull his penis out in front of everyone, and I couldn't believe she would suck it in front of us. I was also still stunned at how big it was.

No one said a word once the door closed and we waited for Que to talk. He closed his eyes for a few seconds and then opened them, pretending like nothing happened.

"Damn, I need a cigarette," he said, smiling while rubbing himself.

We started laughing because we knew Que didn't smoke and that he was trying to make a joke. I laughed, but it really wasn't funny. The laughter broke the tense feeling in the room, and we suddenly became relaxed.

Que looked around the room and finally seemed to notice Raven and I sitting on the couch. He put a large smile on his face and headed our way. The smell of his softly-scented cologne filled our nostrils as soon as he got close to us. He looked like he didn't miss a day at the gym and pampered himself with facials, manicures and massages weekly. Success and money really looked good on him, and he wore it well.

Que always kept his body in shape, but for some reason, he was looking extra buffed. He had on a pair of nice fitting jeans, a black t-shirt, black boots, a large diamond stud earring, and a diamond watch. He was dressed simple but had major swagger.

His skin looked like buttery caramel and his teeth were extremely white. His hair was cut very low, his beard was trimmed perfectly, and his eyes were still very beautiful. Que was looking very handsome, and I had to check myself because I never looked at him in that way before.

"What's up, girls?" Que said, giving us a hug and kiss.

"You tell us," I replied.

"What do you mean?" He asked.

"What the hell was all that about?" Raven asked laughing.

Que laughed but never responded. Instead, he grabbed our hands and pulled us towards the other dancers. As we walked over towards them, they looked Raven and I up and down like they didn't approve of us. Their attitudes weren't anything we hadn't experience before. So, it didn't bother me at all. They were wasting their energy for nothing. I just wanted to dance and get paid, just like them.

"This is Raven and Music, the girls I told you about. They used to dance for Slyy," Que said, introducing us.

"Hello," Raven and I said.

"Hey," the dancers responded in an unimpressed tone.

"I want you guys to treat them good. They are professional and really know their stuff. Maybe they can show you guys a thing or two," Que said.

Raven and I smiled at them, knowing we were in for some bullshit dealing with these dancers. We could tell they didn't like us already, even though they didn't know us.

Women! Can't we be comfortable with ourselves? I thought to myself.

"You girls look beautiful!" Que told us.

"Thanks," we both said.

"You look good yourself," Raven added.

"Your hair really looks good. You both look like models," he said, admiring us.

Each compliment he gave us, the dancers looked at us with more disgust. He complimented us so much, from our physical appearance to what we were wearing, that it started making me uncomfortable.

I was starting to think he was doing it just to irritate them. It didn't help that the dancers were all dressed down in jogging pants, t-shirts, and had no make-up on, which made Raven and I easily stand out.

They all seemed to be in shape and were very attractive even without make-up. They all had short haircuts that made the small diamond earrings in their ears easy to see. Also, we immediately noticed the diamond pendant that said "Q" around their necks and assumed we would be wearing one soon.

"Show Raven and Music the opening routine for the tour," Que told them.

They immediately got in position and waited for the music to start. It was almost like they were robots and only moved on his command. The music started, and they did the choreography like they were on stage in front of millions of people.

The routine was hot, and I was ready to join in. They did it effortlessly with no one making a mistake. Que looked at them hard, trying to find something wrong and daring them to miss one step.

"I have to go to my recording studio for a moment. You guys get to know each other. My assistant Kia will go over everything with you. I will see you guys in an hour," Que said, as he quickly left the room.

Once the door closed, Kia immediately gestured for all of us to come over to her and sit in a circle so we could talk. Que quickly came back into the studio, walked over to Kia, and whispered something in her ear. After she shook her head in agreement, he walked away, while staring at Raven like he could eat her up.

"I want to go over a few things, and then you guys can spend the remaining time getting to know each other," Kia said. "We will be leaving for Atlanta in a few hours, so make sure you take everything with you and put it on the tour bus."

"I saw three tour buses. Which bus are we riding on?" Raven asked her.

"The dancers, assistants, and security rides on Que's tour bus. The band and crew members have their own tour bus," Kia replied.

"Cool," Raven and I said.

"Que rented a mansion in Atlanta that we will all live in until the tour starts," she informed us.

"Wow! That should be fun living in a mansion," I commented, while smiling.

The dancers looked like they were very shocked at me speaking. Every time Raven and I responded to Kia, they looked at us strangely.

"Once we get to Atlanta, I will give you an itinerary for rehearsals. Que runs a tight ship and he is very strict, so I need you to follow directions. You will meet your personal assistant when we arrive there and she will be your point person. Just so you know, I only work for Que," Kia said with authority.

"When do we discuss pay?" I asked.

"Que will personally speak with you guys regarding pay. I will keep you posted on updated information. Get to know each other, and I will let you know when it's time to leave," she said, then headed for the door.

"What's up, girls?" Raven said to the dancers, trying to break the silence.

"Hey," one of the dancers responded.

"What's your name?" I asked.

Another dancer took the lead and introduced us to everyone. She even added a little history about each of them, which I didn't need to know but accepted the information anyway.

"Que gave us all nicknames that we go by. My name is Swagg because he said I have Swagger on stage. This is Sweets because she dances sweetly. This is Flex because she is extremely flexible. This is Sexy because she is so sexy when she dances. Last but not least, this is Heat because she brings the fire when she dances. And you saw Tipp earlier. He called her Tipp because she can work the hell out of some point shoes," Swagg said.

"Wow! Do you ever use your real names?" I asked.

"No. Que wants us to use the names he gave us at all times," Flex stated.

"How long have you guys worked with Que?" Raven inquired.

"Flex and Heat are new and have been with Que for six months. The rest of us have been working with him for three years," Sweets replied.

"How is it touring with Que?" I asked.

"As long as you can deal with being seen but not heard, it's cool!" Heat quickly answered.

"I heard you guys toured with Slyy. What was that like?" Swagg asked us.

"It was cool, just like any other tour," Raven said, not wanting to give them information.

"Which one of you grew up with Que?" Swagg asked curiously.

"I grew up with him," I responded.

Once I said that, they immediately started asking me questions about Que. What type of person was he growing up? What did we do as kids and did we ever date? They seemed to really want to know how well I knew him. After so many questions, I started feeling like they were interrogating me instead of trying to get to know me. The more I told them funny stories about Que when we were young, the more questions they asked.

"Okay, that's enough questions," Raven said in a sassy tone.

"One last question, which one of you is the big-time model?" Swagg asked.

"That would be me," Raven replied proudly.

"Have you been in magazines? What cities have you been to?" Flex inquired.

"We're going to rehearse for three months and be on tour for seven months. I think you guys will have enough time to get to know me then," Raven said, not trying to answer any more of their questions.

We had been talking for about thirty minutes before Kia interrupted us by sticking her head in the door.

"You guys can get ready to get on the tour bus. Raven and Music, wait here because Que wants to talk to you," she said, than closed the door.

After the dancers left the room, Raven and I sat and waited for Que. An hour passed, and we were still waiting. We were starting to think they forgot about us. When we opened the door, security was standing right there. We asked him if Que was coming, and he told us that he was on his way and to continue to wait for him. Finally, after waiting two hours, Que walked into the room.

"When are we going to see the rest of your house?" I quickly asked.

"I will show you the house when we're finished talking," Que said, as he grabbed a chair to sit down.

"I didn't know you were living this large!" Raven commented.

"It's a lot of things you don't know about me," he replied, as he tried to downplay his success. "I wanted to talk to you guys separately since you're the new dancers on my tour. Everyone else knows the rules."

"Rules," Raven said.

"I have rules. Is that a problem?" He asked.

"No," I quickly responded.

"First, I want to say thank you for dancing on my tour. I'm glad you guys are here," Que said, before continuing in a serious tone. "My assistant will tell you everything you need to know. So, you have to learn to be patient and wait to be instructed on what to do."

"Okay," Raven and I replied, unsure of what he meant.

"I love your hair, but I don't like it for my tour," Que said sternly.

Confused, Raven and I looked at each, but we didn't comment because we didn't know where he was going with his statement. So, we let him continue talking.

"You guys are going to have to change your hair. You both need to dye your hair black or brown. I hate blonde hair!"

"What!" I said loudly.

"Music, I can't believe you cut all your hair off, but I was going to ask you to cut it anyway. Raven, I actually liked you with short hair, so you need to take that weave out," Que demanded.

"Are you serious?" Raven asked, completely taken aback.

"Yes, I'm serious," he responded without hesitation.

"We're just starting to rock these hairstyles! I don't want to change my hair," I said, upset.

"I'm sorry, but if you're going to dance on my tour, you need to change your hair before we leave," he said, trying to sound as nice as possible.

"Que, where are we going to get our hair done at two o'clock in the morning?" I asked, irritated.

"I have a salon in my house. My people will take care of you," he said casually.

"Why do we have to change our hair? We look fierce!" Raven said, snapping her fingers.

"You do look good, but this is what I want," Que insisted.

"I paid a lot of money to get my hair done," Raven argued.

"Whatever you paid to get your hair done, I will give it back to you."

"Well, you owe me four hundred and fifty dollars, and I want it now. I only get the best weave, and it ain't cheap," Raven said, holding her hand out.

Que reached in his pocket, pulled out five crisp one-hundred-dollar bills, and handed them to her. He put the money directly in her hand and squeezed tightly.

"Thank you," Raven said, acting unimpressed by his actions.

"Money is never a problem for me, so keep the change," Que replied, flirting with her.

"Que, this is ridiculous!" I said.

"Music, don't make this difficult. Just change your damn hair so we can leave," he told me.

I was so pissed off, I didn't say a word. Que could tell I was upset, but he didn't seem to care.

"Here is five hundred dollars for you, too, Music. So, changing your hair should not be a problem. You only have to change your hair color," Que said, while handing me the money.

"Did you make all your dancers change their hair?" I asked.

"Actually, I did. They wear their hair the way I want them to," he replied arrogantly. "You guys can't get special treatment just because you know me."

"We don't want special treatment. We just don't want to change our damn hair," Raven said.

"Well, cutie, you either change it or you have to leave," he responded without blinking.

"Damn, Que," I said shocked.

"It's business; nothing personal," Que said.

Amazed by his attitude, Raven and I just stared at him. We saw one side of Que on Slyy's tour, but now we were starting to see another side of him. I really wanted to dance for him because he was known to have elaborate shows and I wanted to experience it, but he was already making it very difficult.

"Are you guys cool?" He asked.

"Whatever!" I said.

"Music, you're my girl. You're like family to me. But, I won't allow you to talk to me like that on my tour. I'm your boss. The other dancers don't talk to me like that, so don't give them any ideas."

"Fine," I said, understanding his authority.

"Raven, you were late when my assistant came to pick you up, and I hate people being late. Don't let that happen again. Okay, sexy!" Que said, winking at her.

"Sorry, it won't happen again," Raven responded, trying to respect his power.

"I wouldn't want to fine you guys if you're late. Raven, you're too cute for me to take your money."

"Can we discuss what we're getting paid to dance?" I asked.

"We will discuss it when we get to Atlanta," Que said, sounding annoyed that I was asking about money.

"Why can't we discuss it now?" I asked.

"I'll discuss all business when we get to Atlanta. You can wait, right?"

"I can wait, but don't mess with my money, Que," I said.

"I'm not going to cheat you out of your money. I'm your boy. You know you can trust me," Que replied, trying to assure me.

"I trust you, but don't screw me," I said.

"What's with this tough attitude?" He asked.

"I'm just not taking any shit from anyone," I said.

"Whatever, little Mike Tyson, just keep that attitude under wraps when you're dealing with me. Are you guys going to be able to hang? You know my tour is totally different from Slyy's tour. On my tour, you have to do what I tell you to do."

"We can hang. If we can handle Slyy's tour, we definitely can handle your tour," Raven told him.

"Cool. I'm glad we got an understanding," Que said. "Music, guess who's going on tour with us?"

"Who?" I asked curiously.

"Doug," he said, smiling.

"Doug who?" I asked.

"Don't play dumb. Your old boyfriend, my cousin," he replied, laughing.

"Oh my God! I didn't know he was working with you," I said, surprised to hear his name.

"He's going to be my tour manager."

"That's cool," I said nonchalantly.

"He's the only one I trust to run my business on the road."

"I haven't spoken to him since he cheated on me years ago," I responded with slight irritation.

"I don't want any drama. Can you handle working with him?" He asked.

"Yes, I'm over him!" I said, not wanting Que to know that I didn't want to see him.

"I can't have any tension on my tour."

"I promise there won't be any problems," I assured him.

Raven knew Doug broke my heart when he cheated on me. She also knew I was over him but hadn't seen him to really have closure. Sure, I was worried about seeing him, but mentally, I felt strong since I didn't have feelings for him.

"Why did you make that dancer suck your dick in front of everyone and still fire her?" Raven asked him, trying to changing the subject.

"I don't like desperate people. If you're willing to do something like that, then you'll do anything to make it in this business. I don't want that type of person around me," he replied.

"That was wrong what you did to her," I said.

"I do what I want on my tour and that will never change. You either like it or you can leave. I'm the boss around here."

"You are so mean. What happened to my friend?" I asked.

"I'm still your friend, but this is business. You just need to get used to me being your boss," he told me.

I guess he was right. I had never worked with him and didn't know how he was going to be as my superior. I guess he was trying to tell me in so many words that I needed to respect him and know that I couldn't pull the friendship card. Like he said, it was business and nothing personal. I just needed time to get used to this new union.

"I'm ready to work as your employee, but I still don't think I need to change my hair. You know we look good, so why would you want anything else?" I asked, smiling.

"You're changing your hair and it's not up for discussion. When you guys are finished, we'll leave," he said.

"Why can't we wait until we get to Atlanta to change our hair?" Raven asked.

"I don't want to look at that blonde color all the way to Atlanta. Now, come on so I can show you the rest of my house first," Que said, as he grabbed Raven's hand.

While walking through the house, we were amazed. We knew he was definitely classified as wealthy. The house had seven bedrooms, nine bathrooms, two offices, a recording studio, a dance studio, a basketball court, an infinity pool, a movie theater, two kitchens, a game room, a hair salon, and a barbershop.

We were so impressed, we didn't want to leave. We wanted to stay in his house and experience the glamorous lifestyle. Once Que finished showing us around, he took us straight to the hair salon for our makeovers.

"Do you always get what you want?" Raven asked him before he left the hair salon.

"Always. Is that a problem?" Que asked, smiling.

"No, because I always get what I want, too," Raven said, smiling back.

"Really? Well, you getting what you want might not work on my tour. I'm the only one in that position around here," he replied.

"Oh, I'm going to give you what you want," Raven responded flirtatiously.

"Good," Que said, then closed the door behind him.

"I will get what I want also," Raven said out loud once the door closed.

CHAPTER 3

It only took two hours to dye my hair black and Raven's hair brown. The hairstylists actually did a great job and we were very pleased. They took Raven's weave out and she continued to rock the short haircut she always did. They kept my hair short, spiked it up, and made us look like rock stars.

Once we were done, we were eager to head to the tour bus. Before we could reach the door of the salon, Que's security stopped us.

"You guys need to wait in here until I speak with Que," he told us.

"Are you serious?" Raven asked.

"Very serious, so please don't leave this room until I tell you to," security replied firmly.

"I'm getting tired of waiting around all the time," I said.

Raven was too annoyed to say anything, so she played in her hair while we waited. Waiting around was something we had been doing ever since we had been at Que's house, and it was getting very annoying. I couldn't believe we couldn't move one step until Que instructed us to. He warned us that we would have to do everything he told us to do, but I didn't take him seriously. Now I understood that he meant exactly what he said.

"Que wants to see you guys in his recording studio before you go to the tour bus. Grab your luggage and I will escort you there," security told us after we had been waiting for an hour.

We followed security to the studio and waited by the door for him to open it. Security stood to the side of the door and didn't move to open the door for us.

Raven and I rolled our eyes at him and then opened the door.

As soon as we walked in to the outsized, dimly-lit recording studio, the piercing music busted our eardrums and the smell of vanilla-scented candles filled the room. Que was sitting in a chair, leaned back with his legs stretched out, relaxing as he listened to music.

"This is a nice studio," Raven said, interrupting his calm mood.

"That song is hot!" I added.

"Your hair looks great and much better than before," Que commented, nodding his head to the music.

"Thanks," Raven and I said simultaneously.

"I want you to hear some of the songs for the tour before we leave for Atlanta," he told us.

Que played a few songs off his album and told us how he wanted his tour to be. The song was so loud that the walls appeared to be shaking. His tour was going to be intricate and expensive, and he seemed to be excited. Raven and I danced around the studio enjoying the music, while Que continued telling us the details of the tour. We were so energized; we couldn't wait to start rehearsing.

"How are you guys coping?" He asked, turning the music down and becoming very grim.

His question changed the entire mood in the studio, and we stopped dancing instantaneously. We knew he was talking about Slyy's murder, but we would never say it out loud. We had an agreement to never discuss it with anyone or ourselves. I hated whenever we even hinted about his death because it terrified me.

"We're doing great," I said somberly.

"Have you heard anything?" Que asked softly.

"The police still think Akira killed Slyy," Raven replied, as she looked at the floor.

"I kind of feel sorry for her, but shit happens," Que said dispassionately.

"This is wrong, allowing an innocent person to go to jail for a crime she didn't commit," I said.

"It's tons of innocent people in jail," Que said.

"We're going to hell. I mean, you're going to hell," Raven told him.

Not happy with her comment, Que stared at Raven for a second and then said, "I found out that the police are talking to everyone that was backstage that night. They have already spoken to some of the dancers and band members, so I know we will be next on their list."

"Oh my God! What are we going to do?" I asked.

"You're going to stay calm and stick to the plan," he said.

"Are you getting nervous?" Raven asked Que.

"No. They have to prove that I killed Slyy, and no one saw me but the two of you," he whispered.

"How did I become a part of this? This is getting scary," Raven said.

"Don't be afraid. As long as we stick to the plan, everything will work out. My tour came at a perfect time because it will keep us busy and make it difficult for them to locate us right now. It also makes us look innocent because we're moving on as usual." Que said.

"I guess you're right. I wish I could be as calm as you are about this situation," I said.

"I'm calm because I know if you stick to the plan, you will have nothing to worry about. You guys can't leave this tour because you have to look busy and as normal as possible. So, no matter what, you must finish this tour. By the time the tour is over, Akira's trial should be over and everything should be back to normal."

"I hope so," Raven said.

"You guys have to stop being so damn scary. You look guilty. Chill out!" Que said, upset.

"Okay! We will work on being more like you. Not giving a damn," I said sarcastically.

"I heard things are getting crazy in his camp. They are fighting over his money and he has a daughter," Que informed us.

"He was also older than he claimed to be," I said.

"It seems like he was a big-ass dirty liar. Who knows what else he was hiding or lying about," Raven added.

"All his dirt is coming out. I still can't believe what he did to you, Music. He deserved what he got," Que said, staring up toward the ceiling.

"I don't want to remember," I replied.

"He can't do that to anyone else," Raven stated, as she looked at me sadly.

"Let's continue what we agreed to do and everything should work out. Agreed?" Que asked.

"Agreed," Raven and I replied.

"I just wanted to check on you guys and make sure you were cool and we were still on the same page. I hope I can trust that you will keep your mouths shut." Que said.

"We won't say anything," Raven responded quickly.

"It's over, so let's forget about it," I said.

"I just wanted to make sure you guys didn't go back on what we discussed. I don't want that situation discussed on my tour or anywhere else. Don't fuck with me," he said seriously.

"We're all on the same page," I assured him.

"The secret will always be safe with us," Raven added.

We all looked at each other intensely for a moment and then gave each other a big hug. We were confirming our agreement to never mention Slyy's murder again. We hugged for a few seconds before Que went back to listening to his music.

I could feel Que was worried not knowing what was going to happen with the investigation. Although the news didn't say they had any leads on the murder, we knew it didn't mean they didn't.

"Can I really trust this secret with you guys?" Que asked, while turning down the music.

"You can trust us," Raven replied, looking directly in his eyes.

"Damn, Raven, you look good!" Que said, smiling as he tried to change the tense mood in the room.

"You're just now noticing," Raven responded sarcastically.

"Come over here and sit on my lap so I can take my mind off of this situation."

Raven did exactly what she was told. She was also trying to work her magic and get in his pockets. Her plan was to quickly put it on him so tough that he would easily give his money to her. She sat on his lap and he quickly started rubbing her thighs. As his hand moved further up between her legs, I became nervous, fearing he would discover her big secret. But, Raven never moved and acted relaxed.

I knew Que was trying to see how far he could get with her. Once he noticed she wasn't going to stop him, he immediately stopped. He grabbed her face, licked her lips, and stuck his tongue in her mouth as he kissed her wildly.

Oh God, I said to myself, as my heart dropped. He had no idea he had just kissed a man. *Damn these secrets.* Que and Raven acted like I wasn't in the room, which caused me to feel uneasy. I cleared my throat trying to make them stop.

"I'm sorry, Music. Your girl looks so damn good that I couldn't control myself," he said, while kissing Raven's neck.

I looked at Raven, who gave me a devilish smile while her hand was caressing Que's dick in his pants. Raven and Que were both my friends, but I didn't know who to be loyal to. I didn't want to be in the middle of their love affair, but it seemed like I was all up in it. Que would kill me if he knew that I knew Raven was a man and didn't tell him, and Raven would kill me if I told Que she was really a man. I don't know what to do.

"Okay, break it up," I told them.

"Don't be jealous," Raven said, smiling.

"Trust me, I'm not," I replied, rolling my eyes.

"It's time for us to leave anyway. I'll meet you guys on the tour bus in fifteen minutes," Que said.

After we grabbed our luggage and headed for the door, Raven stopped and turned around to look at Que.

"I can't be carrying my luggage. I'm a lady," Raven said.

"You're right, baby. You shouldn't carry your luggage," he told her.

"Well, we have been carrying our luggage ever since we got here," I said.

"That won't happen anymore. I will take care of it," Que assured us.

"Thank you, baby," Raven said, then walked over and gave him another kiss on the lips.

"Yuck," I said, disgusted.

Que and Raven laughed at me as we left the studio and headed for the tour bus. This time, the security guards were carrying our luggage for us. Raven's relationship with Que would definitely get us some perks.

After Raven and I boarded the tour bus, we quickly tried to figure out which bed we were going to sleep on. All the dancers had their bed selected and dared us to ask them to move.

We smelled Que's favorite vanilla-scented candles as soon as we walked on. The bus was very familiar and posh just like we remembered. The front area had a black and white theme with large fluffy couches, a large-screen television, and a huge kitchen area with a table for four, and a bathroom equipped with a shower.

The bus looked exactly the same as Slyy's tour bus, except the back master bedroom had been turned into a full recording studio. Que actually slept in one of the bunk beds.

We found two empty top bunks and claimed them by putting our bags on the beds. Then we headed back to the front of the bus to relax.

"Ladies, we will be leaving in twenty minutes, so make sure you have every-thing out of the house," Kia said as soon as she walked on the bus with Que.

"Road trip," Que yelled, excited as he kicked his shoes off, and turned on a movie.

Everyone spoke as he got settled in and security took Que's bags and put them in the back closet that was reserved for him. Then he came back to the front with me and Raven's bags in his hand.

"What are you doing with our bags?" I asked.

"Your bags don't belong on the top bunk. They're going on the other bus," security said.

"Why?" Raven asked Que.

"They should have told you that you guys are riding on the crew bus," Que said.

"The crew bus! I thought all the dancers rode on the bus with you?" I asked, baffled.

"Calm down, Mrs. Mike Tyson. Don't bite my ear off," Que said, cracking up with laughter.

"You're not funny," I said, angry.

"You two are new to my tour and have to prove yourself before you can ride on my bus," Que said, looking uninterested at what was going on.

"What's up with this situation?" Raven asked as she started to get upset.

"Remember, its business and nothing personal," he replied with a smirk.

"Why are you treating us this way?" I asked.

"Everyone that is new to my tour has to go through an initiation, and this is part of it. Can you handle that?" Que asked, frowning.

"What if we don't want to ride on the crew bus?" Raven asked, testing him.

"Then you will be taking the public transportation bus back home," Que replied without even looking at her.

I looked at Que trying to figure out what game he was playing. Maybe he was trying to make some point to the other dancers. Either way, I was already tired of the games and was ready to go home. With everyone staring at us, I started feeling embarrassed, while Que acted like he didn't care and started watching the movie.

"Come on, Raven. Let's get on the crew bus," I said, pissed off as I grabbed

Raven's arm and pulled her to the door.

"Since we can't leave his tour, he is trying to disrespect us," Raven mumbled.

"Let's just get this initiation over with," I told her.

Humiliated, we walked off the bus and followed security to the crew bus. The closer we got, the more we knew this bus was not going to look like Que's tour bus because it was a much older model.

After security opened the door, we followed behind him slowly. The bus was full of sweaty, funky men and smelled like dirty socks and old cigarettes. The bus was aged, and the decoration made me feel like I was visiting my grandmother's house. The bus was laid out exactly like Que's bus except it was outdated and the back area had couches.

Raven and I were appalled and didn't want to stay on the bus. The crew was looking at us with smirks on their faces. I guess they were used to Que's initiation for new people and were waiting for us. They were amused by the whole thing.

One of the crew members showed us to the two vacant bottom bunk beds, while security put our bags down and left quickly. The beds didn't even have a DVD player or television. He then introduced us to the new music director named Johnny, who was also riding on the crew bus. We spoke to him, and he had the same irritated look on his face as we did, although he seemed comfortable with the situation.

Johnny was very handsome and seemed quiet and laidback. He was being initiated just like we were and was also assigned to a bottom bunk. The bottom beds were always the worst ones to have. You felt every bump from the road, and it was always extremely hot. Plus, you had to get on the floor to crawl in. We were not happy with this situation but tried to stay optimistic.

Raven and I were so used to getting pampered from Slyy's tour that we were livid we had to ride with the crew. We always knew that Slyy spoiled his dancers better than any other artist. I'm sure Que was getting a kick out of making us suffer.

The crew was very nice to us and showed us how to work everything on the bus. They seemed to be having a blast laughing, drinking, and talking. If the bus didn't suck so much, we would actually enjoy riding with them, but it was late and we were tired.

"Why would they let us get comfortable on the nice, plush bus and then send us to this raggedy-ass bus?" Raven asked, pissed off.

"I don't know what type of game Que is playing," I said.

"Que is on some bullshit!" Raven said.

"I'm not going to let him get to me. Let's do our job and get this money," I told her.

"Oh, I'm going to get his money alright. He is really going to pay for this little charade," Raven replied angrily.

"I don't know who Que is anymore!" I said, shocked.

"You've never worked with him. That's why you don't know him. Let's just play the game and act like it's not bothering us. He's trying to break us, and I can't be broken," Raven said.

"I will play the game for now, but this is getting old fast."

"Let's deal with this initiation because it will be over when we get to Atlanta."

"Que is destroying my excitement about being on his tour."

"I'm seeing a side of him that I don't like, but I know how to handle him," Raven said.

The bus driver started the bus and we headed for Atlanta. It was now five o'clock in the morning, and I was extremely tired. Our plan was to sleep the entire twelve-hour drive to Atlanta and pray when we woke up that this nightmare would be over.

The crew tried to get us to stay up with them, but we were exhausted and couldn't hang any longer. We said goodnight to everyone, crawled in our bunk beds, closed the privacy curtain, and went straight to sleep.

I took a quick look at Johnny before he turned his light out. He was definitely eye candy, and I knew I would have a good dream.

CHAPTER 4

Raven and I woke up at the same time and immediately headed to the front of the bus. Everyone was still asleep, and we were happy we had the front area to ourselves. We grabbed a couple of bottles of water out of the refrigerator and sat down to watch television. The bus driver told us that we were in Atlanta and not far from the house Que had rented. We were so ready to get off the stinky bus, we could have screamed.

"We really got to make the best of this tour because it seems like it's going to be crazy," I said, trying to prepare myself.

"You're right because Que is crazy," Raven replied, laughing.

"He likes to annoy the hell out of people."

"Each tour has different types of craziness."

"So far this tour is the winner for the strangest."

"Are you going to be okay with Doug being on tour with us?" Raven asked.

"I'm not going to let him bother me. I'm over him," I said confidently.

"We're always a part of bizarre situations. It's so draining," Raven said, while staring out the window.

"How are you holding up?" I asked.

"I don't know," Raven replied without hesitating.

Raven knew I was talking about all the secrets surrounding Slyy's murder. It seemed like our life had been crazy ever since we started dancing. We both had dealt with issues, and it seemed to never end. All the drama was stressing us out, and we were doing our best to act normal.

"You seem sad. Are you okay?" I asked her.

"I'm just thinking about how my life is always filled with chaos and no happiness," Raven said sadly.

"Your life is no different from anyone else's," I told her.

"My life is fucked up and I'm messed up in the head."

"Raven, don't go down that road. Let's try to stay positive," I said trying to keep her from feeling depressed.

"It's hard living in a man's body. I've struggled all my life with this. I'm going to have a sex change once this tour is over," Raven revealed.

"If that's what you want to do, then you know I got your back."

"I really like Que and want to be in a relationship with him. I hate keeping my life a secret from him. I'm also tired of taking men's money. The money is good, but I'm lonely," Raven said.

"Maybe you should stop trying to take men's money and look for real love. Things will get better," I said, trying to comfort her.

"I wonder if my childhood was different would I be a different person," she stated, while continuing to stare out the window.

I knew we were going to start the conversation about her life like we always did. It always made me feel miserable when I talked to her. I wanted to help her and save her from the pain, but I knew there was nothing I could do but listen.

Raven never knew her biological father, and her mother wouldn't tell her any information about him. Her mother always told her that her father was dead, and this made her feel like a piece of her life was missing. Raven really wanted to know more about her father to find out about herself.

As a child, she always felt she was a girl living in a boy's body. Her mother understood her feelings and helped her to become a girl so she could live her life the way she wanted to. Raven appreciated her mother's support.

When Raven was young, her mother's boyfriend molested her and her secret didn't seem to stop him. He continued to molest Raven for years until one day he left town and was never seen again. Raven was worried because she thought he would reveal her secret, but she also knew he didn't want anyone to find out he was gay. So, she knew her secret was safe. Once Raven got older, she always thought he left town to be free and live outright as a gay man in another city.

"Do you think that since you were molested by a man for so many years that could be the reason why you are gay?" I asked.

"No. I was gay before he ever touched me. I've never been attracted to women. I only wanted to look like them," Raven said.

Raven confided in her auntie and told her about being molested, but she never told her auntie she was a man. She kept her secret to herself because she knew the only way to keep her secret was to never tell anyone. If I never walked in on Raven taking a shower, I would have never found out she was a man, and I'm sure she would have never told me.

Her auntie was a different type of woman and made a living being a gold digger. She didn't have any respect for men and continued to carry that hatred throughout her life. She had also been molested as a child, and this was why she could relate to Raven. She hated men and taught Raven to hate them, also. She showed Raven how to manipulate them.

Being a man herself, Raven knew exactly how men thought, which made it easy for her to be the coldest gold digger around. She learned from her auntie that men were only good for sex and money. Raven never respected men, and this really encouraged her to always dress like a woman.

Her auntie taught her how to look and smell good at all times so the men would come running. Raven was always on point and you never saw her look a mess. She was well put together and men loved this about her. She shared this information with me to help me be well put together, too. I love her for teaching me about style, class and etiquette.

Raven has always been a very caring and helpful person, even though she was a con-artist. She has a great heart and is always there when I need her. She had been the sister I never had. We shared everything together and would always have each other's back.

Even though I knew Raven was a man, she definitely acted like a female at all times. She truly had turned into a woman, inside and out. It was scary watching her because sometimes I forgot who she really was. Although she lost her mind on Slyy's tour and totally treated me like a stranger, I still forgave her. I gave her another chance because she's the only real friend I have and I don't want to lose her.

It had been a while since I've seen her get her feelings involved with a man. I was used to her not giving a damn about anyone and letting material things feed her emotions. She seemed to really like Que, but I knew she would drain his pockets first before she started to love him.

Raven hated men and hated that she was a man. I felt sorry for her. Even if she had the sex change, I don't think it would change her mentally. I never knew how she could hate men so much, seeing that she was attracted to them. She was getting out of control and losing herself. She was more focused on getting money than doing what she loved to do, which was dance. Once you follow money, you will do anything to keep it. I just hoped she didn't crash and burn.

"I don't want you to be miserable," I told Raven.

"I want to be happy," Raven said sadly.

"We both need to make changes when this tour is over. You go and get your sex change, and I'm going to a psychiatrist," I told her.

"A shrink!" Raven said, shocked.

"I'm having a hard time dealing with the rape, beating, and murder," I whispered.

"Do what you need to do to get better. Don't let him steal your power."

"He's dead and still affecting my life. If I could do it all over again, I would beat his ass the first time he touched me. I hate him," I said softly.

"You should hate his ass. I was worried about you before because you were acting like you had sympathy for him. I'm happy you've snapped back to reality. He deserved to die."

"You're right. That's why I'm going to a doctor and get myself together. You should do the same if that makes you happy."

"I've had the money for the procedure for awhile, so I'm going to schedule my appointment soon."

"I'm going to be right there with you," I told her.

"Thanks, Music. I love you."

"I love you, too. We have to stick together and take care of each other."

"I'm glad you're in my life. I trust you and will never do anything to hurt you. I will always have your back and lookout for you," Raven expressed.

"Thanks. You know I got your back, too."

Raven continued to look out the window. Suddenly, tears rolled down her face that she quickly wiped away. I hugged her, trying to comfort her and let her know that everything would be okay. I knew she was sad, but I also knew she was very strong and could bounce back from anything.

An hour later, we were pulling up to the house that Que rented for the next three months to rehearse. The house was incredible and had a wonderful lakefront. I could see the boat dock, infinity pool, and several terraces. There was also a guesthouse behind the mansion. The house sat on acres of land by itself with no neighbors in sight.

I was thrilled to live like royalty for the next three months. Que really knew how to do things right and take care of his staff. I was ready to rehearse and knew this would definitely keep our minds off of things.

Raven and I couldn't get off the bus quick enough. We stood outside of the bus and waited to go inside the house, but no one exited the other buses. After we were waiting for about an hour, we got back on the bus. By then, the crew members were awake and sitting in the front area.

"What are we waiting for?" I asked, irritated.

"We can't move until Que tells us to," one of the crew members said.

"Are you kidding me?" Raven asked.

"What is Que doing?" I asked, aggravated.

"He's probably still sleeping," another crew member replied.

"This is so bizarre," Raven said.

I couldn't believe we couldn't make a move until Que told us to. All we had been doing was waiting for his command. This was already getting old, and I didn't know how much more I could take.

"If you're going to stay on this tour, you have to learn to deal with it. You'll get used to it," a crew member told us.

Since we had nothing but time to waste, we started questioning the crew about how long they worked with Que and how it was working for him. They weren't trying to give up no real information about him. They gave scripted answers, and we knew they were not going to tell us what we wanted to hear.

Que had his staff wrapped around his finger, and if we wanted to continue dancing for him, it seemed like we would have to get wrapped around his finger, too.

While we waited, we turned the television channel to a local news station and started listening to what was going on in Atlanta. They started talking about things happening in the entertainment business and announced there was new information on Slyy's case. Raven and I looked at each other as our hearts dropped because we didn't know what they were about to say.

Slyy's attorney had a press conference and stated that everyone wanted to know the details about the case, but they would have to wait. They didn't give too much information, but Slyy's age was confirmed.

He was really forty-eight years old, which was a shock to Raven and I because we thought he was in his thirties. They said he never wanted anyone to know his real age, but the media had dug into his personal records and retrieved his birth certificate.

They also mentioned they had reviewed his life insurance and legal documents and found that Slyy had a daughter who was believed to be in her twenties. The reporters went crazy when they heard that information, because Slyy never acknowledged having any kids.

The attorney said they would be looking for his daughter to discuss the details of his estate. One of the reporters started asking questions, which led to all the reporters bombarding the attorney with question after question.

Raven and I sat there with our mouths wide open. I couldn't believe he was forty-eight. He really looked like he was in his late thirties. Then I started wondering if he ever had plastic surgery to look so young.

"I can't believe he lied about his age!" Raven said.

"He never told us his age, so I guess he never really lied," I told her.

"He lied!" Raven said.

"I can't believe he has a daughter! Her father is a rapist," I whispered in Raven's ear.

"He's a lying bastard," she whispered back.

"You never really know who people are. I wonder what else he was lying about," I said.

"When they find her, she's going to get paid!" Raven said.

"I wonder if he was taking care of his daughter," I said.

"If they are just finding out he has a daughter, I doubt if he was taking care of her financially. That cheap asshole."

We had so many questions, which led to a conversation with the crew. They started telling us things they had heard about Slyy. We tried to think of every female entertainer that could be his daughter. A few hours had passed, and we were still talking about Slyy when Kia walked on the bus.

"Get your things together and be outside the bus in ten minutes," Kia said and then quickly left.

Our personal belongings were already together. We had been ready to get off the bus ever since we stepped on it. The crew scattered around to get their things together, while we sat and watched them. Ten minutes later, we were standing outside of the bus waiting for our instructions.

"This is getting ridiculous," I expressed.

"I can't keep waiting and waiting," Raven said.

"I feel like a child. I don't know if I can deal with this the entire tour," I told her.

"Well, you better get used to it quickly, because this is how the tour goes down all the time. Hurry up and wait," Johnny said.

"I thought you were the new music director on the tour. How do you know what happens around here?" Raven asked.

"I was his music director for one of his tours before, but once that tour was over, I started working with someone else and missed his last tour. Whenever you miss his tour and come back, he treats you like a stranger. You have to start all over," Johnny informed us.

"That's messed up. How do you deal with that?" I asked.

"I just think about the money and that makes it better. I know what to expect now, so it's not a problem for me. Hopefully, you'll get paid what you deserve," Johnny said.

"We haven't discussed pay yet," I told him.

Johnny wrapped his arms around me and Raven's shoulders and walked us to the side of the bus. "Make sure you get all your money. Don't let him pay you a low salary. Don't settle," he said seriously.

"Does that happen a lot?" Raven asked.

"The other dancers never worked with anyone before, so Que pays them such a low salary that they can't afford to take care of themselves. They accept the low pay because they are so excited to work for him," Johnny said.

"I grew up with Que. So, I'm not that excited to be working for him that I'm not going to get paid what I deserve," I replied.

"I've seen you dancing on Slyy's tour and you look good. I know you're used to being treated like a professional, so just get what you deserve," Johnny said with a sexy grin.

"How is it working on Que's tour?" Raven asked.

"It's a crazy tour. Que likes things done his way. He likes to control every-one," he responded.

"Control!" Raven said, shocked.

"If you can deal with that, you can handle this tour," Johnny told us.

"We can handle anything," Raven said.

"Just keep to yourself and you shouldn't have too many problems," he said.

"Thanks for letting us know," I said.

"No one else will tell you the truth about his tour, but I will," he expressed strongly.

"And why are you telling us this?" Raven asked with a raised eyebrow.

"Since you've worked on Slyy's tour, I know you're used to being treated with respect. Everyone in the business knew that Slyy pampered his staff and paid them well. You have to demand respect on this tour or you will get ran over. When you feel like you can't get another job, then you will allow Que to treat you however he wants to, and he will take advantage of you," Johnny said seriously.

"Does Que show you respect?" Raven asked.

"Definitely," Johnny quickly answered.

"Why? What makes you so different?" I inquired.

"Because I do my job, I demand respect, and I'm the best music director and keyboard player in the business," Johnny said with confidence.

"Thanks for the information, but I'm still wondering why you're telling us this since you don't know us," Raven said, looking at him suspiciously.

"The music industry is not about all this foolishness. It should be about doing something you love and getting paid for it. I'm just trying to help you. So, you can take the information or not," Johnny responded, raising his shoulders.

"Thanks, Johnny," I said, trying to stop Raven from interrogating him.

"No problem. I'm here if you need to talk," Johnny said, then winked at me.

Johnny left with a swagger in his walk. We could still smell his cologne lingering, which smelled so good I wanted to continue sniffing it. He was very cute with deep dimples and jet black hair. His beard was groomed low and perfect.

His voice made your panties wet instantly from its smooth, deep tone. His dark complexion made him look like an African goddess. His skin was so pretty and smooth looking that I wanted to see how he looked naked. He looked like he tanned all day long, which made his skin have a perfect, dark chocolate glow.

He was dressed casual with a black t-shirt, fitted jeans, and black shoes. His jeans were hanging just low enough to see the rim of his underwear. His muscles filled his t-shirt perfectly, and his low, deep voice made you want to listen to him all night long.

Johnny made me melt when I talked to him, and I was starting to really feel him. I had to keep it cool because I didn't want him to think he had me already, even though I was happy he was on the tour and couldn't wait to get to know him.

"Johnny is so fine," I told Raven.

"Music got a boyfriend!" Raven started singing.

"He is sexy," I said.

"Yeah, he is attractive," Raven agreed.

"Back off. This one is mine."

"Girl, I don't want him! You know I want Que. You better get him before those other bitches take him," Raven said.

"I'm not worried about them. If he wants one of them, then he definitely is not my type," I said.

Kia interrupted our conversation and said, "Follow me," as she walked towards the house.

The house Que rented for us to rehearse in for the next three months was amazing. It was so large that I didn't think I would be able to find my way around. The house was larger than Que's house, and had all the amenities and more.

We followed Kia into the large, posh mansion and waited in the spacious foyer area. Once everyone was inside the house, Kia made an announcement.

"We will all stay in this house until the tour starts. There are three levels. Que and his security will stay on the entire third level of the house; the women will stay on the second level; and the band and crew will stay on the first floor. The remaining staff will stay in the guest house. There is a large rehearsal studio, recording studio, swimming pool, conference room, basketball court, and dance studio in the back building for everyone to use," Kia told everyone.

"Do we get our own bedrooms?" Raven asked.

"This house is gigantic, but not large enough for everyone to have their own bedroom. So, you guys will be sharing rooms. Go check your rooms out and get settled. We will have a meeting in one hour in the conference room," she said.

We didn't waste any time trying to find our bedrooms. Raven and I were not used to sharing rooms with anyone, so we wanted to make sure we would be roommates. We moved quickly. Some people took the stairs and some took the elevator.

Raven and I grabbed one of our small bags and left the large bags behind so we could run up the stairs to claim our bedroom. Once we got to our level, we separated and tried to look in all the rooms to see which one was better.

The second level of the house was wonderful. There were three bedrooms and one large recreation room. Each room was very spacious and had a large master bathroom. We noticed there were only one king-size bed, a couch, chair, and a flat-screen television in each room.

All the rooms were decorated the same and were the same size. Raven and I took the room closest to the stairs right on the corner, but we still couldn't figure out where everyone would be sleeping.

There were twelve women on the tour: six dancers, two stylists, and four assistants. Everyone was in each room trying to figure out what was going on, when the elevator doors opened and Kia walked out.

"I know you guys have noticed there are only three bedrooms and twelve women. There will be four people to each room. All the assistants will share a room, four dancers will share a room, and the remaining two dancers and two stylists will share the last room. No one is allowed to sleep in the recreation area. That room is for us to lounge and relax in. We need the space seeing that we are all sharing a bedroom," Kia said.

Not saying a word, everyone stood in silence.

"Two people will share the bed, and the other two will share the sofa bed. Get settled in, look around the house, and be in the conference room in one hour," Kia concluded.

After Raven and I looked at each other, we immediately headed to the room we selected on the corner and grabbed the bed. There was no way we were sleeping on a sofa bed for the next three months. We didn't want to share a room with anyone, but was happy we would be sharing the room with the stylists instead of the dancers because we felt like there would be no competition or attitude.

The two stylists were twin sisters named Chloe and Claire. They were very bubbly and seemed very nice. They were two white girls that thought they were black. You could tell they had mastered trying to be someone other than themselves.

They had long red hair and wore black-framed designer glasses. Chloe wore her hair curly, while Claire wore hers straight. They were tall and very thin, and of course, they were dressed uniquely stylish. They each wore a large necklace around their neck with a diamond pendant spelling out their name. So, we knew who was who.

"I guess we will be your roommates," Chloe and Claire said in unison.

"I guess so," I said.

"You can call us both CeCe, because when you speak to one, we both will answer. It's a habit, and it makes it easier on the people around us," Chloe and Claire said.

"Okay," Raven and I said, imitating them.

"You are the new guys, so we welcome you," Chloe said.

"I hope you guys don't mind sleeping on the couch," Raven said, knowing she really didn't care.

"It's not a problem. These sofa beds are actually very comfortable," Claire replied.

"Those are nice chains you have around your neck," I commented.

"Thanks. Que bought them for us because he said he couldn't tell us apart. Also, he requested that we wear our hair differently so he can always know who we are," Chloe said.

"You always have to wear the necklaces?" Raven asked.

"We can't take them off or we will be fired," Chloe said with no concern.

"That doesn't bother you?" I asked.

"No, it's not a problem. Besides, to work on this tour you have to do what Que tells you. We don't mind doing what we are told as long as we're getting paid," Claire said bubbly.

Raven and I went downstairs to get the rest of our bags and get settled in. We had thirty minutes to check the house out, so we didn't waste any time. The house was so huge we were getting lost. We covered every inch of it except for Que's level. We were not allowed on his floor unless we were invited. His security stood on guard at the elevator and stairs of his floor.

Que was doing it big, and for some reason, he felt like a stranger to me. I was trying to get used to all the rules and craziness so far, but it was becoming stressful. I couldn't even talk to him, which was weird to me.

On this tour, Que was definitely the star and I had to treat him like one. That was hard for me because I didn't see him that way. He was still my friend I grew up with, my friend who always had my back, and my friend whose secret I would always keep. I still loved him like a brother, but I just didn't like these arrangements.

We were five minutes early when we found the conference room. Several people were already in the room because no one wanted to be late. We found a seat and waited to hear what the meeting would be about.

"This house is so cool," Raven whispered.

"Que is spending a lot of money to rent this place," I said.

"Obviously, he is loaded," Raven replied.

"Johnny looks good sitting over there," I whispered.

"Be cool! You don't want to seem too eager. Make him come to you," Raven said, trying to train me.

"I'm not going to say anything to him. I'm just going to admire him from afar," I responded, while smiling.

"We need to figure these people out first," Raven said.

"You're right," I agreed, as I continued staring at Johnny.

When Johnny looked up and saw me staring at him, he gave me a look that said he wanted me just as much as I wanted him. His stare was so strong and seductive that it made me a little uncomfortable. Que quickly interrupted our moment when he walked into the room.

The assistants gave everyone a glass full of champagne, and we waited for Que to speak.

"I want to thank everyone in advance for being here. This will be a successful and exciting tour. Let's celebrate. Drink up." Que said, as he took a sip from his glass.

"Now, let's get down to business. We have three new people. Johnny, the new music director, has worked with everyone in the music business, and he is the best. Most of you already know him because he has worked with me before. Music and Raven are the new dancers who used to dance with Slyy. Stand up and meet everyone," Que told us.

Johnny, Raven, and I stood up and said hello to everyone, then sat down quickly as the assistants passed out a sheet of paper. Once I sat back down, I saw Doug, my ex-boyfriend. Our eyes connected, and instantly, I felt relived. I was happy I didn't have any feelings left for him. I simply smiled at him and he smiled back.

I was happy I could look at him and not want to kill him. I had my closure and truly didn't have any feelings left for him. Doug then winked at me, and I nodded my head to let him know everything would be okay.

"The paper you just received is some of my rules for the tour. You must follow these rules or you will be fired. The main rules you need to remember, are to never be late for rehearsals and do what I tell you to do. As long as you remember that this is my tour and I run everybody that's a part of it, we won't have any problems," Que said.

The room remained quiet while he spoke.

"The dancers will have their own personal assistant. So, meet Macy. She will be your assistant for the rest of the tour. She gets her instructions from me and will tell you everything you need to know. You don't move unless she tells you to," Que said, looking directly at me and Raven.

Everyone said hello, and then she came and sat down next to us. She seemed nice, but I knew if she was working for Que, I would need to watch her. Macy was very tall with short curly black hair. She also had a necklace around her neck with her name in diamonds. She was jazzy and very loud. She definitely looked like she didn't play and wouldn't take any bullshit from us, but at the same time, she seemed like she was a lot of fun.

"Rehearsals will start tomorrow. We will rehearse every day until my show is perfect. If you are fucking up on my tour, you will be fired! The assistants will keep you posted on what is going on. Talk to them if you have questions," Que told us.

He had everyone's attention, and nothing but silence filled the room whenever he was speaking.

"I'm taking everyone out to eat to celebrate! Meet me on my tour bus in ten minutes," he said, while holding his glass high in the air.

Que took us out to eat at a very expensive restaurant and told us to order anything we wanted from the menu. The entire entourage filled the restaurant completely. We did exactly what we were told and ordered only the best. Lobster, steak, champagne, and exotic dessert were mostly what everyone ordered.

Que didn't even blink when they handed him the pricey bill. He just handed them his black credit card without hesitation, smiled, and asked us if we'd had enough to eat and drink.

After dinner, he took everyone to a local nightclub. He was really treating us first-class, wanting us to have a good time. That's when I got the chance to sit down and talk to Johnny, and it seemed like we had a lot in common. He was very cool, and I couldn't help but stare at his luscious lips. We talked the entire time we were at the club and enjoyed our dance together.

Raven was enjoying Que's company, and the dancers were trying to fit in. Johnny and I stayed to ourselves, enjoying good conversation and expensive champagne courtesy of Que. I was becoming emotionally connected to Johnny fast. I didn't want to get involved with someone on tour, but this was happening and I couldn't stop my feelings.

By the time we arrived back at the house, it was ten o'clock at night. With everyone tipsy and exhausted, we were eager to go to our rooms and get in the bed.

Johnny and I took our time and continued talking. We walked slowly and even grabbed something to drink from the kitchen on the way to our room. We didn't want to leave each other, but we both were extremely tired and needed to rest.

"You looked nice tonight," Johnny said.

"Thanks. You looked good, too," I said, smiling.

"I had a good time at the club with you," he added, grabbing my hand and holding it tightly.

"Thanks. I enjoyed being with you, also," I said, flirting back.

"I think you're beautiful and I want to get to know you better," he told me.

"That sounds cool," I replied, blushing.

"It's going to be hard for us to see each other while we're rehearsing, but let's try to make time. Can I get your number so we can text each other during rehearsals?" Johnny asked, stopping before we reached the stairs.

"Sure," I said, as we exchanged numbers.

"I'll talk to you tomorrow," Johnny said, while squeezing my hand goodbye.

"Talk to you later," I said, grinning as I walked away.

"That man, that man, that man," I babbled to myself.

He had me with his sexy voice, pretty smile, luscious lips, beautiful complexion, dreamy eyes, and muscular body. He was smart and didn't seem impressed by the industry or the people in it. He had class and knew how to handle himself. He was definitely a real man, and he had me already.

CHAPTER 5

I was deep in sleep when I felt someone hitting me and calling my name. I turned over thinking it was Raven, but saw that it was Swagg standing over me.

"Wake up, Music!" Swagg said, while nudging me in the arm.

"Why?" I asked, annoyed as I rubbed my eyes.

"It's time to rehearse, sweetie," she said sympathetically.

"Rehearsals don't start until tomorrow," I told her, while yawning and turning over.

"Que wants everyone to rehearse now!" Swagg said powerfully.

"Are you serious?" I asked, becoming livid.

"Yes! Now get up!" Swagg said, irritated but understanding my frustration.

"What time is it?" I asked, still trying to wake up.

"It's one-fifteen," she replied.

"In the morning?" I asked, shocked.

"Yes! You need to get up and meet us in the dance studio right now!" Swagg said.

I sat up in the bed hoping this was a bad dream. When I looked at Swagg, she was staring at me impatiently, so I knew she was serious. I looked over at Raven, who was still asleep.

"Wake up, Raven," I said, pushing her.

"Stop, Music! I'm tired!" Raven said irritated.

"Get up. We have to rehearse."

"What time is it?" She asked.

I knew she was feeling the same way I was. She looked up and saw Swagg standing over us and then she saw the look on my face and knew something was wrong.

"Why the hell do we have to rehearse now?" Raven inquired, puzzled.

"You guys need to hurry up before you're late," Swagg said, then exited the room.

"Is this bitch serious?" Raven asked, livid.

"Yes, so I guess we better get up now," I said angrily.

When I looked over at the sofa and noticed Chloe and Claire were not in their bed, I knew this wasn't a joke. Raven and I dragged ourselves out of bed, put some clothes on, and headed to the dance studio.

Ten minutes later, Raven and I reluctantly walked into the studio where the dancers were already stretching. Swagg signaled for us to find a spot and join them. We stretched for an hour, and once we were done, Swagg started teaching us a routine.

Raven and I never said a word; we just went with the flow. It was too early in the morning to be dancing, especially after having a huge dinner and several drinks. Raven and I kept a frown on our face the whole time. The other dancers didn't seem to mind and appeared comfortable with the impromptu rehearsal.

I heard of sleepwalking before, but I had created something new because I was sleep dancing. I was so tired I could hardly keep my eyes open. I was not used to rehearsing at this time of day and especially when I was woken up out of my sleep.

Three hours into rehearsal, Swagg told us to take a five-minute break.

"Why are we rehearsing at this time?" Raven asked.

"I don't know," I said.

"Are you guys okay?" Swagg asked.

"Yeah, we're fine," Raven replied, looking at Swagg strangely.

Raven noticed Swagg was running the rehearsal, and therefore, she needed to know more about her and her position.

"I know you guys are struggling with the late rehearsals, but you'll get used to it. We rehearse at this time every day," Swagg told us.

"Why so late?" I asked.

"Because Que works during this time and sleeps during the day. Everyone has to be on his schedule," she responded.

"He could have told us that we were going to be rehearsing so we wouldn't have eaten or drank so much," Raven said.

"He likes to shock people. You have to always be ready to rehearse when you're working with Que," Swagg replied.

"I see it's never a dull moment working with him," Raven said sarcastically.

"You'll get used to it. Just try to hang in there," Swagg said.

"Are you the choreographer?" Raven asked, trying to find out more information about her.

"No. Que choreographs everything. He shows me, and then I teach you guys. I'm the head dancer on this tour, and I run the rehearsals," she informed us.

"Wow! How did you get that position?" Raven inquired, trying to see if Swagg was sleeping with Que.

"I've been dancing with him the longest, and he trusts me to run his tour the way he likes it," Swagg replied with confidence.

"That means you guys are very close," Raven pressed.

"We're family," Swagg said, realizing that Raven was trying to get information.

"That's cool. Now I know I can come to you if I need help with my dance moves," Raven responded, trying to be nice.

Raven knew she couldn't piss Swagg off, but she also wanted to know her competition. She was determined to get Que, and she wasn't going to let Swagg stand in her way. So, she decided to become her best friend for the time being. Dancers always wanted the head dancer spot, and they would stab you deep in your back to get it.

While Raven was talking to Swagg, Johnny had sent me a text wondering if I was in rehearsal like he was. Que had everyone rehearsing and working at the same time. We exchanged our frustration through the texts. Then Johnny expressed that he couldn't wait to see me, and before I could respond back, Swagg was telling us it was time to start rehearsing again.

Swagg was like a drill sergeant; she was definitely following Que's instructions. Raven and I looked at each other because we knew Swagg was going to be a problem for us. We knew she was Que's eyes and ears on the road and would tell him every little detail. After rehearsing for eight hours, Que finally gave the okay for us to leave.

We arrived back in our bedroom at ten o'clock in the morning. Once I finished showering, I immediately got in the bed. Before going to sleep, I sent a 'good night' text to Johnny and he sent one back saying, 'I want to see you. Good night'. He made me smile and anticipate trying to see him later that day.

It felt strange getting in the bed when I should have been just waking up. We had to totally change our schedule. We would now sleep during the day and work overnight.

Raven and I made a promise to adapt to whatever Que threw our way. We felt like he was trying to break us down, and we weren't going to let him. No matter what, we were going to get our sleep. We were there to rehearse for a tour and that was what we were going to do.

Chloe and Claire had just made it back to the room, also. The entire staff worked the same schedule as Que. The twins were used to it but seemed exhausted, as well.

"How are you guys holding up?" Chloe asked, as she plopped down on the bed.

"We're okay," I replied.

"It was rough when we first started, but it will become easier," Claire said.

As we were talking, Kia walked past our room, and I jumped up to talk to her.

"Kia, can you tell Que that I need to speak with him?"

"Sure. About what?" Kia asked in a snippy tone.

"About our salary," I responded.

"Okay, I will let him know," Kia said, then walked away.

We had started rehearsal and Que still hadn't spoken with us about what we were getting paid. I didn't want to make the mistake of not taking care of business. I wanted to make sure we were taken care of.

I got back in the bed trying to get some needed rest, but once again, my sleep was interrupted. Kia woke me up an hour later saying Que wanted to talk to me. *Does he ever sleep?* I thought to myself. I was annoyed again, but eager to speak with him.

After quickly waking Raven up, we went to see Que in our pajamas. I had on a pink tank top and short set, and Raven was wearing a short tank top gown that stopped right below her butt. We didn't try to cover up or change our clothes because we were eager to discuss our salary.

As soon as we arrived on Que's floor, his security immediately stopped us. We told him we had an appointment with Que, and once he confirmed our visit, he signaled for us to enter. When we walked in, Que was sitting on the couch watching a movie as he popped some pills in his mouth and washed them down with water.

"Hey Que," Raven said.

"What's up, baby!" Que said, excited.

Raven walked right over and kissed him in the mouth. Once again, they acted like I was not in the room. They continued kissing until I interrupted them.

"Okay, that's enough," I said.

"What's wrong, Music?" Que asked.

"This is a business visit, not pleasure. I want to discuss my money, and then you guys can continue your freak show," I replied snippily.

"Calm down," Que said.

"I'm tired and want to go to sleep," I responded in a tone that clearly let him know I was upset.

"Okay, let's discuss your salary so I can get back to Raven's sexy ass," Que said, as he squeezed Raven's butt.

Raven knew she was putting me in a weird situation, but she didn't care. She had her eyes focused on Que's money and making him fall in love with her. The more I saw them kiss, the more uncomfortable I became.

"What is the weekly pay rate?" Raven asked Que.

"The dancers get paid five hundred dollars a week," he said.

"Five hundred dollars!" I yelled, completely taken aback.

"That's what I said," Que responded casually.

"We can't survive off of five hundred dollars a week," Raven said, offended.

"We got paid $2,500 a week with Slyy," I added.

Raven looked at me and frowned because she knew Slyy only paid us $2,000 a week. I frowned back at her because it was time for a raise.

"This is not Slyy's tour," he said.

"Que, I can't dance for that amount. I got bills to pay," I told him seriously.

I was totally confused, upset, and tired. I couldn't believe he would get us all the way to Atlanta and drop this low-salary bomb on us. Que knew we got paid a lot more than five hundred dollars a week on Slyy's tour, so I didn't know why he was trying to be so cheap.

"Music, what kind of bills do you have?" Que asked, frowning.

"The same type of bills you have. Rent, car note, and so on," I snapped.

"Watch your fucking tone," Que said.

"Sorry. I'm just shocked you're trying to pay us this low salary," I said, trying to control my temper and not be insubordinate.

"Get rid of your car note, cable, telephone, and other bills while you're on the road. You really don't need an apartment because you're going to be gone for almost a year," he told us.

"Are you serious?" Raven asked, surprised by his comment.

"Yes," Que said nonchalantly.

"I need to get paid $2,500 a week plus per diem or I can't dance for you," I said in a tone that expressed my disappointment.

"Music, you're going to leave my tour?" Que asked, shocked.

"This is business, nothing personal," I replied, using his words.

Que didn't respond; he just laughed. I didn't find it funny and stood my ground. I was prepared to leave his tour. Raven never said a word and looked at me trying to figure out if I was bluffing.

"Que, stop being so cheap," Raven said, trying to soften the atmosphere.

"My dancers get paid five hundred dollars a week, so why should I pay you more?" he asked.

"Because we're worth it and we're the best," Raven replied confidently.

"I got the best dancers now for five hundred dollars a week," Que said with a cocky tone.

"Well, I can't work with you," I responded unwillingly.

"We got paid five hundred dollars for per diem on Slyy's tour," Raven said, dissatisfied.

"Do you know how many dancers are willing to work for free to dance on my tour?" Que asked.

The room was suddenly quiet. There was nothing left to say. Que was standing his ground and we weren't taking pennies for our salary.

"Why did you think we would work for less?" I asked, trying to make sense out of the situation.

"I thought you would do this for me," Que said.

"We need to get our regular pay plus per diem. So, please do this for us," Raven begged.

"I can't pay you guys that amount and not the other dancers," he told us.

"They don't have to know. My salary doesn't have anything to do with them," I said.

"I don't want people to think I'm showing you favoritism," he responded.

"It's not favoritism. It's business!" Raven quickly said.

"You need to give us our money. I'm not playing," I said jokingly.

I walked over to Que and playfully grabbed him by his neck, pretending to choke him. Raven joined in, and we tackled him to the floor and pretended to fight him. We kept telling him to give us the money. Que thought our stunt was amusing and he was cracking up laughing.

"Damn, you guys are demanding!" Que yelled.

"Give us the money!" Raven shouted.

"Damn, I like this!" Que said in a sexual tone.

"You're nasty. Get off of me," I told him.

Raven never said a word and stayed on the floor with Que. I stood up and was done playing around because it didn't seem like the little wrestling match was working.

"Are you going to pay us what we're requesting?" I asked.

"What are you going to do for me?" Que asked with a devilish look.

"I'm going to do my job and dance my ass off!" I said.

Que looked at Raven and kissed her. Then he looked at me and smiled. Raven never said a word. She just seemed happy to be lying on the floor next to him.

"If you give me a kiss, I will pay you guys what you want," Que told me.

"What!" I said.

"Give me a kiss, and I'll pay you guys your pay rate," he repeated.

"Music, give him a kiss so we can get our money!" Raven yelled.

Here it was, the moment some people find themselves in. He wanted me to do something I didn't want to do, even though he would give me what I wanted. I knew he was not talking about a kiss on the cheek, and I was not prepared to kiss him on the mouth. He was my brother, my family, someone I had never gone down that road with. *Why in the hell is he asking me to do this?*

"Is it that hard to give me a kiss? I'm your boy!" Que said, then licked and puckered up his lips.

I've got to do what I've got to do to get paid, I thought to myself. I walked over to Que, kneeled down on the floor, and leaned over to do something I've never done with my friend. I knew it was wrong, but I wanted to dance on his tour. So, kissing him wouldn't be that bad. I headed directly for his lips, when he grabbed my face and immediately stopped me before our lips touched.

"Damn, Music, you were really going to kiss me!" Que said, shocked.

"I need my money!" I replied.

"You're acting desperate. Don't be one of those girls that would do anything to get paid," he told me.

"I was just going to peck you on the lips," I said, humiliated.

"You know a peck is not all I wanted. It always starts that way. You do something small, then that leads to something big. I'm shocked at you. Don't ever do that shit again!" Que snapped.

I was embarrassed that I allowed myself to become someone I said I would never be. The money was leading me and I found myself chasing it.

"Damn," I mumbled to myself.

"You should have learned from Slyy's tour. You let him abuse you because you were desperate to stay on his tour," Que said.

"Shut up," I replied, as tears instantly formed in my eyes.

That pain was still there and didn't seem like it was going anywhere. I didn't like him bringing it up because I was trying so hard to forget about it.

"Don't get upset. I'm just telling you the truth," Que said.

"That's enough," Raven told him.

"Music is my girl, and I'm going to let her know when she's fucking up," he replied.

"I'm going home!" I said.

"You're not going anywhere. I'm going to pay you guys your salary plus per diem. Damn!"

"Okay, but don't talk about that situation ever again!" I demanded.

"Calm down. I'm not trying to hurt you," Que assured me.

"I was about to kiss you. I'm desperate and messed up in the head!" I said, disappointed and ashamed by my actions.

"Stop stressing out. Just don't let that happen again. You're not that desperate chick that will do anything to make it," he said.

I was so upset with myself that I didn't know what to do. I was just happy I didn't do that in front of his dancers and staff.

"Don't mention this to anyone that I'm paying you guys more than the dancers," he told us.

"No problem," Raven said.

"Are you still going to give me a kiss?" Que asked, as he approached me while licking his lips slowly.

"No! Get away from me!" I shouted, forcefully pushing him away.

"Damn, you really need to loosen up! I'm just kidding around," he said, smiling.

Que grabbed me and playfully kissed me on the cheek. He kept kissing me until I fell on the couch. He was laughing so hard he started crying. This broke the ice and made me start laughing with him.

Raven and I left the studio pleased that we were getting what we deserved. I left wondering who the hell I had become.

CHAPTER 6

Time was going fast. A week had past already, and as usual, we were at rehearsal. It was two o'clock in the morning, and it didn't bother Raven and I anymore. We had adjusted to the weird schedule.

We had so many routines to learn that I was not looking forward to it. Que was very hands on and choreographed all of the routines. He was a great dancer and shockingly an amazing choreographer. He paid attention to every little detail and no mistakes got past him. He always demanded perfection.

Que wanted to make sure his tour was going to be the talk of the industry, so he continued to put pressure on us. His music was number one on the charts, and everyone wanted to meet him, interview him, or work with him. He was at the top of his game and had become very successful, especially since Slyy wasn't there to hold on to the number one spot. Now Que was number one, and he refused to give that position away to anyone.

I was starting to hate when he would come to our rehearsals because that meant we would be doing a routine over and over until he said it was just right. He didn't give Raven and I any slack, and I was starting to feel he was really making us work for our higher salary. He always gave us a hard time at rehearsals and made it obvious when we made a mistake.

Que finally was feeling some sympathy for working everyone so hard. We had been rehearsing for a week straight and were getting burned out, so he decided to give us a day off. We were much in need of a break. As quickly as I got excited about our day off, Que told us that we had to enjoy our day inside the house because we were not allowed to leave.

I was disappointed because I was looking forward to getting out and enjoying Atlanta. However, the house was so big with so much to do that we didn't get bored. Some people were watching movies in the theater, while some played basketball and went swimming. Raven and I called our families and friends to update them on our adventurous life on tour.

It was eight o'clock in the evening when Que ordered pizza for dinner. We tried to make the best out of feeling like we were prisoners, so we enjoyed the food. We ate pizza, drank beer, and got to know each other better. However, I was only interested in getting to know one person, and that was Johnny.

I hadn't seen Doug around the house and was kind of happy we didn't bump into each other. I knew I would have to talk to him sooner or later, but I think he was avoiding me just like I was trying to avoid him.

"What's up, Music?" Johnny asked, as he walked over to me.

"Hey Johnny," I said, blushing.

"This is some good pizza," Johnny commented, stuffing his mouth.

"It's good with lots of calories," I replied.

"I'm glad I don't have to watch my figure."

"The way Que is working us I could eat this whole pizza and burn it off at rehearsal in one night."

"How's everything going so far?" He asked me.

"Cool. I'm just getting used to this crazy schedule," I replied, then stuffed a slice of pizza in my mouth.

"It takes time to get used to it, but soon, it won't bother you," Johnny said, looking directly in my eyes.

"I can handle anything," I responded.

"You can handle anything?" Johnny said, curiously raising one eyebrow.

"Well, I try."

For a second, we just looked at each other. I wasn't sure if he was feeling me the same way I was feeling him, or if he was looking at me because I had pizza hanging from my mouth. I immediately wiped my mouth just in case.

Johnny stopped staring at me and continued to eat his pizza. There was definitely some sexual tension between us, and I was ready for it.

We continued talking and laughing like old friends. We didn't pay attention to anyone else in the room, even though everyone seemed to be doing their own thing. Suddenly, my perfect conversation was interrupted by Que.

At first, no one noticed when he and Doug walked in quietly and chilled in the back of the room. Once everyone saw him, they begin to acknowledge him. I didn't move and continued talking to Johnny. I still looked at Que as my friend, and I wasn't impressed by him like everyone else. Sure, he was my boss, but he wasn't a superstar to me. Besides, it was my day off; I was off the clock.

Raven never acknowledged him either. She sat in her seat and continued to eat her pizza until Que walked over to her and started a conversation. He never stopped looking around the room while talking to her.

"It's time for rehearsal!" Que stood up and announced.

"Rehearsal!" everyone said in unison, surprised.

"I thought this was our day off?" Raven asked.

No one else dared to question Que about having to rehearse, but it didn't stop Raven from asking.

"My show is not where it needs to be, so you guys need to rehearse," he said.

"This is senseless," Johnny whispered to me.

"See you guys in ten minutes," Que said, than left the room abruptly.

I looked over at Raven, who twisted her lips disapprovingly at his command. I couldn't figure Que out and didn't understand why we couldn't have one day off. It seemed like he saw everyone having a good time and he didn't like it.

"I will talk to you later," I told Johnny.

"See you later," he said, as he stood up to give me a hug.

I was just getting to know Johnny and didn't want to go to rehearsal. When he gave me an extra long hug, I didn't want to let go of him. I felt like he wanted to kiss me, but he moved away fast.

Everyone dragged themselves back to their room to get changed for rehearsals. Our personal assistant, Macy, was right on our heels, following us to make sure we were following instructions.

"Once you're dressed, wait in your rooms. I will let you know when Que is ready for you," Macy told us.

"Shit! I'm really tired of being locked in this house and waiting around all the time!" Raven screamed. "I can't take this. All we're doing is rehearsing and sleeping, and this is boring. I need to go out. I need to have sex!"

"Have sex with Que," I said, laughing.

"We're not on that level yet. I'm still trying to figure him out," Raven replied.

"There's always masturbation," I said, laughing some more.

"I don't masturbate. I need a real person. I'm going to start fucking anyone that walks by me," Raven said, joining me laughing.

"Just don't try to fuck me."

"Now you know you're not my type, but I will fuck one of these men running around this house," Raven whispered.

"Chill out."

"Girl, I can't keep tying this hard-ass dick down. I'm horny!"

"I'm horny, too," I said, playfully hitting her on the legs.

"You better stop touching me before I fuck you," Raven said, then fell on the floor laughing.

"You really need to stop playing around. Save all that for Que," I said.

"He's making me not like him," Raven responded.

"We have a long time to deal with this mess," I reminded her.

"I'm happy we're getting paid the salary we want, because I couldn't deal with this if we weren't," Raven said.

"Let's just suck it up and deal with it, because we can't leave this tour no matter what is going on. Once this tour is done, our nightmare of going to jail will be over."

"You're right," Raven agreed. "But now that I think about it, jail might be a good thing."

"What!" I said, stunned.

"At least they're having sex in jail, and right now, I need to be fucked or fucking somebody," Raven stated jokingly.

"How can you crack jokes?" I asked.

"I have to make jokes, because if I don't, I'll go crazy," Raven said.

"I need a man!" I yelled playfully.

"I saw you talking to Johnny," Raven said.

"I like him a lot," I confessed.

"Que stopped your conversation with Johnny," Raven said, laughing.

"He's a hater," I said, smiling.

An hour and a half had passed, and we were still waiting in our room. Everyone had moved to the recreation room and were either watching television or falling asleep. This tour was either going to stress me completely out or make me a very patient person.

"Okay, ladies. Que is ready for you guys to start rehearsing," Macy announced.

Just like the trained puppies we had become, we got up and headed for the dance studio. Que was training us to jump at his every beck and call. The only thing we hadn't asked yet was how high.

CHAPTER 7

Rehearsals were taking a toll on our bodies, and soaking in the tub was not helping our aching bones. Our bodies needed a break. I was afraid my body was going to shut down soon. I was mentally and physically drained. All these impromptu rehearsals were killing me. Que worked us extra hard. The only thing we had time to do was rehearse, sleep, shower, eat and then start all over again the next day.

"Can you please call your mother? Because now she is ringing my cell phone off the hook," Raven said, annoyed.

"I can't deal with her right now," I said.

"Do you want me to answer her call?" Raven asked.

"No, just ignore all her calls. I'll talk to her when I'm ready," I replied as we headed to rehearsal.

When we walked into the dance studio, we saw Que and Doug sitting front and center. This made me a little uncomfortable because I hadn't spoken to Doug in years, and it felt strange being in the same room with him watching me.

"Are you going to be okay being around Doug?" Raven asked.

"Yeah, I'm cool. I'm over him," I said.

"That's good, because that would have been very uncomfortable being on the tour with his cheating ass," Raven responded with relief. "I hear that Doug has been very busy," she added, smirking.

"Busy doing what?" I asked.

"He's been busy sleeping with every woman on this tour. I heard he slept with all the dancers, and he's currently dating Sexy."

"Wow! He has been busy. Do they know I use to date him?"

"Unfortunately, they know," Raven said.

"Damn," I said, annoyed. "That explains why Sexy has been looking at me strange."

"You want me to say something to her? You know I will slap the hell out of her," Raven said, upset.

"No, I will handle it. I'm going to have a talk with her. I don't want her stressing over me. If Doug has been busy, then you know Que has been very busy, too," I replied.

"Yes, I heard that also. He's sleeping with some of the dancers, but he hasn't slept with me, you, or Flex," Raven informed me.

"You know we won't ever be sleeping together, but you know he's working on sleeping with you and Flex," I said sarcastically.

"I don't mind sleeping with him because I don't want to be his girlfriend like the rest of them. I just want his money!" Raven replied.

"I see how you act around him. You want more than his money. You really like him."

"You're right. I do like him," Raven admitted. "I hope he can act right so we can be in a relationship."

"I can tell Que really likes you, too," I said.

"How?" she asked.

"He's being distant towards you. When we were younger, that's how I knew he liked a girl. I think he's really into you."

"The feeling is mutual," Raven said, smiling.

"There's only one thing in the way," I told her.

"What?"

"The one eyed snake," I said, laughing.

"That might not be a problem," Raven replied.

"Are you trying to say Que is gay?" I asked.

"No. I just haven't figured him out yet," Raven said.

"Que doesn't sleep with men. He loves women too much."

"If I ever feel the insides of Que, you will be the first to know," Raven responded sassily.

"Oh God! This is a messy situation," I said, disgusted.

"Why?"

"Everyone on this tour has had sex with each other. I smell trouble," I said, shaking my head.

"I haven't slept with anyone yet," Raven told me, smiling.

"You're trying to sleep with Que, but he's not going to sleep with you. Trust me, I know my friend," I said, trying to convince Raven.

"We'll see."

"Raven, you better be careful with trying to turn straight men gay," I warned her.

"I never turn men gay. They were already gay before they met me," she said.

"You're a hot mess."

"Life is messy," Raven said.

Que interrupted our conversation and told everyone to get in position for the first song of the tour. Before doing so, Sexy walked straight up to Doug and kissed him on the lips. I felt like she was trying to prove a point to me. Only she didn't have to prove that point to me because I didn't care.

After we were in position, Que started the music. I must say when you are threatened to do something right, you make a point to be impeccable.

Que was waiting for us to miss a step. Even though we did the routine perfectly, he still complained that we were not feeling the music. He made us do it over and over again. Doug never said a word. He just sat, watched, and agreed with everything Que had to say.

"You guys need to be low to the floor when you do that move. Do it again!" Que shouted.

He started the music again and we started over. We tried to get as low to the floor as possible. We had done this same routine over ten times, and he still was not happy with our performance.

"You guys look crazy being that low to the floor. Do it again!" Que yelled.

I was going crazy trying to understand what he wanted us to do. One minute, he told us to get low to the floor, and the next minute, he said we were too low to the floor. He was starting to piss me off.

I was so sick of doing the same routine over and over again. He was not making any sense, and it seemed that he enjoyed making us repeat the routine. I couldn't take it anymore, and I wanted to get some clarification on what he wanted from us.

"You guys look horrible. What the hell is going on?" Que shouted.

No one said a word. I just looked at Que like he was crazy.

"I can find better dancers! You're all fired!" Que yelled and walked out of the room.

"What!" I said out loud.

"What is going on?" Raven asked.

"I guess we're fired," Swagg said unhappily.

"Are you serious?" I asked.

"He has fired us before," Swagg said in a laidback demeanor.

"What is this all about?" I asked, confused.

"I'm so tired this silliness," Raven said, upset.

"What did you guys do when he fired you before?" I inquired.

"We have to give him time," Swagg said.

"We have to kiss his butt," Sexy blurted out.

"Let's go to the room and make a plan to get our job back," Sexy said.

"Are you kidding me?" Raven asked.

"Yeah, you have to do it," Swagg said.

"Why do you guys put up with this?" I asked.

"This is the best tour to be a part of. Dancers are dying to work with Que, and we want our jobs," Swagg replied.

"We have to do this together. He will only accept it as a group," Sexy said.

"Please, Music and Raven, we need you guys," Swagg pleaded.

Raven and I never said a word. Instead, we followed them back to their room to make a plan to get our jobs back. I still was in shock that we were fired. I couldn't believe Que was serious. We watched as the dancers tried to come up with a plan, but we couldn't join in with them because we thought it was absurd. It was amusing to me, and I was curious to see what was going to happen.

"I'm ready to leave," I whispered to Raven.

"You've dealt with worse," Raven said.

"Yeah, but this is just stupid," I said.

"We can't leave this tour, remember? Just deal with it so I can get my money," Raven told me.

"Oh, this is for you?" I asked.

"No, it's for the both of us. It's not that bad," Raven said.

"Oh, it's bad. We are grown ass women playing these childish games," I said.

"I'm going to take all his money for putting us through this," Raven whispered.

Raven was right; it could have been worse. I definitely had dealt with worse situations.

"Okay, I will deal with this," I said, giving in.

"Good. Now let's get a plan to get our jobs back. This is so stupid it should be fun. Let's be dumb asses like the rest of them. I always wanted to know what it felt like to act stupid," Raven said, laughing.

We still couldn't come up with a plan to get our jobs back, so we let the dancers think of one. They decided to do what they had done before, which was to give Que a strip show and then tell him how much he was appreciated. It was the dumbest thing I've ever agreed to do in my life. Well, one of the dumbest thing. I felt like we were belittling ourselves in the name of our job and Que's ego. But since he wasn't beating my ass or raping me, I considered it.

I tried to call Que on his cell phone, hoping we could laugh at this situation, but he never answered. After several phone calls and no answer, I realized he was really upset.

Swagg suggested we also make his favorite lemon cake and give it to him when we stripped for him. Raven and I couldn't believe they were really serious, but by the looks on their faces, I knew they truly wanted their jobs back and would do anything to be rehired.

"Are you really going to do a striptease for Que?" I asked Raven.

"Yes, and so are you. So, get to stripping, bitch," Raven said, laughing.

Two hours later, we took the cake to the recording studio where Que was working on a new song. His security immediately stopped us at the door. Swagg told security that we really needed to speak with Que, and security told us to wait while he went into the recording studio. We waited like little puppies waiting to be fed.

Thirty minutes later, security came back out and told us that Que would speak to us. He told us to wait in the dance studio for him. Swagg and the other dancers were excited that Que was willing to talk to us and they appeared to be relieved.

Raven and I still felt stupid by the whole situation. We were waiting to see how this was going to play out. We had never experienced anything so childish and ridiculous that this had become entertaining to us.

Feeling embarrassed and degraded, Raven and I followed the dancers into the dance studio. We were trying to be a part of the crew, get our jobs back, and get Raven her money, so we waited patiently with them.

"You better dance like you're swinging from a pole," Raven said teasingly.

"Let's just get this over with," I said annoyed.

"I don't know about the rest of you, but I'm going to get paid for my strip-tease," Raven said.

"Just remember we don't have to get naked," I told her.

Although it felt strange to be giving my friend a striptease in front of people, it also felt even stranger to dance with no makeup on and no sexy clothing. We had on fitted workout shorts and tank tops with gym shoes. This felt wrong.

After three hours of waiting for Que, he finally walked into the dance studio looking just as exhausted as we were. It was seven o'clock in the morning, and I was sleeping like a baby. Raven poked me in the side to let me know that Que and Doug were in the room.

Swagg took the lead and started talking, while Que pulled up a chair and sat down.

"Que, we're so sorry for not understanding your creation. We really want to be here and we apologize. We even baked your favorite cake and prepared a striptease for you just the way you like it. Please give us our jobs back," Swagg begged like child.

I looked at her and frowned. I couldn't believe she was begging him like that. It was embarrassing, and I didn't want any part of it. I didn't know what type of striptease he liked. I felt like they were setting Raven and I up for failure. Raven poked me in the side because she was just as flabbergasted as I was. I couldn't wait until this was all over.

Que never commented. He just waited patiently in the chair for us to continue begging.

"We got the routine and we know what you want. We just needed to get our heads right. We will make you proud," Swagg said.

Que looked like he was unmoved by Swagg's speech.

"Does everyone feel this way?" Que asked softly, as he reached for the cake and grabbed a large chunk from the center with his hand.

"Yes, everyone feels the same. We're all sorry for our actions," Swagg said, trying to sound sincere.

"Well, I need to hear an apology from everyone," he replied, while putting more cake in his mouth. He looked at Doug and offered him a piece, but he declined.

I wanted to get up and walk out of the room. I couldn't believe he was still allowing this to continue. I could tell Swagg was used to dealing with Que by the tone of her voice. Since Raven and I were the new dancers, I knew he particularly wanted to hear it from us.

All the dancers started telling Que how sorry they were and how they wanted to work with him. When it was time for Raven and I to say something, we were at a loss for words.

"Do you have anything to say?" Que asked, looking directly at me.

I looked at him and hesitated for a moment. He looked at me with an irritated expression and closed his eyes slightly while waiting for me to say something.

"I'm sorry, Que," I said, not knowing what I was sorry for.

"That's it?" He asked, aggravated.

"I'm sorry for not giving you what you wanted. I really want to dance on tour with you. Please forgive me," I said, hoping that was enough for him.

Que never said a word and continued eating his cake. Then he quickly turned and looked at Raven, who spoke fast to get it over with.

"Que, you know I love you, and I would never do anything to hurt you. I'm sorry for fucking up. Tell me what to do to make it better," Raven said sincerely.

It appeared that Que loved her answer because he quickly smiled. Doug never said a word. He just continued sitting there enjoying every minute of it.

"We can do the strip tease for you," Swagg said with a sexy, seductive tone.

"I'm a little tired right now and want to go to bed, so maybe later," he told her.

Relieved, I whispered, "Thank God," not knowing Que and everyone else heard me.

"Music, you didn't want to do the striptease for me?" He asked.

"I didn't say that," I responded.

"What are you saying?" Que said, frowning as he continued eating the cake.

"I was going to do it," I said softly.

Que knew I didn't want to do the striptease for him, and now everyone else in the room knew it, also. He didn't like that the attention was now on me; he was fuming inside. He looked at me like he was deeply thinking of something.

"Oh, you're going to give me my striptease," Que said.

I didn't dare respond to him. I knew he hated when he felt like you were talking back to him, and I knew he was not happy with me at that present time. I was hoping I could speak with him later to clear the air.

"You guys need to give me what I want all the time. Don't fuck up my show. Do what I tell you to do," Que snapped.

He took a deep breath, ate more cake, and then continued speaking.

"I accept your apology. Now get back to work," he said.

"Now?" Raven asked.

"Yes, now! You want your damn job back, right?" Que asked.

"Yes," Raven replied, perplexed by the tone of his voice.

"You missed rehearsals today, so you have to make that day up. You got any other questions, Raven?" Que asked, fuming because he didn't like Raven questioning him in front of everyone.

"No," she said softly, while putting her head down.

Raven was truly upset with him embarrassing her in front of everyone. She didn't know who he was, but she knew if he wanted to get with her, he would have to stop humiliating her in front of the other dancers. She was the head bitch, and he needed to learn that quickly.

"If you want your job back, start rehearsing now!" Que shouted and then left the room.

"I'm in hell!" I said out loud once the door closed.

"I don't know how you guys deal with this," Raven told the other dancers.

"You deal with it by putting your pride to the side. After that, it doesn't bother you. You just do what you have to do and move on," Swagg replied.

"Let me see the first number of the show. I will be back in ten minutes," Que said, as he stuck his head in the door.

We didn't waste any time rehearsing. Ten minutes later, the doors to the dance studio opened. Que, Doug, and five other men entered the room. We kept rehearsing until Que told us to stop.

"Let me see the first song of the show," Que said seriously.

His guests took a seat and waited for the show. We didn't know who the guests were, but they looked very important and some of them looked familiar. Knowing Que, they probably were reporters he respected and music moguls he trusted. This way, he could have them critique his show and spread the word about how great it was going to be.

The music started and we did the routine like we were performing in front of millions of people. Que had a look on his face that told us that he was not impressed with our performance. He made us do the routine three times.

By then, we were extremely tired and hoping he didn't tell us to do it again. There was no way we could do the routine for the fourth time perfectly and with energy. The first song was so high impact that we were trying to catch our breath discreetly.

"You guys are not low enough! We've been through this before. Now get low, and your ass better touch the floor!" Que shouted.

I couldn't believe he was starting this again. It was obvious we couldn't please him and he didn't know what he wanted.

"Let me see you do that move!" Que yelled.

The music started and we got as low to the floor as we could, trying to follow his directions. We knew we were not going to get it correct, so we prepared to be embarrassed in front of his guests. Que was definitely about to make a scene.

"Can you understand English?" Que yelled.

We didn't dare answer him. We remained quiet and looked directly at him while trying to swallow our pride.

"I'm going to sit on the floor, and I want you guys to get as low as I am at eye level. I want you to do that dance move across the room until you get directly in front of my face and I tell you to stop," Que said, as he sat on the floor irritated.

"You guys are going to get this right. Start from the other side of the room, one at a time," Que demanded.

The music started and my heart dropped. He was completely embarrassing us and breaking us down. I just prayed that he didn't tell me to do the dance move first. It was very hard to open your legs, squat so low that your butt was almost touching the floor, shake the top part of your body continuously, and walk across the room while doing it. I had to get myself together.

"Sexy, you're first, and you better rock that move," Que said, pointing to her.

Sexy looked at me, still trying to compete and prove a point. She was jealous that I used to date Doug, and she was having a hard time with me being around him. I was so tired of her constant stares and smart remarks that I knew I needed to say something to her before things really got out of hand.

After she stopped looking at me, she started doing the dance move, trying to get as low to the floor as possible. As soon as she reached the middle of the room, Que stopped her and told her to go back.

"Do it again. You're not low enough. If you're not low enough, you're going to start over and keep doing it until you get it right," he told her.

Sexy started over again. This time, she stayed focused and made it across the room directly in front of Que's face. She kept doing the move in front of him, and he got so close to her face that their noses were touching. She never took her eyes off of him, and he finally told her to stop.

"That's how you do it! Swagg, you're next, and if you fuck up, you're going to do it again!"

We were all so scared and didn't want to do the move over. We tried to stay focused and prepared to do it only one time. Swagg did the move with no problem, and he didn't ask her to repeat it. He pointed at Raven next.

Raven started out doing the move, and as soon as she took two steps, he told her to do it again. She never even made it to the middle of the floor. Que continued telling her to do it again until she finally became frustrated. It showed on her face and she hesitated to do it again.

"You don't want to do the move anymore?" Que asked.

Raven never responded.

"Do you hear me, Raven?" Que asked, aggravated.

"I heard you," Raven replied.

"Do the fucking move again or get the fuck out!" Que shouted, looking directly at her.

Raven was so confused by his treatment. One minute, he was kissing her, and now he was telling her to get the fuck out in front of everyone. She didn't know how to handle the situation, so she just got lower to the floor and did the move again. She finally made it across the floor and was staring directly in Que's face. He continued to let her do the move in front of him as he got closer to her face like he was going to kiss her.

"You better not stop doing the move! Keep dancing!" Que yelled.

Raven never stopped. She kept squatting low to the floor, trying her best to do it correctly. Her legs started shaking and tears were running down her face. She was in pain, but she was not going to let Que defeat her.

"You're a trooper. You can stop," Que said, amazed at Raven's strength.

Raven fell to the floor and looked at him with tears running down her face. She felt overwhelmed, puzzled, and mistreated.

"You're next, Music," Que said, pointing at me.

I was so terrified that I wanted to run out of the room. I knew he was going to make a fool out of me just like he had done Raven. I took a deep breath, squatted as low as I could, and let my butt sweep the floor.

I went into a trance and was determine to give him what he wanted. I was not going to let my pride get in the way because his guests were watching. I was determined to only do the dance move one time. I had paid attention to the other dancers that went before me and tried to study everything he said they were doing wrong so I wouldn't make the same mistakes.

I hit the floor doing the move with a vengeance. I had to let everything inside of me go. Still focused, I made it to the middle of the floor, and Que never said a word. I was looking directly at him, while he stared back at me with a scowl on his face.

I made it across the room and directly in front of his face. That's when he tried to break my pride down. He kept telling me to keep going while he got closer to my face. He was so close to me that I could smell the spearmint gum he was chewing. I looked directly in his eyes and continued to stay focused.

My legs started shaking and my cheeks tightened. Que looked at me like he was a sergeant in the army and he was there to break me in. He kept frowning while slowly leaning his head from side to side. After a minute of continuously doing the move, my legs gave out and I fell to the floor. I was tired and grabbed my legs in pain.

"That's how you hang in there, baby!" Que said, energized.

I lay on the floor looking up at him and wanting to slap the hell out of him. He never even tried to help me up. He immediately looked at Heat and told her that she was next. I scooted myself out of the way and continued to lie on the floor in pain. I didn't even try to talk to Raven because we both were in pain and feeling degraded. We didn't have any words to say at that moment to each other.

Heat started and finished the course like a professional. He didn't have one bad thing to say to her and didn't even make her continue doing the move once she reached him. Next, he pointed to Flex and told her to start dancing. He stopped her a few times, looking like he was disgusted with her performance.

"Now that you guys understand what I want, let me see the first routine of the show again," Que told us.

I cringed at the thought of doing the routine again, and by the looks of the other dancers, they felt the same way. My eyes filled with tears as I got into position. Que sat down next to his guests and waited for us to begin. As soon as we started our routine, Que started frowning, showing that he was not happy with what we were doing.

He stood up, grabbed his chair, and threw it directly at us. We quickly jumped out of the way. His guests never moved and appeared to be used to his sudden temper tantrums. The look on my face showed that I thought he had lost his mind.

"Sweets, you're fucking up!" Que shouted. "Do it again!"

We jumped back into position, the music started, and we began the routine over again. I tried my best to continue giving a hundred percent, but my body was tired and hurting in places I didn't know I could have pain. I looked at Raven, who looked like she was struggling just like I was.

"Sweets, you're still messing up steps. Everyone sit down except Sweets. Do it alone," Que demanded.

I felt sorry for Sweets, but I was happy we got an opportunity to sit down. My legs were still sore and getting stiff. Sweets did the routine alone and only messed up one time. I thought she did a good job considering the pressure and being tired from doing it so many times.

"You fucked up again! Sweets, you're fired!" Que said.

"Why?" Sweets asked, shocked.

"I told you not to mess up a step and you did," Que told her.

"I only missed one step. I know the routine. I'm just tired," Sweets pleaded.

"No excuses. You got to go," he said nonchalantly.

"Are you serious?" Sweets asked.

"Goodbye, Sweets."

"Please let me try again," Sweets begged.

"Stop begging because that's not sexy. You're fired!" Que said.

Surprisingly, while security escorted Sweets out of the room, she didn't put up a fuss. Honestly, she looked like she was tired of dealing with Que and was ready to go home.

We all looked on in distress. Que was no joke. We had worked for him almost a month, and he had already fired all of us once. It was getting crazier every day. I didn't want to know what would happen next.

"Go get some rest and be ready for rehearsal tonight," Que told us, as he walked out of the room with his guests following behind him.

It took us only a few seconds to leave the room. Raven and I were so confused, tired, and humiliated that we didn't say a word to each other. There was nothing to discuss about what had just happened. We were both baffled and surprised at all the drama that continued to go on.

"I hate this!" Raven yelled, as we both laughed while heading to our room.

CHAPTER 8

My body was aching from rehearsal and I was mentally drained. I took a long hot shower, put on some comfortable pajamas, and jumped in the bed. Raven was in the bed before I could get in.

"Are you going to talk to Sexy?" Raven asked, yawning.

"Yeah, I'm going to talk to her soon," I replied.

"You see how she's been looking at you. I'm going to hurt her if she looks at me funny again," Raven said, pretending to hit someone.

"She shouldn't be threatened by me because I don't want Doug. I want Johnny," I said, smiling.

"Well, get her straight before I do."

"I'll talk to her tomorrow," I told her.

"Good night," Raven said before closing her eyes.

Thirty minutes later, I was still lying in bed staring at the ceiling. As tired as I was, I couldn't go to sleep. Chloe and Claire had the room singing as they snored in harmony. Raven was sound asleep looking like a little baby. Even when she was sleeping, she looked like a pretty woman.

Unable to sleep, I decided to get up and go in the recreation room to watch television, hoping that would make me sleepy. I grabbed a blanket and pillow, and as soon as I walked into the room, I saw Sexy sitting on the couch watching television. She was unable to sleep, also. When I saw her, I immediately turned around and headed back to the bedroom.

"You don't have to leave on my account," Sexy said.

"I didn't want to disturb you," I responded.

"You're not disturbing me. This room is for everyone. Have a seat."

As friendly as she was being, I still sensed a little animosity in her voice. I felt like she didn't want me to be there as much as I didn't want to be in the room with her.

"What are you watching?" I asked, trying to make conversation.

"The news because nothing else is on," she said, trying to sound sociable.

I knew this was the perfect time to talk to her since we were alone and able to have a private conversation. Yes, it was perfect timing, but I didn't feel like being bothered. I was tired and just wanted to go to sleep.

"I think we should talk," I finally said.

"Talk about what?" She asked.

"I wanted to talk to you woman-to-woman. I feel the negative vibes you're giving me, and I know it's because I've dated Doug," I said, sounding sincere as possible.

"Music, I don't have a problem with you," Sexy replied, trying to convince me.

I ignored her response and continued. "Doug and I are not a couple anymore and have not been for years. I just want you to know that I don't want him. So, you don't need to feel intimidated by me. I know Doug has dated everyone in this house except Raven, and that has to be hard for you to deal with. I just don't want you to be worried about me. If I'm making you uncomfortable in any way, please let me know."

"I'm cool," Sexy said unenthusiastically.

"If you don't like me, that's cool. But don't have a problem with me because I used to date your man." I said.

Sexy looked at me and took a deep breath. I didn't know what she was thinking, but she looked like she was trying to figure something out.

"I'm stunned you're telling me this," she finally said.

"Why?" I asked.

"Because most women wouldn't say anything. I don't know if you're telling the truth or not, but I like the effort you're giving," she said.

"I can respect that. You don't know me, but time will show you the truth. I don't want him. Been there done that. Not interested anymore," I told her.

"It is hard being around all the women my boyfriend has slept with. I'm not sure if he is still messing around with them," she stated sadly.

"Well, that's something you shouldn't worry about unless he gives you a reason. Don't stress out," I said, trying to comfort her.

"When I heard you were coming, I wasn't happy. Doug told me that you were the one he wanted to marry. You being here did make me uncomfortable," she confessed.

"Thanks for being honest. I can understand why you felt that way. This is a strange situation, and I know it's hard for you."

"Doug and Que have dated everyone on this tour. They are the biggest dogs around," she informed me.

"So why are you dating Doug?"

"The same reason he's dating me; for the sex. Once I find me a good man, Doug will be history," she said.

I didn't know why she was telling me this information, but I really didn't care. I felt like she was trying to see if I would run back and tell Doug. If so, she was wasting her time.

"Do your thang, girl."

"You're pretty cool," Sexy said, amazed.

"Thanks. Now you don't have to worry about me trying to take your man," I said, smiling.

"I guess not," Sexy responded, smiling back at me.

Even though I felt like we had made peace between each other, I knew we were still going to have problems. I knew it wasn't that easy to clear up the situation, and I was going to watch her like a hawk. Sexy was that type of woman you definitely couldn't trust or believe anything she said. I knew her type all too well. I would never trust her, but I was happy we could pretend to be civilized with each other.

We finished talking and started watching television until we both fell asleep on the couch. The next day, I woke up and looked at Sexy, who was still asleep on the couch. Trying not to wake her, I got up quietly and went to my bedroom. Raven was just waking up and getting out of the bed.

"Where were you all night, hoe?" Raven asked.

"I slept on the couch in the recreation room," I said, throwing a pillow at her.

"Why?"

"I couldn't sleep, so I went to watch television and ended up falling asleep. Sexy was in there and I had that talk with her," I said.

"How did it go?" Raven asked, extremely curious.

"It went good. I told her how I felt and she appreciated it," I replied.

"You know she's full of shit," Raven said, twisting her lips.

"I know, but she knows how I feel. Hopefully, I won't get the funky looks now."

"I'm glad you guys talked, but you know not to trust her, right? Now get dressed so we can discuss our plan," Raven said.

"What plan?" I asked.

"You know what I'm talking about. The operation called 'Get Que's Money Fast'. He's a hard person to figure out, and with him treating me like crap, it's not working for me. I need him on my team fast."

"I don't want any parts of your plan. You're all alone on this one," I told her.

"I knew you were going to say that. You're such a square," Raven said, laughing.

"Shut the fuck up!"

"Wow, you're using such vulgar words. I know you've been hanging around Que too long, because fuck is his favorite word. I just wish he would stop saying it and start doing it to me," Raven said.

"You are so crazy," I said, laughing.

"I'll meet you at rehearsal. I'm going to try to see what Que is up to," she said and then walked out of the room.

Another day of rehearsals and we were feeling tired, upset, sore, drained, frustrated, hot, and overwhelmed. It was a normal day and we were on our usual schedule. Rehearsals and Que's craziness were kicking my butt.

CHAPTER 9

I was now on Que's strenuous work schedule and I didn't have to use an alarm clock to wake up anymore. Raven and I started waking up a couple of hours before rehearsal so we could relax, eat, and pretend we were living a normal life.

Like clockwork, I was up two hours before rehearsal, and Raven was already up and in the shower. Not wanting to waste any of the time I had set aside for my two-hour break, I rushed in the bathroom once I heard the water stop.

After showering, I put on cotton boy shorts, a fitted t-shirt, and socks to relax in because there was no need to put on my designer clothes to walk around the house in for two hours. I still kept it sexy with some lace thong underwear and a spray of my soft-scented perfume.

It actually felt good not to dress up or put make-up on. I was starting to get used to the clean casual look, but missed getting dolled up. Raven on the other hand hated every minute of it. Even though she looked pretty without make-up and still continued to look like a woman, she felt naked and struggled daily. She put on mascara and eye liner everyday just to feel normal and there were some days I did the same.

It's hard not wearing make-up when you are used to wearing it every day. We had an image to uphold and we couldn't just look a hot mess daily. A little make-up did the trick and made us feel like our usual self and kept us looking cute.

We had learned how to make the two hours work for us and get things done. We still had to take care of our bills at home and take care of ourselves. Since we couldn't leave the house, we paid our bills online, did our own hair, waxed our eyebrows, and gave ourselves manicures, pedicures, and facials. Even though we didn't have to look well put together, we couldn't just let ourselves go.

Once a week, Raven and I had a pamper day before rehearsals. The other dancers looked at us wondering why we were pampering ourselves. No matter what, we were determined to keep our bodies looking great.

I couldn't wait to get to the kitchen to get something to eat because I was hungry. With all the exhausting rehearsals, I had been eating more and thankfully not gaining any weight, only losing pounds. Que made sure the two huge refrigerators were always fully stocked with the type of food we requested. He also hired a chef to prepare our meals three times a week.

It was nice being able to have food cooked for us. Even when the chef wasn't there, he left pre-made food in the refrigerator for everyone. He made sure the food was always cooked healthy and fat-free, but sometimes, I just needed something fattening like cake, cookies, and cheeseburgers.

"Hurry up, Raven, so we can get something to eat," I said.

"I have a taste for some ice cream," she replied.

"I see you're craving sweets, too," I said, while putting on some lotion.

"I always crave sweets when it's that time of the month," Raven said.

"I hate that because I always gain two to three extra pounds. Wait a minute! What are you talking about? You don't have a period," I said, laughing while shaking my head.

"All women have a period, Music! That is what you do with these," she said, then pulled a tampon out of her luggage and waved it in the air.

"Why do you have those?" I asked, cracking up laughing.

"The same reason you have them," Raven said, joining me in laughing.

"Girl, you are too much!"

"I'm a woman having a period. What's so strange about that?" Raven asked.

"You've officially lost your mind. Come on so we can get something to eat," I said, still shaking my head.

Once we got to the kitchen, we noticed everyone had the same cravings we did. They were devouring all the sweets in the kitchen. As soon as we filled our plates with salad, salmon, and potatoes, we joined them to satisfy our sweet tooth. I ate my salmon and salad and had just put a spoonful of strawberry cheesecake in my mouth, when Macy walked in the kitchen.

"Que wants to see you, Music," she said.

"Okay. Do I have time to finish my dessert?" I asked.

"No, he wants to see you now."

"What is this about?" I asked Raven.

"I don't know, but I can't wait for you to tell me," Raven said, while stuffing chocolate ice cream in her mouth.

"I'll be back," I told her.

"Whatever it is just remember we can't leave this tour. So, just deal with whatever he is serving. Don't let him get to you," Raven said, trying to keep me strong.

I followed Macy to Que's bedroom and she instructed me to walk right in. When I opened Que's bedroom door, he was sitting on a large black suede comfortable-looking chair positioned right in front of his bed watching the huge flat-screen television mounted on the wall. The familiar smell of Que's favorite vanilla-scented candles escaped the room as soon as the door opened. He turned around in the chair when he heard me come in.

"What's up, Que?" I asked, closing the door behind me. I didn't know how to act around him anymore because he was a stranger to me. So, I was now nervous to be around my own friend.

"What's up, Music. Have a seat," he said, motioning for me to sit on the edge of his large, king-size plush bed. "So, how are you doing?" He asked, as he swiveled the chair around and looked directly at me.

"I'm good. Why?"

"I'm just checking on my girl. I want to make sure you're handling things," Que said seriously.

"You're rough on us, but I can handle it. At least these rehearsals are keeping my mind off of things," I replied.

"I'm glad you can handle everything. I told you that if we keep working, we will soon forget and everything will be over," Que said, nodding his head at me.

"Yeah, you were right," I agreed.

"How do you like the choreography for my tour?" Que asked.

"Everything is great. You've always been a great dancer, but I didn't know you were a choreographer. You're actually really good. The show is going to be hot."

"I got skills," he said proudly.

"I can't wait for the tour to start," I said.

"Do you trust me?" Que inquired.

"Huh?" I asked, confused by the switch of conversation.

"Do you trust me?" He repeated.

"Yes, I trust you. You're my boy," I said, wondering where he was going with this.

"I know that I can trust you with our little secret," Que continued, lowering his voice as he pushed the chair closer to me.

"Your secret is safe with me," I stated softly, assuring him.

"Good because your trust is my freedom."

"Don't worry about that. I won't let anything happen to you. I have always had your back, and it won't change now," I said seriously.

"Thanks, Music. I'm glad I can trust you," Que said, relieved.

"Your word is my freedom, also. I have just as much to lose as you do. So, I need to make sure you can keep the secret, too," I told him.

"No doubt. I got you," he said, then leaned in and gave me a hug.

We hugged each other like we were scared to death, not knowing what was going to happen. We hugged, sealing our trust and knowing we needed each other.

"Let's play a little trust game," Que said, as he quickly pulled away from me.

"I never knew you liked playing so many games. I'm really sick of this," I said.

"Well, you need to show me that you trust me."

"Come on, Que. I'm tired of all this crazy stuff," I said, annoyed.

"This will be your last initiation, and this is the most important one. Can you handle it?" Que said, smirking.

"What is it?" I asked, rolling my eyes at him.

"Put this blindfold on," he told me, while handing me a black scarf.

Wanting to get whatever it was he had planned over with, I snatched the scarf from him and wrapped it around my eyes. Que made sure I couldn't see out of the blindfold.

"Don't tickle me. You know how I hate that," I said.

"I'm not going to tickle you. I'm not even going to touch you," he said.

"Good. Now hurry up with this little trust game," I said.

"Lean back on the bed," Que instructed me.

"What?"

"No talking. Just do what I tell you to do and this initiation will be over fast," he demanded.

All I could hear was Raven's voice telling me to do whatever needed to be done to stay on the tour. Que was really testing me, though, and I wasn't sure if I could pass the test. I agreed to his instruction and lay back on the bed with my legs hanging off. It seemed like several minutes had passed before he said something to me.

"Do you trust me, Music?" He asked again.

"Yes."

"Do you really trust me?"

"I said yes. Now get on with this damn game," I said, sounding totally annoyed.

"Good. Do what I say and all this will be over in a few minutes."

I took a deep breath and exhaled really hard and long. I was actually getting nervous not knowing what was about to happen. I had time to really think if I truly trusted Que, and I felt like I did. I didn't think he would do anything to harm me, so I relaxed. I soon felt a hand on my thigh, which made me jump.

"What's going on?" I asked, quickly sitting up.

"If you trust me, lay back down," he said calmly.

"I'm not playing, Que. Don't touch me!" I said, as I lay back down.

"I'm not going to touch you."

A few minutes passed and then I felt the hand rub my leg again. I remained quiet and calm, thinking it would be over soon. I closed my eyes tightly behind the blindfold and tried to think about something else, like my strawberry cheese-cake I was going to eat soon.

The hand rubbed my thigh softly and moved between my legs. I then felt another hand on my other thigh, and still, I remained calm. I didn't know if this was a good thing to be enticing me by rubbing on me. I had been on lockdown in this house and was hot and horny. However, I didn't want to get caught up in whatever was about to go down.

"I can't do this," I said, sitting up. Que knew we didn't get down like that, and I couldn't believe he was trying to touch me in that way.

"Music, you can't go home and you said you trust me. That's what's wrong with you. You're too perfect. Now lie back down and play the little game with me," he said.

I thought about what he said and laid back down. I took another deep breath and gave in to Que. I was ready to play the game with him. The hands immediately started rubbing me again. This time, they moved quickly. Both hands started rubbing my thighs, quickly moving my shorts and panties to the side, while someone began licking between my legs like they were licking on a lollipop.

When I attempted to get up to stop the charade, someone held me down and started kissing my breast wildly. That's when I realized there was someone else in the room with us. This really made me scared and I started freaking out.

As much as I fought to get up, the person between my legs never stopped licking me, continuing like their life depended on it. The other person struggled to hold me down while I forcefully tried to get up. Suddenly, I heard Que's voice from a distant.

"Okay, you guys can stop," he said.

When I finally broke free from the person's hold and snatched the blindfold off, I jumped up off the bed. Que was leaning back in the chair with a smirk on his face. In the bed where I had just been lying were Sweets and Tipp dressed in only their panties and bras.

"What the fuck are you doing?" I asked.

Furious, I swung hard and hit Sweets in her mouth, while Tipp caught part of my swings and got hit on the side of her head. I kept beating Sweets and Tipp until Que pulled me off of them. They never fought back, and only covered their faces and heads to shield them from the beating they were receiving.

"Calm down Music. You know Tipp and Sweets," Que said breathing hard from trying to stop me.

"Let me go, Que," I yelled, while struggling to get free.

"You really need to calm the fuck down!" Que yelled, as he held me tight and sat me down on the chair in front of the bed.

"What the hell does this have to do with trust?" I asked, still trying to break free from his hold.

"They wanted to taste you, so I let them," Que said, still struggling to hold me down.

"You let them!" I shouted, as I fought him hard to break free.

"I thought you would enjoy it, and it looked like you did."

"I didn't enjoy these bitches licking my pussy!" I shouted.

"Stop being so uptight," Que said, raising his voice.

"I'm getting out of here," I said angrily, jumping up and heading for the door.

"Wait a minute!" He yelled.

"What the hell do you want?" I shouted back.

"Don't take another step. Sit your ass down and let me talk to you," Que shouted, as he gestured for Tipp and Sweets to leave.

I stood still and waited for them to leave the room. Before the door closed, Swagg stood up from the corner of the room where she had been sitting and watching the whole time. Smirking, she walked out without saying a word. I was so angry that I didn't even notice her in the room. I knew Que had completely lost his mind and really didn't know me at all if he thought I would like that.

"Sit down!" Que shouted.

"No. You asshole!" I shouted back.

"I'm sorry. I didn't know you would get so upset."

"Well, I don't like women licking my pussy. I'm not gay!"

"You don't have to be gay to like it," Que said calmly.

"You're sick!" I replied, while staring directly into his eyes as I gritted my teeth.

"You trusted me, and that's what's important here. You passed your initiation."

"This has nothing to do with trust! I don't trust your freaky ass!" I said with anger showing in my eyes.

Que never said a word. He just looked down at the floor. His demeanor had changed since Swagg, Sweets, and Tipp left the room. He appeared to be sincere, but I didn't trust him anymore. I turned around and headed for the door.

"Wait, Music!" Que said, as he got up to catch me before I left. "I'm sorry," he said genuinely.

"Why would you do that to me? You set me up and you had Swagg watching. What is going on?" I asked.

"That's just how I get down. I thought you would be cool with it, but I guess you haven't changed. I'm a freak, and I see that you're not."

"You could have just asked me to find out for yourself instead of trying to set me up," I said.

"I didn't set you up. It was an initiation!" Que yelled.

"I'm so mad right now I could punch you in your mouth!" I snapped.

"And I will knock you the fuck out, so don't hit me!" He warned me.

"Bastard! I'm out of here," I said, snatching my arm away from him, opening the door, and slamming it hard behind me.

I walked back to my room knowing I would never trust Que again. I couldn't wait to get back to the room to tell Raven. I hope he wouldn't try to initiate her the same way. If so, he would get the shock of his life.

Raven was completely stunned when I told her what happened to me in Que's bedroom. She was upset that he would set me up like that and more confused on who Que really was.

"Que is freaky!" Raven said.

"He is stupid," I said, still angry.

"What type of game is he playing?" Raven asked, upset.

"He set me up with Swagg watching the whole scene. It was not an initiation."

"Que, Que, Que. He's a nasty man," Raven said, deep in thought.

"Que has lost his mind, and I know you're next on the list to be initiated," I told her.

"I thought Que fired Sweets and Tipp," Raven said, confused.

"That's what I thought, too, but obviously he's making them work to get rehired."

"What the hell was Swagg doing watching?"

"I don't know, but you know she's his sidekick," I said.

"Que is really scared about killing Slyy, but he wants us to think he's fine. I think he's trying to get something on us because we can pin that murder on him. He needs some dirt to use against us," Raven said, still in deep thought.

"Really?"

"I know Que is your boy, but this is about murder, his career, and his life being taken away from him. He doesn't want to lose everything he has worked so hard for, and I know he doesn't trust us as much as he says he does," Raven responded.

"I think you're right. I can still see the weird look on Swagg, Tipp, and Sweets' faces when they walked out of the room," I said, now in deep thought myself.

"He would have never done that to you if he wasn't scared. He has always protected you and now things have changed. This motherfucker is going to pay big," she said.

"What should we do?" I asked.

"We need to think. He's very slick at his game, and I'm sure he has already planned everything out. We got something big on him so that will always be our ammunition."

"Do you think he'll try to harm us?"

"I think he will kill us if we run our mouth," Raven replied.

"Then we need to get him before he gets us," I said seriously.

"Bitch, now you're thinking!"

"Can you use another word instead of calling people bitches all the time?" I asked.

"Whatever, bitch. You're thinking the way you need to be. You can't be naïve in this situation. You got to be just as dirty as he is. The good thing is he thinks he has you wrapped around his finger. But, you will prove him wrong."

"I told you that I'm not taking any more shit from anyone!" I said.

"People wouldn't believe this type of foolishness goes on," Raven said.

"Something's are unbelievable," I added.

"This is so crazy and I'm tired of it. I really want to go home, but I know it's best that we stay here. Plus, I really want to do his tour. It's going to be hot and is the most talked about and anticipated tour yet," Raven said.

"I want to go home, too, but I feel the same way you do. The tour is going to be hot. My cousin Sydney told me most of the shows are sold out and people are begging for them to add more."

"Let's just do this tour and be done. We've dealt with worse things than this. We can handle this," Raven said.

"Yeah, we can handle anything, right?" I asked, waiting for confirmation.

"Right!" she agreed. "I really liked Que, but now I'm going to drain him dry. He won't have a penny left when I'm done with him. He better remember I have some juicy dirt on him, so he doesn't want to play with me," Raven said.

"Don't do anything stupid," I told her.

"I'm not. We're going to finish this tour as planned, but we will watch our back every step."

"You know you're next," I said.

"I know he's going to try something with me, but I'm going to get him before he gets me. He's messing with the wrong chick," she replied.

"He knows I will never say anything about that night," I said, reminiscing back for a moment.

"But, he doesn't know if I will say something," Raven responded.

"Let's not react right now. We're going to sit back and see what happens next."

"I got something for his ass," she said, then gave me a high-five.

Raven and I sat thinking about what was going on, but still couldn't figure Que out or what would be his next move. We knew we needed to act normal and keep rehearsing until we were able to come up with a plan.

I knew Que was afraid, but I didn't think he would turn on me because of his fear. Raven and I were the ones that could send him to jail and end his career, and he was not comfortable with that.

After what he did to me, I wanted him to suffer. He crossed the line, and now I had the power to scare the hell out of him.

CHAPTER 10

We were still rehearsing on the same tight schedule, two months later. Que was still consistently being hard on us, and Raven and I learned to keep our mouths closed to get what we wanted. Same old schedule, same old routines, and same old drama every day. I was ready for the tour to start and be over with.

My mother had stopped calling so much and even gave me a break. I continuously got calls from a number I didn't recognize and I never answered it. I figured it was a detective trying to get some information about Slyy's murder, and I was avoiding all calls pertaining to that. If I didn't know the number, I didn't answer the phone.

Que pretended like nothing happened in his bedroom with me, Sweets, Tipp, and Swagg, so I acted like nothing happened either. Things were back to normal, and it seemed like Que was focused on the tour and done with playing games. He hadn't tried to initiate Raven, so we assumed he had given up, but we were still watching our backs.

We repeated the same work schedule every day. Rehearsal started at twelve o'clock in the morning and was over eight hours later or longer, depending on how Que was feeling that day. Once we left rehearsals, we showered and went straight to bed. We had turned into robots and were being controlled by Que's command.

Que's show was perfect and guaranteed to be the hottest concert around. There was a buzz in the media about how great his show was going to be, and people were waiting and anticipating an elaborate tour. Some of the special effects in the show were leaked to the press, and his fans were now excited to attend the concert. All information leaked to the media was done by Que. He set the entire publicity stunt up, and it was working because all shows were sold out.

Things had calmed down a bit and nothing too crazy was going on around the house. We were all getting along because we had no choice but to deal with each other. We also knew Que wouldn't deal with any problems with the dancers. The closer the tour start date got, the more serious things became. No games were being played by Que.

Raven and I started hanging out with the other dancers, which made the atmosphere in the house more pleasant and actually fun. During our off time, we went swimming, watched movies, and helped each other with the choreography.

We really wanted the show to be hot and we were determined to make Que happy. We had worked too hard to have a horrible show. Our reputation was also on the line, and we wanted great reviews so we could move on to the next tour highly recommended.

Que hadn't said anything to Raven and was very distant. He knew he was extremely hard on her, and I guess he felt like he needed to give her a break. He was more focused on business than getting with her.

Raven was feeling rejected, which is something she's not used to. Her feelings were involved and she couldn't turn them off. All she needed was for him to show her some attention because he just abruptly stopped. He had put a halt to her plan and she needed to get things back on track. She hadn't given up on him; she just needed time to work her magic.

Que ate, slept, and drank the music industry every day, all day long. It seemed like he never did anything normal and his lifestyle was driving us all crazy. He was a control freak and needed attention all the time. His life was consumed by money, power, and sex.

I had learned so much more about Que in the short amount of time since joining his crew, and I didn't like this side of him. He already showed me the many sides of him: the killer side, the controlling side, the temper tantrum side, the insecure side, the bossy side, and the disrespectful side.

We definitely didn't have a life. Que kept us on lockdown and focused on the show. I was burnt out and needed some normalcy. Sure, this crazy schedule kept my mind off of things, but it didn't keep me from feeling lonely.

Raven was working hard trying to get with Que and I was trying to get with Johnny. However, I'd been too tired and busy to talk to him or even see him. Que was also working the band, crew, and staff just as hard as the dancers. I didn't see Johnny much, and the only time I got a glimpse of him was usually after we finished rehearsals.

By this time, I was too exhausted to say anything and usually gave him a tired wave or a quick hug. Even though our hellos were quick, there was still a strong attraction between us. We always stared at each other seductively. Sometimes our hugs got longer and the stares got more intense.

We continued to text and call each other, as things started to get interesting. All we talked about was how much we wanted to see each other. The distant was making us want each other more. I just wanted to get some time to spend alone with him, but it seemed like that would never happen.

We didn't have any personal time because all of our time was given to Que. He wasn't paying us enough for what he was putting us through, and you could tell it was taking a toll on everyone. People were starting to look worn down and weak.

People on the outside looking in at our situation would probably tell us that we were crazy to be complaining. All they would see is that we were working with Que and living the good life in a mansion. We needed a couple of days to relax because we deserved it, and I feared if it didn't happen soon, someone was definitely going to snap.

CHAPTER 11

My body was throbbing from rehearsal when I woke up. I couldn't believe it was nine o'clock in the evening. I had planned on sleeping late and waking up at eleven o'clock, an hour before rehearsal. Now that I was up, I couldn't go back to sleep.

I had three hours before rehearsal and didn't want to waste one minute. I knew Raven had gotten up early, too, because she was already in the shower. After we both showered, we headed to the kitchen to get something to eat. When I entered the kitchen, Johnny was sitting at the counter eating a sandwich.

While rehearsing, there was no reason to look cute because we never went anywhere and was too tired to do anything. Therefore, Johnny always saw me in the raw. No make-up, hair hardly combed, and sporting jogging pants and t-shirts. I figured if he still was attracted to me in my current state then when I got made up, he would go crazy. Raven and I was actually getting comfortable with not dressing up and putting on makeup all the time.

"Where is my sandwich?" I asked, flirting with Johnny.

"You can have a bite of mine," he said, holding the sandwich in the air.

"What's up, Mr. Johnny?" Raven said, smiling.

"What's up Raven?" Johnny responded.

After she and I made a turkey sandwich, we joined Johnny. We sat at the counter and pretended we were at a restaurant eating. Even though it was a beautiful house we were living in, we were sick of not being able to leave.

"Que added another song to the show. Did you guys learn it already?" I asked Johnny.

"We started on it yesterday. I'm so tired of him adding songs. He will keep adding songs until he feels the show is where he wants it," he said.

"Looking past all the drama so far, the show is going to be outstanding," Raven said, excited.

"Are we ever going to get out of this house?" Raven asked, not waiting for a response. "Look, I will talk to you guys later. I'm going to go see how I can break out of this hellhole," Raven said, laughing as she walked out of the kitchen.

I knew she was trying to give us some privacy, and I appreciated her courtesy. She knew Johnny and I hadn't had time to talk since we had been there. I gave her a wink to say thank you as she left the kitchen.

"Have you finished your initiation?" Johnny asked.

"What?" I asked, shocked, thinking he knew about what happened in Que's bedroom.

"Everyone goes through initiation. I was just wondering if you passed."

"Yeah, I passed," I said, as I looked down at the floor.

"Are you okay?" He asked.

"I'm good," I said softly.

"It's just an initiation. It doesn't define who you are. Just forget about what happened. It's over. So, just move forward, do the tour, and get your money," Johnny told me.

"You're right. Did you go through an initiation?" I asked.

"Yeah. I told you everyone does."

"What did you have to do?" I probed.

"You didn't tell me what you had to do, so I'm not going to tell you. Looking at you, I know it was something you don't want to do again. So, let's leave it at that," Johnny said, smiling.

"No problem," I replied, wondering what type of initiation he had to go through.

"How are your rehearsals going?" He asked in a sexy voice.

"My body is aching," I said, rubbing my neck.

"I can help you with that ache."

"You can?" I asked.

"Let me show you."

Johnny jumped up, walked behind me, and started rubbing my neck softly. His strong hands quickly rubbed my pains away. Closing my eyes, I tried to enjoy the massage.

"How does that feel?" He asked softly.

"That feels good. I hope your girlfriend won't get mad," I said trying to find out some information about him.

"I don't have a girlfriend, but my boyfriend will be upset."

"Boyfriend!"

"I'm just kidding. I'm not gay. Trust me, I'm just kidding," Johnny assured me.

"That's not funny," I said, then turned around and hit him in his chest.

"Would it have mattered if I was gay?"

"That would be a problem," I told him.

"Would you have been mad?"

"Yes," I said slowly.

Johnny stared at me, then grabbed my hands and started rubbing them. I looked at his beautiful brown eyes and succulent lips. I was in a trance and mesmerized by his strong grip.

"You don't think I'm gay, do you?" Johnny asked, while squeezing my hand.

"No, I hope not."

Johnny leaned in and kissed me on my lips. His lips were so soft that I felt like I was in heaven. I closed my eyes and allowed the pleasure. He then stopped and looked at me.

"I hope that kiss proves I'm not gay."

"You could be on the down low," I said while smiling, but praying to God he wasn't.

"No, I'm not on the down low. I only date women," Johnny said seriously.

I couldn't say a word because he had hypnotized me with his eyes. He continued kissing me, and it became very passionate. We stopped and gave each other a long deep hug, feeling every inch of each other's bodies.

It had been awhile since I've had sex with a man and I was yearning for some attention. I didn't want to let Johnny go, but I didn't want to seem desperate either. The truth is I was desperate, and at that very moment, I didn't care if he noticed.

"I'm sorry," Johnny said, as he immediately stopped hugging me.

"Sorry about what?" I asked.

"I didn't mean to kiss you. I don't want to jump the gun."

"It's cool. I wanted you to kiss me," I told him.

"Good, because I know every man in this house is trying to get with you and I wanted to show you how I felt about you before they got their claws into you."

"Well, you definitely showed me how you feel."

"I probably went a little too far, but I just couldn't help myself. I wasn't sure when I was going to see you again, so I didn't want to miss this opportunity of putting my bid in. I've been thinking about kissing you for a long time, and it was worth the wait," Johnny said, then leaned in and kissed me again.

"I...I...I..." I said. All I could do was stutter. Nothing more would come out.

Johnny grabbed me gently by the back of my neck and pulled my head back. He kissed my neck so softly that it sent chills down my body. I moaned as I tasted his neck. It seemed weird to be kissing and caressing him since we hadn't even been on a date. However, the feelings we had for each other were mutual, and being on lockdown made us feel like we needed to capture the moment, just in case it never happened again.

The sexual tension between us was going to be a problem. I didn't know if we really liked each other or if we were just in lust with each other. I think lust was winning and it felt good.

I felt like I was in jail and was finally getting a conjugal visit. He felt so good that I could have had sex with him right in the middle of the kitchen. We finally took a break from tongue wrestling and hugged each other passionately. I closed my eyes and laid my head on his shoulder.

I took a deep breath and opened my eyes slowly. When I looked across the room, I was startled to see Que leaning against the doorway with a smirk on his face. As soon as I pulled away from Johnny, he quickly left.

I didn't know how long Que had been standing there, but by the look on his face, it told me he had been standing in the doorway long enough to see us kissing. He didn't appear to be too happy watching our display of affection. He kind of looked disappointed when he walked out, but I really couldn't determine what he was feeling.

Johnny never saw Que and didn't notice him leaving the room. He continued kissing me.

"Your lips feel so good," Johnny whispered.

"We shouldn't be doing this," I said.

"Why not?"

"This is work, remember?"

"We're not working at this moment," Johnny said while kissing my neck.

"Que was just in the kitchen and I think he saw us kissing," I said, experiencing a bit of nervousness.

"Really," Johnny said blasé.

"He just walked out and didn't say anything."

"If he has a problem with what he saw, we will hear about it."

"Is that good or bad?" I asked.

"You sound worried."

"I'm not worried. I just don't want any problems."

"I'm not worth it?"

"I don't know. Are you?"

"You will soon find out," Johnny said, looking deep into my eyes.

"We better get ready for rehearsal," I told him, trying to break the thick sexual tension in the room.

"Let's work on seeing each other more often."

"Okay," I responded.

"I'll think of something because I want to taste your lips again."

"We better go," I said quickly.

I kissed Johnny's lips one last time and then quickly grabbed his arm to lead him out of the kitchen. I assured him with my actions that I wanted to kiss him again. Before we left the kitchen, he grabbed me by the small of my back, yanked me close to him, and kissed me again.

Although I was nervously trying to leave the kitchen, I knew Que had already seen us kissing, so why not get another one to hold me over?

I walked into the bedroom smiling from ear to ear. I was feeling good and relaxed. I really needed that time with Johnny, and it changed my attitude.

"What's wrong with you?" Raven asked after getting off her cell phone.

"I just tasted Johnny's lips," I said, blushing.

Raven smiled. "Slutty butt."

"I know you're not calling me a slut."

"What did his lips taste like?" Raven asked with a grin on her face.

"Shut up," I said, laughing. But then I became worried. "Girl, Que saw us kissing."

"Really!" Raven shouted, cracking up laughing.

"I looked up and he was standing in the kitchen doorway, but he never said a word. He's so odd."

"Que needs to be kissing me and stop watching other people."

"He didn't look happy," I told her.

"Well, you better check the rule book. There might be a rule about not dating anyone on the tour," Raven said, looking for her book.

"We're grown and I'm not going to check no damn book," I said peeved.

"If he has a problem, you know he will let you know," Raven said.

"I shouldn't have to be worried about something like this."

"Don't stress over it. Let's see what happens at rehearsal. I will take care of Que for you."

"Let's hurry up so we won't be late because we're practicing with the band tonight," I told her.

When Raven and I walked into the dance studio, the band was working on some songs and getting ready to start rehearsal. We were shocked to see Tipp and Sweets working on some dance moves. The last time I saw them, Tipp was holding me down and Sweets was licking between my legs. It looked like they had paid their dues and were now rehired.

"What's up, girls?" I said, trying to act casual.

Raven didn't say a word. She just looked at Tipp and Sweets like she didn't approve of them being there. They actually appeared embarrassed and uncomfortable around me. I thought I was going to be the one feeling ashamed, but it turned out they were. So, of course, I was going to let them waddle in the pool of disgrace and pretend I wasn't bothered by what happened.

"Music and Raven, this is Tipp," Swagg said, introducing us. She knew I had met her up close and personal, but I went along with the game.

"What's up?" Tipp said very friendly.

"What's up?" Raven and I said dry.

"You guys already know Sweets," Swagg said, smiling.

"All too well," Raven mumbled to herself.

"Que hired them back," Sexy said, excited.

"What happened to your face?" Raven asked Sweets, even though she knew the answer.

"It looks like someone beat your ass," I said sarcastically, giving her a mean stare.

"I had an accident, but I'll be fine," Sweets answered, lying through her teeth when she knew I had hit her so hard in the face that she would never try to lick anyone else.

"When did you get here?" Raven asked Tipp sarcastically, playing the role in front of the band.

"I've been here for two months," Tipp responded, while looking away uncomfortable.

"Two months!" Raven said, shocked.

"Wow, two whole months!" I said, looking at Tipp and twisting my lips.

"Sweets, how long have you been here?" Raven asked.

"I never left," she said.

"Where were you guys?" Raven inquired.

"We were staying in Que's room," Tipp said proudly.

"Why haven't we seen you guys?" Raven asked.

"We stayed on Que's floor and wasn't allowed to leave," Sweets told us.

Why would he fire them and let them stay with him? I assumed Que was making them show him how much they wanted their jobs back.

Raven knew Que was a dog, but now she had feelings for him and was starting to realize what type of person he was. I had never seen her so attached to someone before.

It seemed like the more Que became distant with her, the more she became emotionally attached. When men reject women, it seems like the woman ends up wanting them even more, which I believed was happening to my best friend.

Raven knew she had to erase her feelings for Que. He was not the person she needed to fall in love with. Her feelings were hurt and now she had returned to the original person she was. The person who didn't give a damn about anyone but herself.

"Don't worry about them," I whispered to Raven.

"I'm not worried. I just didn't know he was this ruthless," she said.

"Don't hate the game," I told her.

"I'm not. I'm just waiting on my turn to play," Raven said, thinking.

"I don't want you to get hurt or played."

"I won't get played because I created the game," she responded with a smile.

"I was worried about you for a minute," I said, relieved.

"I'm good. I still like him, but I have to get rid of these feelings. I'm not sure how, but they got to go."

"As long as you're good," I said.

"If I can't beat them, I will join these bitches. They're trying to keep their job, and I'm trying to get my money," Raven told me.

"Let's start rehearsal," Swagg said, interrupting our conversation.

"Since Tipp and Sweets are back, do we have to change our formation on stage?" Raven asked.

"Actually the positions we are in now are not our permanent ones. Que will give everyone their final position the last week of rehearsal," Swagg said.

"Why do we have to wait until then?" I asked.

"Just in case one of you gets fired, we don't have to rearrange things," Swagg said.

"What if you get fired?" Raven asked.

"He will never fire me," Swagg said with confidence.

"Why is that?" I asked.

"Because he won't. Now let's start rehearsals" Swagg said.

Raven and I looked at each other and raised our eyebrows. We didn't know why she couldn't get fired, seeing that Que seemed like he would fire anyone at anytime. Swagg was his right-hand woman, and she felt like she had a permanent spot that wasn't going to be taken away by anyone.

"This is another person I got to worry about," Raven whispered to me.

"I think you should leave this alone," I told her.

"I can't because the game has already started," Raven said.

"Don't start any mess."

"Hot mess. That's my middle name. You're starting to become a mess, too," Raven said, laughing.

I rolled my eyes at her because I knew she was always starting trouble. I didn't know what she had planned, but I knew she was up to something. Things were already crazy, and we hadn't even started the tour yet. What else could possibly happen?

CHAPTER 12

"Let me see it from the top," Que said as soon as he walked in the dance studio with Doug.

We always hated to see Que walk through the doors because we knew he was about to put us through hell. He never gave us a break and rode us until he couldn't ride us anymore.

When we started the choreography over again, I looked at Sweets and Tipp because I wanted to see if they were going to make a mistake. We had been rehearsing every day for over two months now, and I didn't know how they would keep up. I was starting to get upset since I knew it was going to be a long night because of their mistakes. To my surprise, Sweets and Tipp were on point and didn't miss one step.

Raven had her game face on and she knew she had to come to Que a different way if she wanted to be with him. So, she kept a smile on her face and was giving out positive energy. He didn't seem to pay her any attention, but she also ignored him, pretending to be uninterested.

Raven was restructuring and refocusing herself to get to Que. She knew Tipp, Sweets, and Swagg were sleeping with him, but she needed to find out why Swagg was so confident that she wouldn't get fired. She had work to do and decided to forget about what they were doing. Instead, she would work on what she was going to do.

She always considered herself the head bitch in these situations and didn't like it that Swagg currently had that title. She was working hard at trying to take her position and was confident that it was only a matter of time for her to be promoted.

While Raven was trying to figure out her master plan, I was a little nervous. I was waiting for Que to say something about me and Johnny kissing. I tried not to have eye contact with him and just did what I was told.

Que never even looked at me, which made me even more tensed. Once we finished the routine, Que put his hand over his mouth and looked at us. We looked back but didn't say a word. Finally, he broke his silence.

"That was great!" Que said, clapping.

We were so shocked to hear him say those words because he had never been happy with anything we ever done before. He had been making us feel very insecure and not worthy of dancing for him. Now, finally, we got a compliment and encouragement.

"Thank you," everyone said.

"You guys have been working very hard and it's paying off. For doing such a great job, take an hour break," Que said, smiling.

You could feel the relief in the room and the stress level went down quickly. He was finally happy with what we had been rehearsing so hard for. We really needed to hear that from him.

Not wanting to waste one minute of our hour-long break, everyone scattered like roaches. Before Raven and I could get out of the door, Que grabbed me by the arm.

"I need to talk to you," he said seriously.

"Okay," I responded.

"I need to talk to you, too," Raven told Que, while rubbing his arm.

"Okay," he said, looking at her peculiarly. "Let me talk to Raven first and I will talk to you once I'm done," he turned to me and said. Then he led us both to the recording studio.

"Music, have a seat. Raven, you come with me," Que said, taking her into the vocal booth.

Que didn't know that I knew how to work a music board. Since he sat me down next to the board, I couldn't help myself from listening. I slowly slid my hand across the board and pushed the button to hear what was going on in the booth. I made sure the volume button was down low.

Since I could see them and they could see me, I pretended to read a magazine, while peeking at them and watching the door so I could turn the sound off quickly if someone came into the studio. They appeared to be having a serious conversation.

"Is everything okay?" Raven asked Que.

"Yeah, things are good," Que responded.

"Are you mad at me?" She asked.

"No. Why are you asking me that?" Que replied casually, while leaning against the window of the booth.

"I feel like something is wrong. Am I doing what you want me to do?" Raven inquired.

"What do I want you to do?" Que asked, as he crossed his arms.

Raven didn't respond. Instead, she walked over to him, got on her knees, unzipped his pants, pulled his dick out, and stroked it before she started sucking it. I couldn't believe what I was seeing and had to act like I wasn't watching.

Que quickly moaned from pleasure and grabbed Raven's head, moving it back and forth. She went to town. All you could hear was slurping sounds. He kept telling her to slow down, but she never stopped. He fell against the glass window, leaned his head back, and held on to her head as he moaned and groaned loudly.

"Oh shit!" Que screamed, while coming hard.

Raven wiped her mouth and then got off her knees while he was still leaning against the window breathing hard. He didn't expect her to give him a blow job that quickly; it caught him off guard.

"That's what I wanted to do," Raven said seductively.

"Damn, that felt good," Que panted, trying to catch his breath.

"How freaky are you?" Raven asked softly.

"How freaky do you want me to be?" Que answered with a question.

"Do you trust me?" Raven asked, while rubbing his dick.

"Yeah," Que said, closing his eyes.

"Let's play a game. You do what I tell you to do. The only catch is you can't touch me," Raven said.

"What?" Que asked, confused.

"Do what I want and don't touch me with your hands," Raven said, smirking.

"Okay. What do you want me to do with my hands?"

"Hold on to the wall," she told him.

"Okay. I'll play your little game," he said, smiling as he leaned on the wall with both of his hands.

Raven squeezed herself in front of him, got on her knees, and sucked his dick just to get it hard enough to do what she wanted to do. After he was right where she wanted him, she stood up, turned around, arched her back, pulled her shorts and panties to the side, leaned against the wall, and told Que to fuck her hard. A shocked but excited look came over Que's face as he took a condom from his pocket before his pants fell to the floor.

Raven quickly grabbed her dick and balls, pulled them forward and held on to them tightly. Que never suspected anything; he just thought she was masturbating. She told him to hurry up and enter her from behind. He didn't hesitate taking the opportunity to fuck her in the asshole. Not abiding by the "no touching" rule, he quickly grabbed her by the waist to bang her harder.

She allowed him to grab her waist, but paid close attention so he wouldn't touch her anywhere else. He seemed turned on and moved like a happy child in a candy store. He did everything she told him to do and never hesitated to please her. When she told him to put his hands back on the wall, he quickly obliged as she backed her ass into him harder. Que moaned uncontrollably and fucked her like he hadn't had sex in a long time.

I couldn't believe Raven was having sex with him when she knew I could see them. She knew she had to do something drastic to get her plan back in motion, and she knew sex would jumpstart it. Most men couldn't resist a beautiful woman that wanted to have sex with them, and for some reason, they were really turned on when the woman wanted anal sex.

I watched with my mouth open, still trying to act like I wasn't looking. They started sweating and both moaned louder and louder as Raven performed like a porn star. She worked Que and had him stuttering and calling her name. Once they were finished, Que could hardly move.

"Damn, baby, I'm addicted," he said, exhausted.

"I've been trying to show you what you've been missing, but you've been ignoring me," Raven replied, happy that her plan was working.

"The way you just put it down I won't ignore you anymore," Que said, while pulling his pants up.

"This is all for you," she responded, pointing at her body.

"That's what's up," Que said, smiling.

"You can have me anytime you want. Just don't treat me the way you have been," Raven said cautiously, not knowing if she was crossing the line, but she had to get him on her page quickly.

"How was I treating you?" He asked.

"You were ignoring me and embarrassing me in front of the other dancers," she replied with a feisty tone. Then she walked up to him, kissed him, grabbed his dick, and licked his neck.

"You're all good," Que said.

"What does that mean?" Raven asked.

"You won't have any more problems."

"I really like you, Que," Raven said, trying to sound sincere.

"I like you, too, and I really like how you get down," he replied.

"I can get down better than this if you give me a chance. I will fuck you every night, anywhere, anytime, and any way you like it," Raven said with confidence.

"Damn! It's like that!" Que said, excited.

"Yes, that's how I get down with someone I really like," she replied, trying to stress that she didn't sleep with just anyone.

"I didn't know you were this cool."

"I've tried to show you, but you shut me out," she told him.

"Don't take it personal, baby. I have a lot going on right now. Business and money always come first, and I play later."

"A lot is going on when you're fucking everyone?" Raven said, knowing she was wrapping him around her fingers.

"What?" Que asked, shocked.

"I know you're fucking the other dancers and I want you to stop, but I know you won't. So, just fuck me when you want to and give me what I need, and I will make sure you stay happy," Raven said, smiling.

"That's cool," Que replied, returning the smile.

"Remember, I have to be the head bitch and nothing less."

"The head bitch, huh? When can I fuck you again?" Que said, letting Raven know he controlled the arrangements and not her.

"Whenever you want to, and also whenever I see a diamond bracelet on my wrist and five thousand dollars in my bank account," Raven responded with a broader smile.

"All you want is a diamond bracelet and some money in your account. I thought you were going to ask for more than that."

"Oh trust me, it will become more. This is just the appetizer. Can you handle that?" Raven asked.

"Of course, baby! Now suck my dick," he said, sounding like a mean pimp.

Raven didn't have a problem letting him think he was running things. So, she got back down on her knees and began sucking his dick as instructed. *Checkmate*, Raven thought to herself.

I sat there waiting on them for two and a half hours. When I saw they were about to come out of the booth, I turned the volume down and turned my chair around with my back facing them. Then I pretended like I was sleeping when they came back into the room.

"Music," Raven said.

"What?" I asked, pretending to be waking up from a deep sleep.

"Let's talk later, Music. I have a meeting to go to," Que said, as he quickly headed for the door.

"No problem. Is everything okay?" I asked, sounding groggy.

"Everything is perfect. Right, Raven?" He asked, stopping to look at Raven while smiling.

"Right," Raven responded, smiling back.

"You guys better get back to rehearsals because you're late. I will talk to you later, Music," Que said, then left the studio.

"Damn, Raven!" I said as soon as the studio doors closed behind him.

"I told you I'm the head bitch around this place," Raven told me, smiling while we rushed to rehearsal.

"Yes, Ms. Head Bitch, and we will talk later about that little porn scene you just performed," I said, laughing as we entered the dance studio.

~~~~~~~~

After rehearsing for three hours straight, we were finally able to take a break. The other dancers were still staring at us, wanting to know why we were late returning to rehearsal. They knew Que didn't like for people to be late, and since we told them we had met with him, they really wanted to know what we were talking about.

"Take a ten-minute break," Swagg said. After Raven and I collapsed on the floor exhausted, she turned to us and asked, "Seriously, why were you guys late?"

"Raven was talking to Que," I said annoyed.

"I will speak with Que, and your story better check out," Swagg replied, then walked away.

At that very instant, it felt like everything went back to the way it was in the beginning when first meeting them. The dancers instantly gave us attitude and were looking at us funny. This competition for Que's attention was getting on my last nerve, and it was a waste of their time.

I knew Raven was smiling on the inside. Although Que was a little difficult to wrap around her fingers, she knew she had him wrapped tightly now. The only problem she felt she had was the other dancers being in the way, especially with Swagg acting like the leader. After weeks of pretending to be best friends with the other dancers, that vanished within minutes. Once we walked into the rehearsal late, they hated us all over again.

Swagg was always the cool one and it appeared that nothing bothered her. I never really heard anything about her being involved in any mess. Since she ran Que's rehearsals, I knew she had slept with him. I knew Que all too well. She appeared to be innocent, but I knew better.

Swagg had many personalities and always appeared concerned about our feelings, but once Que was around, she became his puppet. If Que told her to treat us like dirt, she jumped into character and was hard on us the entire rehearsal.

When he wasn't around, she pretended like nothing ever happened and tried to inform us on how to deal with it. I started to feel sorry for her because she didn't know who she was and Que was manipulating her mind.

Tipp didn't have too much to say to anyone, but appeared to be very comfortable and not concerned about what people thought about her. I knew Tipp was a freak and obviously sleeping with Que. She appeared to be under a trance when it came to him.

I still couldn't really figure Heat out because she was always very quiet and you hardly noticed she was in the room. But, one thing my mother always taught me was to watch the quiet ones because they are usually the sneaky ones. So, while she's observing others, I will be observing her.

Flex appeared to be out of control. She was always stretching, kicking her legs, and just acting crazy. I took her personality as fun and she enjoyed life. She had an I-don't-care attitude, and she didn't seem to like being involved in drama. She was a little strange, but fun to be around.

Flex knew how to work Que. When he entered the room, she became a different person, quiet and meek. You could tell she went after what she wanted and stayed focused until she achieved it. She was definitely one to watch and stay clear of.

When it comes to dancers trying to make it in the entertainment business, it's so much competition, insecurities, and jealousy that take over, making the journey to becoming successful painful. What make success so memorable are the struggles you experienced while getting there.

You need perseverance and strength to make it in this business, and I had both. However, a person can only handle so much, and I really felt that touring the world might not be worth my sanity.

"What are you thinking about?" Raven asked me, while watching me daydreaming.

"I'm thinking about these dancers. They have totally lost their souls to Que. He is manipulating them. They're like his slaves. That's sad," I said, still staring into space.

"That's their problem, so don't let them get to you," Raven said.

"I'm cool."

"You know I got Que wrapped around my finger," she told me.

"Yes, I saw," I told her.

"You saw what?"

"I saw enough to know that you will do anything to get his attention."

"Girl, you saw us screwing?" Raven asked, shocked.

"Let's just say I saw enough."

"Who cares? You've seen me get screwed before," Raven said, rolling her eyes.

"You're right, but that doesn't mean I want to continue seeing it," I responded with laughter.

"I got him wrapped tight," Raven said, laughing with me.

"The only thing wrapped tightly was your mouth around his dick," I said frowning.

"I'm going to send you my bill for teaching you how to suck a dick correctly," Raven said, unconcerned.

"Now you're acting like a groupie," I told her.

"I'm a dancer, groupie, and gold digger. I don't care what you call me because I'm going to get what I deserve," Raven said.

"You're a whore, so accept it."

"I'm just getting what's mine. Why fuck a man for free when you can get paid for it?" Raven responded.

"Okay, groupie," I said.

"Groupies, video vixens, or dancers, either way the artists want to fuck them all and they usually do, whether they do it willingly or they take it. So, would you rather be a groupie and get fucked just to get a chance to go backstage without getting a penny and being treated like a prostitute? Or a video vixen that fucks the artist just to get more camera time in the music video or be the leading lady. The vixens get paid a little something, but they are not respected and are also treated like dirty hoes. Then there's the dancers that are treated professionally, get paid a salary, are respected for their talent, travel the world, and have a very close relationship with the artist. But, guess what? The dancers get fucked by the artists, too," Raven expressed, taking a breath.

"You're ruthless," I said, interrupting her.

"It's worse for the dancers because the artists feel they have invested in you, so now they own you. They demand that you give them what they want whenever they want it. There are so many dancers they could hire, but instead they hire you and make you work for the salary and respect of being a dancer. Either you fuck them willingly or they will rape you. Right, Music?" She asked, looking directly at me and nodding.

I never said a word and just listened to her make a point.

"So, if they are going to fuck me, then they're going to pay me or I will just take it. If they don't give me what I want, I will steal it. Yes, I have stolen before. I stole Slyy's Rolex watch, diamond earrings, and his money out of his wallet the first week I met him. I also took a hundred dollars out of Que's pockets when I was sucking his dick," Raven said, laughing.

"Dang, you're a thief," I said laughing with her.

"I'm just taking what I deserve. You need to learn this, Music. While Slyy was raping you, you should have been taking all his money. Instead, you did nothing and allowed him to use you. Now you have nothing but bad memories of being raped and beaten, a worn-out pussy, no extra money or diamonds, and a fucked-up mind to go with it. You should have taken all his money, because now you have nothing to show for him fucking you the entire tour," Raven said seriously.

"Your crazy butt was stealing," I said ignoring her statement.

"Music, you need to have an open mind, and maybe you too can have a nice bank account!" Raven stated teasingly.

"You're just nasty!" I said, shaking my head with a smirk on my face.

"Just think, Music! If you wouldn't have fought Slyy and allowed him to fuck you freely, you would be paid right now. Instead, you made him take it from you, and then he beat your ass in the process. You could have just given it to him willingly since he was going to take it anyway, and your bank account would be full just like mine," Raven said, schooling me.

I looked at Raven sadly because I knew she was making sense, and even though I didn't believe in stealing from people, Slyy had stolen from me in a major way. Things might have been different if I had taken that route.

"Que is a dirty man and so was Slyy. They both deserve what they get. They don't care about the money I stole from them because they have tons of it. When I stole Slyy's Rolex, he simply thought he lost it and replaced it the next day. See, it didn't even bother him. A man can't think when his dick is in someone's mouth. Let me teach you how to get paid and be set for life."

"You're really acting like a prostitute and not a dancer. That's why we have such a bad name," I told her.

"Girl, we're all the same. It's just we all have different goals. My goal is for my pockets to stay full," Raven said.

"You're the reason why everyone thinks dancers are hoes and we're losing our respect," I replied, appalled.

"I'm no different from someone working in a corporate office. People sleep with their bosses to get promoted and make more money. They even steal from their company. Whether it is money, office equipment, or supplies, you know you have stolen from your job," Raven said, laughing.

"I never stole money," I said laughing.

"Yeah, but you did steal paper, pens, and a stapler. See, you're no different."

"Shut up," I said, shaking my head and laughing because she was telling the truth.

"I'm no different from any other person working any type of job. They steal. I steal. Hell, we all steal at some time in our life," Raven continued.

"What are you planning on doing to Que?" I asked seriously.

"I'm going to break his pockets, make him fall in love with me, and then kick his sorry ass to the curb," Raven said staring into space.

"Just be careful," I said with concern.

"It will be quick and painless."

"I definitely want to get him back for what he did to me," I told her.

"Good. I'm glad we're on the same page," Raven said.

Before I could question Raven more about her plan on stealing Que's money and heart, Swagg interrupted our conversation and told us it was time to start rehearsing again.

"We will talk later," I told Raven, as I stood up.

"Welcome to the other side," Raven told me, grinning from ear to ear. She was happy thinking I was going to be on the same page as she was.

CHAPTER 13

A few days had passed and we were still preparing for the tour with strenuous rehearsals everyday with the band. We were fitted for our costumes and it was very close to the real show time. We were repeating our routines over and over, and rehearsals were still tiring. Que definitely was a perfectionist, but it was paying off because everyone was on point and there were hardly any mistakes.

After all the rehearsals, we couldn't wait to start the tour. We were ready to show off all of our hard work. Que even shocked us with a couple of surprises that he added to the show.

He had several artists that would join him on stage, and he gave Raven and I solo dances with him. A couple of the other dancers already had solo parts, but we were not expecting to dance solo. The concept was hot, but it meant Raven and I would have to work harder to learn his elaborate scene.

It was hard for me to stay focused at rehearsal thinking about me and Johnny's kissing episode in the kitchen. We were now in the same room together rehearsing, and we kept eyeing each other the entire time, while trying not to be obvious. Que still had not said anything about seeing us kissing, and I was sort of relieved. Now I could relax and anticipate seeing Johnny again since it seemed like Que wasn't going to address it.

We had been rehearsing for five hours. It was five o'clock in the morning and we were still going strong. We were running through the show, and it felt amazing to be a part of such an intricate show that was full of props, explosions, tricky lights, smoke hydraulics, and mystery guests.

Once we learned the technical side of the show, things were running smoothly. Although it took a while to get used to all the tricks to the show, it was exciting, and I couldn't wait to perform live.

In the middle of our routine, Doug walked in the room and stood in the door-way until we finished. Once the song stopped, he interrupted rehearsal.

"Music, come with me," he demanded.

I frowned, not knowing if I should go with him or not. I hadn't talked to Doug and I was now very uncomfortable. I looked at Raven, who raised her eyebrows because she didn't know what was going on either.

Everyone was looking at me, especially Johnny and Sexy, wondering what was going on. Once I started walking towards Doug, he left out of the door and it closed behind him. I immediately stopped because I couldn't believe he didn't hold the door open for me. Not looking back, I opened the door, and when I walked out of the room, Doug was leaning on the wall next to the door.

"What's going on?" I asked.

"Que wants to talk to you," Doug said, then started walking down the hallway.

"About what?" I asked, trying to catch up with him.

"I don't know," Doug said aggravated.

"What's wrong with you?" I asked confused by the tone of his voice.

"You can talk to Que, but you haven't said one word to me since you've been here," Doug said, stopping in the hallway.

"We haven't had time to talk to each other. What did you want to talk about?"

"Music, I want you back," Doug said, as he grabbed my shoulder.

I knocked his hand away. "Are you serious?"

"Now that I've seen you, I know I want you. I'm sorry for hurting you," he confessed, trying to sound genuine.

"Doug, please! It's over. I don't want a cheating man."

"I know you want me back."

"I don't want you. You got Sexy. Why do you want me? Oh I know, because you need to sleep with every woman on this tour. Well, you won't be screwing me anymore," I said, fuming.

This was the first time I've spoken to him since I walked in on him sleeping with another woman. It felt good to release all that anger within me. Doug was a dog, and he was now trying to conquer me again.

"I miss you," Doug said.

"You hurt me deeply and I would never take you back," I replied sadly.

"I'm sorry!"

"It's over. Now go be with Sexy and leave me alone," I told him.

"Why are you doing this?" He asked.

"What! Are you seriously asking me that?"

"I want you."

"Well, I don't want you. Now move so I can go talk to Que," I said, pushing him out of my way as I headed for the recording studio.

"You're probably fucking Que!" Doug yelled down the hallway.

I stopped, turned around, and frowned at him, but never responded. He didn't even deserve a comment for that statement. He knew I had never had sex with Que, but he was always jealous of our relationship.

I turned back around and kept walking. When I opened the door to the recording studio, Que was sitting at the sound board. As soon as he heard the door open, he spun around in his chair and quickly stood up.

"What the fuck are you doing with Johnny?" Que shouted angrily.

I actually thought since time had passed that he wasn't going to talk about it. Now that he was shouting, he completely caught me off guard and I didn't know what to say.

"Why were you kissing him in the kitchen?" Que yelled.

"It just happened!" I shouted back nervously.

"You looked like you were about to have sex with him. I didn't know you get down like that," Que yelled.

"Get down like what?" I said.

"You just met him, and now you're fucking him?" Que yelled louder.

"We're not fucking!" I yelled back.

"Well, what the fuck is going on?" He continued yelling.

"We like each other," I said.

"You shouldn't be kissing him in the kitchen out in the open. No dating on my damn tour," Que shouted.

"Stop yelling at me!" I shouted back.

"Stop acting like a nasty bitch!"

"Kissing someone makes me a nasty bitch? Since when? You're fucking just about everyone on this tour and I'm the bitch? You keep us locked up in this house and we feel like prisoners! You're the only one that's fucking around this house. You get off playing these games with everyone and you want to control our every move. Fuck you!" I shouted letting out everything I was feeling inside.

"Damn, Music, you're really trying to curse me out! Johnny is a dog and has fucked everyone in this business. I'm just trying to protect you."

"Asshole!" I yelled.

"Stop going off on me like that," Que said, laughing.

"I don't like the person you have become. You're a freak and just crazy! I don't remember you being this way when we were younger."

"As you can see, I'm not a little boy anymore. I'm a grown man."

"I remember you having to control every situation when we were kids. You were a spoiled rotten kid and wanted everything to go your way. I guess some things never change. I just don't remember you being such a dog because you always treated women with respect," I said, calming down a little.

Que and I could argue one moment, and the next minute, we would act like nothing happened.

"I still treat women with respect. I just want what I want when I want it. How did we get on me anyway? This conversation was about you and Johnny," Que said, raising his voice again.

"I'm just worried about you. You've really changed."

"Don't try to use my words," he replied.

"Why do you have to sleep with every woman on this tour?" I asked him.

"I haven't slept with you," Que said with a grin.

"We're family and will never sleep together. You need to keep your little dick wrapped up."

"My dick ain't little. Have you seen it?" Que questioned.

"Shut up!"

"Are you still upset about the initiation?" He asked.

"Yes!" I said quickly.

"It's over now. I told you I'm sorry."

"Whatever," I responded.

"Are we cool?" Que asked.

"Yeah. Whatever Que."

"You're still my little sister and I love you," he expressed, but I didn't respond. "You can't stay mad at me forever."

Que and I had the type of relationship where we could say anything to each other. We truly acted like brother and sister and had been there for each other since we were kids. Que was always over-protective of me since he didn't have any sisters of his own.

Now that no one was around to witness our conversation, I was able to speak to him like I usually did, and I knew he would accept it. I knew I couldn't talk to him like that around other people, so I let it loose and said everything on my mind while I had the chance.

Que took two pills out of his pocket, popped them in his mouth, and washed them down with some water before speaking. "Since I'm already sleeping with everyone, maybe we should sleep together."

"What?" I asked, aggravated.

"I'm just kidding. But, if you ever want to, just let me know and I will fuck you," Que said, looking at me with a serious expression.

"You need to keep that little dick in your pants," I said shaking my head.

I was annoyed that he kept asking to sleep with me. That was something he had never done, and now I felt like he was crossing the line. While trying to erase his disrespectful comment from my mind, I started looking at all the pictures on the wall.

"Come here so I can show you how it feels. You might like it."

When I turned around to roll my eyes hard at him, I saw Que sitting in the chair with his dick in his hand stroking it. He was right; his was not a little boy anymore and his dick was huge.

I couldn't believe he was sitting there with his dick out, hard as a rock, stroking it in front of me. However, I had to remember that he allowed Tipp to suck his dick in front of everyone and he didn't seem to care.

Before I could say anything, Doug walked into the room, saw Que rubbing himself and quickly turned around trying not to look. He looked shocked and hurt at the same time.

"The band will be here in five minutes to record the hook for the song," Doug said slowly.

"Send them in here in twenty minutes," Que told him, as he continued stroking his dick.

"Okay," Doug said, as he looked at me disappointed before leaving.

"That's just great! Now Doug is going to think I'm sleeping with you. Put your damn dick back in your pants before I beat the hell out of it with my shoe!" I yelled.

"Calm down. Who cares what Doug thinks?" He replied, while trying to put his hard dick back inside his pants.

"What's wrong with you, Que?" I asked, totally baffled by his actions.

I looked at him as he took his time zipping his pants. Frustrated, I picked up a magazine off the table and threw it directly at him. He dodged it and started laughing hard.

"Relax," Que said.

"Don't treat me like one of your bitches!" I replied, upset.

"You need to relax and enjoy yourself sometimes. You're too uptight."

"I don't know who you are anymore. You're a nasty dog!" I yelled.

"Who the fuck are you talking to like that? You're the nasty bitch! You fucked Slyy, and now you're fucking Johnny!" Que shouted.

"Slyy raped me, and I'm not fucking Johnny!" I yelled.

"You were about to fuck him if I hadn't walked into the kitchen," he shouted.

"I haven't fucked him yet!" I yelled back.

Looking at Que's face, I could tell he didn't like me talking to him in that tone. He also didn't like that I said I was going to have sex with Johnny.

"Shut the fuck up!" Que yelled angrily.

"You shut the fuck up!"

"Bitch!" Que said under his breath, as he got up to grab some CD's off the table while trying to calm down.

"I'm a bitch? You're a murderer! You killed Slyy!" I shouted to the top of my lungs.

As soon as Que heard me say he killed Slyy, he rushed over to me, grabbed me by my shirt, and pushed me against the wall. I hit the wall so hard that it knocked the breath out of me.

Surprised by his actions, I blinked my eyes a couple of times before taking my knee and shoving it in his balls. He screamed out in pain. He then grabbed my shirt again and hit me in the chest while continuing to hold his position. I took both of my hands and grabbed his hands to try to stop his tight grip.

"What the fuck did you just say?" Que asked with a killer look in his eyes.

"Get off of me!" I said, trying to break loose.

"We agreed never to mention it!" Que said, fuming.

"You're crazy!"

"Have you been running your mouth?" He asked, enraged.

"No! Now let me go!"

While we were yelling back and forth at each other, we didn't hear the band members walk into the room. When they saw me pinned against the wall by Que, they rushed over to break it up with Johnny leading them.

"What's going on?" Johnny asked, while he and the other band members along with security pulled Que off of me.

"Get off of me!" Que shouted.

"Man, what are you doing?" Johnny asked in total shock.

Que was furious that Johnny was interrupting and asking him questions. He didn't even want Johnny talking to him. He also knew he couldn't tell them why we were arguing and why he had me pinned against the wall.

"Stay out of this!" Que told Johnny.

Just as he was told, Johnny quickly shut up. He stared at Que and then back at me with a frown on his face and his hands balled up.

"Are you okay?" Security asked Que.

"I'm cool. Everybody get the fuck out of my studio!" Que yelled so loud it startled them.

Security didn't move. Instead, they looked at Que to make sure everything was fine. Que nodded his head, giving the signal that everything was okay. As the band and security started leaving the room, I followed behind them.

"Music, don't you leave this motherfucking room!" Que yelled.

I felt like a prisoner who had almost gotten away. I stopped, closed my eyes, and took a deep breath because I didn't want to continue this fight with him. Johnny immediately stopped walking and turned around when he heard him tell me to stay.

"You better keep moving, man!" Que said, as he gritted his teeth.

Johnny stood there and thought about what Que had just said. He wasn't moving fast enough, so security pushed him out the door. It was obvious Johnny wanted to step in and help me, but he didn't know if I was worth him losing his job, especially since he didn't know what was going on.

My heart dropped when the door closed, leaving just Que and I standing face to face. He stood there looking at me furiously. I didn't know if he was going to continue where he left off, but I was prepared to fight. When he reached for my shoulder, I went off, pushing and hitting him.

"Stop, Music! This has gotten out of hand. You know I will never hit a woman," he said.

"No, you don't hit women. You just punched me in my chest," I said out of breath from fighting him with everything I had.

"I can't go to jail because you can't keep your mouth shut. My life and career is in jeopardy, and I'm not going to lose either one. My albums are number one, my concerts are sold out, I'm producing songs for every major artist, and my clothing line makes over fifty million dollars a year. I can't have you fuck that up! We're family and I don't want to hurt you, but if you mention that again out loud, I might have to kill you," Que said, looking at me with a look I had never seen before.

Appearing to be in deep thought, he grabbed his head and rubbed it hard. I couldn't say a word. I looked at the strange expression on his face, which reminded me of the look Slyy had right before he beat me.

I watched Que stab Slyy in the neck, kill him, clean up the murder scene, and then act like nothing happened, so I knew he would have no problem killing me. I also didn't know how he was able to deal with killing Slyy so easily, which made me think maybe he had killed before. Que had a lot to lose, and he wasn't going to allow me to get in the way of continuing his successful career.

"What if someone overheard you? I'm sorry for losing my temper," Que said sincerely.

"It's okay," I said softly.

I didn't believe a word he said. Que had never put his hands on me and was the one who always protected me. All I could think about was how much he had change and how I really didn't know him anymore. My lifelong friend was now a stranger to me. He had turned into a controlling person, a dog, a murderer, a possible drug addict, and a freaky sex-crazed man. I was now afraid of him.

"Are we cool?" Que asked.

"Yeah," I said.

"Music, don't repeat that again. We can't make any mistakes."

"Okay," I said.

"I'm so sorry for putting my hands on you," he told me again, trying to make things better.

"I don't know you anymore," I said, as a tear rolled down my cheek.

"I'm the same person. I haven't changed," he replied.

"You've changed."

"Let me make this up to you," Que said, sounding very apologetic.

"I'm cool," I responded, because there was nothing he could do to make the situation better.

"Good. Now go back to rehearsal so you won't miss anything."

"Okay."

Before I could walk out of the room, Que hugged me from behind and wouldn't let me go.

"I'm so sorry, Music. I will never hurt you again. I'm your brother and the one that protects you. You can still trust me. Slyy's death has just been very hard on me. I'm trying to act like it didn't happen, but I know it did. I'm scared to death. I don't want to go to jail," Que whispered in my ear.

I turned around and saw that he had tears running down his face. I had never seen him so afraid before. Honestly, I was happy to hear that he had feelings, because I was starting to think he was a heartless killer. Now, I knew he was just as scared as Raven and I.

"I'm scared, too. I'm glad to hear how you feel. Raven and I have been having a hard time dealing with this. It's just good to hear that you're suffering too, because we didn't think you had a soul," I expressed, sounding relieved.

"I'm scared, Music. My life and career can be over any day if they find out the truth," Que said, crying.

"I will never tell your secret. We will always be family. I don't want to go to jail either," I said, wiping the tears from his face.

"I'm so sorry for hurting you."

"I'm cool. That was nothing," I said trying to downplay the situation.

"Don't hate me," he said.

"I don't hate you. I'm going to go back to rehearsals now," I told him.

"Okay. I'll talk to you later," Que said, as he sat down, put his hand on his head, and hung it low.

I walked back into rehearsal and pretended like nothing happened. Johnny stared at me the whole time and the band members had a funny look on their faces. Sexy was staring at me upset that I had left the room with Doug and had been gone for an hour, and Raven had a look on her face that told me she wanted to hear all the details.

"Is everything cool?" Raven whispered as I got into position.

"Yeah, I'll tell you about it later," I whispered back.

I finished rehearsal like nothing had happen. I was used to working during a crisis. In this business, you learn to put your personal feelings or problems to the side and finish the job. The show must go on no matter what.

After a couple of hours, rehearsal was over. Raven quickly pulled me to the side to hear every little detail. Johnny walked over and gave me a hug. He whispered in my ear that he would call me later. Then he kissed me on the cheek and walked out of the room. He wasn't hiding his affections and was letting it be known to everybody that we were involved. After everyone had left the room, I told Raven everything that happened between me and Que.

"I can't believe this shit," Raven said.

"He's crazy," I stated.

"I'm going to beat his ass," she told me.

"Don't worry about it. He's just as scared as we are. He doesn't want to go to jail either," I whispered.

"It's funny how you can get raped, beaten, and now slammed against a wall, yet you keep going like nothing has happened. One day you're going to snap." Raven said.

"I'm a strong person, but I can only take so much. It's a shame that I'm used to chaos," I said.

"You need to stop taking bullshit from these men. Make his ass pay," Raven said, fuming.

"I'm still wondering when you're going to get initiated," I said.

"I had my initiation when I sucked Que's dick. I've already passed."

I huffed. "That's not fair."

"I told you to get with the program. Then you won't have to deal with that bullshit," Raven responded.

"Wow," I said, shaking my head.

CHAPTER 14

When Raven and I headed to rehearsal the next day, I tried my best not to run into Johnny because I was too embarrassed and not ready to explain what happened with Que. Hopefully, it would pass without a word having to be said.

Once we got to rehearsal, only a few band members and dancers were in the room. Usually by the time we arrived, more people were there. It was twenty minutes before rehearsals started and no one else had shown up. That's when Raven and I knew something was wrong.

"What's going on?" I asked Heat.

"I don't know. I'm surprised everyone is not here by now. Maybe it has something to do with Johnny getting fired," she replied.

"Johnny got fired!" I said, stunned.

"I heard he got fired this morning." Heat said.

"What happened?" Raven asked.

"I don't know," she responded.

"Did he leave the house already?" I asked.

"Not yet, because I saw him in his room when I was on my way here."

As Raven and I looked at each other frowning, my heart dropped. We knew Que was crazy, but we didn't think he was foolish enough to fire his music director a week before the tour started. If this was true and Johnny had gotten fired, I knew Que fired him because he was trying to help me.

I suddenly became emotional, and Raven had to hit me to calm me down.

Finally, Swagg walked into the room ten minutes after rehearsal was supposed to start.

"Guess what, guys?" Swagg said, smiling from ear to ear.

"What!" We said stunned.

"We got the night off," Swagg announced, still grinning from ear to ear.

We didn't believe her because we hadn't had a day off since we started rehearsing almost three months ago.

"I'm serious! Que gave us tonight off. He said you can leave the house if you want, but you must be back before eight o'clock in the morning. Rehearsal will start tomorrow as normal. I've already informed the rest of the group. That's why they're not here now. Go and enjoy your night off," Swagg said, looking totally ecstatic.

"What made him give us a night off?" I asked Swagg.

"Since we only have one week left before the tour starts, he wanted you guys to have a break," Swagg said.

Before Swagg could finish explaining, everyone had grabbed their stuff and was headed for the door. Raven and I walked slowly behind the others as we headed to our room. Some people walked right out of the house and started enjoying their freedom.

"I can't believe he fired Johnny!" I told Raven, as we walked to the room.

"Wow! Que is serious," Raven said.

"I feel like it's my fault," I said sadly.

"It's not your fault. You can't control Que."

"I feel like it is my fault because Johnny was trying to defend me."

"Let's go to his room and see if he really got fired," Raven said.

"Okay. Let's go."

Quickly, Raven and I headed to Johnny's bedroom and couldn't wait to find out what was going on. I was nervous to see him, but needed to get some answers. As soon as we got to his door, it opened quickly and his roommate walked out.

We looked in the bedroom and saw Johnny putting clothes in his luggage, which confirmed he had gotten fired. Raven gave me a sad look and gestured for me to go in the room.

"Go in there and find out what's going on. I will wait out here," Raven said, as she started talking to his roommate.

I walked into the room slowly and closed the door behind me. Johnny looked up at me, and then he put his head back down and continued closing his luggage.

"What's going on, Johnny?" I asked with concern.

"You tell me," he said upset.

"Where are you going?"

"I was fired, so I'm going home," Johnny said annoyed.

"Why?" I asked softly.

"I didn't get an explanation. I was just told I was fired and needed to leave today. A car will be here to take me to the airport in a few hours," he calmly informed me.

"This doesn't make any sense," I said, baffled.

"It's very clear to me," he replied.

"Does it have anything to do with the situation between me and Que?"

"You tell me," Johnny said, sounding irritated.

"Please don't treat me this way. I don't know what's going on," I said sadly.

"I assume it has something to do with you and Que," Johnny responded, then sat in a chair and stared at me.

"I'm so sorry, Johnny."

"It's not your fault. I've been tired of Que's bullshit anyway. So, if I got to go, then I'm gone, and this time I won't be back," he said, taking a sip from his beer.

"What are you going to do?" I asked.

"I'm the highest paid producer in the world, and I've worked all my life. I've written number one songs for just about every artist in the business, and I've won a few Grammy Awards. So, I really don't need this tour. When I get bored, I work on tours as a music director during my time off. I'm just upset about him acting like a spoiled bitch," Johnny replied, then took a longer sip from his beer.

After inhaling deeply, I blew it out and closed my eyes for a second. "I'm happy this isn't affecting your money," I said, relieved.

"I financially don't need to do this tour. I live in a five-bedroom house and drive a Bentley," he said with an air of cockiness.

"I guess you're paid."

"Look, are you going to tell me what the hell was going on between you and Que?" Johnny asked, getting mad.

"Can we discuss that later?"

"Yeah, that's what I thought," Johnny said, frowning.

"If you think Que and I are sleeping together, you're wrong. He's my friend. We just got into a bad argument." I said.

Seeing the way he was looking at me, I knew I had to tell him something.

"What would make him try to hurt you like that?" Johnny asked, looking for answers.

"Can we please talk about this later?"

"Yeah, whatever," he said, while looking at me strangely.

"I really like you, Johnny, and I don't want you to go home."

"Well, I'm going," He said.

"I see you're upset, so I'm going to leave. It's not my fault that you're leaving, but I'm sorry you got fired," I said, then started walking toward the door.

"Wait, Music," Johnny said, then stood up and walked towards me.

"Be mad at Que. Not me," I told him.

"I just thought you guys were sleeping together because it looked like a lover's spat," Johnny said.

"I told you that we're not sleeping together, but if you want to keep thinking that, then fine. I'm out of here."

"Well leave!" Johnny said angrily.

"I'm gone!" I yelled.

I swung the door open and began to walk out. He snatched me back inside, closed the door, and started kissing me. He pushed me up against the wall, ripped my shirt off, and quickly turned me around to face the wall. He was kind of rough, but not too forceful.

"Wait. What are you doing?" I said softly, trying to stop his quick movements.

"I want you now before I leave," he expressed.

"Not like this," I told him.

"Why not? Are you scared Que will find out?" Johnny said, as he suddenly stopped.

"This has nothing to do with Que."

"Then let me make love to you before I leave," he said, then started kissing me again.

I wanted to make him stop, but I was too hot and horny to resist. Plus, if I was never going to see him again, I wanted to make sure I felt every inch of him. It didn't seem like he was going to take no for an answer, so I decided to give him want he wanted, willingly.

I grabbed his shirt and ripped it open, popping all the buttons off. After pulling his shirt off, I removed his pants while he removed my clothes quickly. He immediately lifted me off the ground, with my legs dangling across his shoulders as he parted my valley with his tongue. He walked over to the wall, and I leaned my back against it while he licked me until I started shaking.

He slowly put me down and moved me to the bed. I rubbed his body, amazed at how great he looked. I kissed his neck, chest, and stomach. Then, I inserted his big, hard dick inside my mouth. He started breathing really hard as he grabbed my head tightly. I lay down and showed him how flexible I really was by stretching my legs open to a perfect Chinese split.

"Damn," Johnny said, amazed and turned on by my flexibility and my Brazilian wax.

He quickly put a condom on and rushed his dick inside me fast and deep. I let out a long moan and begged him to stop, even though I really didn't want him to. I was impressed with how long, thick, and fulfilling his dick was. It was almost too much to handle.

"I want to fuck you first, and then I want to make love to you. Is that okay?" He asked softly, but with authority.

I hesitated before nervously saying, "Okay."

I was a little tense as he held my hands down and fucked me so hard that I started crying. He slowed down and then turned me over doggie style, fucking me even harder. He picked me up from the bed and carried me across the floor to the window, while his throbbing dick was still inside me. After turning me around, he sat on the edge of a chair, I straddled him and we continued fucking.

Once he came, we sat on the chair holding each other. A few minutes later, he got up and went to the bathroom. I waited for him to finish, and I went in to freshen up next. When I came back out, he was lying on the bed and gesturing for me to come and lay down beside him.

As I lay next to him, he expressed how great I felt and how much he cared me. He told me that he was not into sharing, and therefore, he didn't want to share me with anyone. He said he wanted a commitment and would like us to have a relationship.

Without waiting for my response, he stared into my eyes and told me that he wanted to make love to me. I was still tired from being fucked all over the room and didn't know if I was up for another round. However, I wanted him and couldn't get enough. I was sore and needed a break, but couldn't resist him inside me again.

While rubbing my body so gently, he kept whispering in my ear how he was going to marry me one day. He made love to me so gently. Once we were done, he looked at the clock and jumped up because the car would be there in twenty minutes to take him to the airport. Although he didn't financially need to work on the tour, I knew he didn't want to leave.

"I hope this isn't the last time I will see you," Johnny said, while getting dressed.

"It won't be," I said unhappily.

"Please don't play me. I really want to be with you when this tour is over," he confirmed.

"I want to be with you, too," I said, hugging him.

"Good. Let's keep in contact while you're on the road, and once the tour is over, come see me before you go home so I can make love to you again," Johnny said seriously.

"Thanks for standing up for me," I told him.

"No problem," he said.

"I'm really sorry you got fired."

"Don't sweat it. This was all worth it now that I met you and have you in my life," Johnny replied, smiling.

"Thanks," I said, returning the same warm smile.

"You're going to tell me what happened between you and Que, right?" Johnny asked.

"Yes, of course," I responded, assuring him.

"Good, because I think I have a right to know," Johnny said, as he fastened his belt buckle.

"I don't want you to leave," I told him.

"I don't want to leave you, baby, but I got to go. I will see you when you guys come to LA. I'll call you when I make it home," he said.

Then he kissed and hugged me goodbye and left the room.

Tired of waiting on me, Raven returned to our room. Once I entered, she immediately started badgering me for details, so I gave her the play-by-play of me and Johnny's sex scene.

"Johnny seems like a cool person," Raven commented. "Make sure you keep in contact with him."

"Oh, I'm not going to let him get away, but we will see how it all plays out. Time will tell if he's really serious about me or if he was just spitting game," I said, hoping he was telling the truth about his feelings.

My cell phone rang, and thinking it was my mother calling, I ignored the call. When it continued to ring, I picked it up and was prepared to press the ignore button until I saw Johnny's name on the screen. I quickly answered.

"Hey, baby. You miss me?" Johnny asked, sounding excited.

"Yes, I miss you. Come back and get me."

"Are you serious? You know I will have this car turn around and come to pick you up," he replied.

"Good answer," I said, blushing.

"Matter of fact, pack your bags and get out of there. I don't want my girl working for Que's crazy ass," Johnny said.

Not taking him seriously, I waited for him to laugh and say he was just joking. However, when I didn't respond, he got quiet.

"Johnny, are you still there?" I asked.

"Yeah, I'm here," he said sounding disappointed.

"You know I can't leave right now. I just want to finish what I started," I explained.

"No problem. I just want you with me," he expressed.

"I'm happy to hear that because I want to be with you right now," I said.

"Well, I'm pulling up to the airport. I will give you a call when I get home. Hey, stay out of trouble, and if you need me, don't hesitate to call me. You know I'm here for you."

"Thank you. Have a safe flight and please make sure you call me when you get home," I said.

"Bye, sexy," he said, then hung up.

I threw my head back and enjoyed the wonderful feeling I was experiencing. My telephone rang, and thinking it was Johnny again, I picked it up without checking the caller ID.

"Where have you been?" My mother asked.

"Damn!" I mumbled to myself.

"Hello," my mother said.

"Hi, Mom," I replied, irritated.

"Music, I have been trying to call you. I even called Raven trying to reach you. I know you're ignoring me, but I really need to talk to you. You've run from me long enough."

"Mom, I can't talk right now. Que has us in rehearsal all day long, and it's been crazy around here. Can I talk to you when the tour is over?" I asked.

"Music, I need to talk to you now," my mother demanded.

"They want me back in rehearsal. Sorry, I got to go, Mom. I will talk to you when the tour is over. Love ya. Bye," I said quickly and hung up.

Raven looked at me because she knew we did not have to go to rehearsal since we had the day off. She also knew I didn't want to talk to my mom.

"Your mother is very persistent. I think you should hear what she has to say. I think something is wrong," Raven said, concerned.

"Girl, my mother does this all the time when I won't listen to her. It's nothing that important, trust me. She can wait until I feel like dealing with her."

I checked my voicemail and deleted all ten of my mother's desperate messages. There was one message from my cousin Sydney, who called to say hello and to inform me that my mother had been blowing her telephone up too.

She said my mother really needed to talk to me and she thought I should give her a call. I planned on talking to my mother, but not until after the tour was over. So, she would just have to wait until then. In the meantime, I would continue to ignore all her calls.

CHAPTER 15

Raven left the room thirty minutes before rehearsal to go visit Que. I drugged myself down to the studio to get through another long exhausting night. I was really missing Johnny and didn't want to see Que's face. Johnny gave me something to smile about and the motivation to keep going.

I walked into rehearsal and Macy was waiting for everyone to tell us we were rehearsing at another location. She told everyone to get on the tour bus to be driven to the new place. Once I got on the bus, Raven was already sitting down waving for me to sit next to her. Everyone looked tired but excited to be getting out of the house.

"Que said we are going to a larger rehearsal space where a mock-up of our entire stage is set up. We are going to rehearse there for the next week until we leave for the tour," Raven said.

"Cool. Did Que say anything about firing Johnny?" I asked.

"No, he didn't even want to talk about it," Raven said.

We walked into the rehearsal room and were impressed at the stage. We saw the drawing of the stage and bits and pieces of it at the house, but never seen the entire stage set up and ready to go.

We had our routines down, so we were going to use this time to work with the props. The show was going to be very detailed with tons of excitement. We worked with the stage manager all night long learning how to use the different props for the show.

The band rehearsed a few songs and perfected the intro, and the additional last minute songs Que added to the show. I was shocked to see a new music director sitting in Johnny's seat never missing a beat. I guess the saying is true, that there is always someone waiting in the background for your spot and Johnny spot was already filled.

Raven knew I was upset with Que and missing Johnny at the same time. She also knew that I could put my feelings to the side and rehearse. I was turning into a different person and she knew touring was the cause of it. Que showed up to the rehearsals three hours later and demanded we start the show from the top.

"Let's get started and don't fuck up one move because I'm not in the mood for no bullshit," Que said as soon as he walked onto the stage.

We quickly jumped into place and waited for our cue. We ran through the entire show without any mistakes, just adjustments. We were flying through the air, popping up from the floor, sliding onto the stage and hanging from the ceiling.

Things had to be perfect or you could be seriously hurt. I hadn't said a word to Que since he had been in rehearsal and it seem like he was trying to avoid me. I had a solo dance I had to do with Que and was dreading when the time came to rehearse the number.

I waited backstage to do my solo performance and I had to take a deep breath to relax. I needed to be sexy and seductive for this number. This scene was created to tease the men and make the women jealous, and I wasn't in the mood for any of it, but I was going to be professional and do my job. This was a love scene and I was to portray the sound of music, which he fell in love with.

The music started and I entered the stage laying on a piano that was suspended in air. The piano slowly came down and landed softly on the stage right in front of Que. A crew member put a bench in front of the piano as soon as it landed. I didn't want to look at Que but I knew if I didn't do what we rehearsed he was going to make me do it over and I wasn't about to do that.

Que started playing the piano to the slow seductive love song, still never looking at me. I did my dance on the piano and slowly slid off while walking around him. Que stood up and started singing to me staring into my eyes.

I continued to play my part, knowing I wanted to hit him, but I kept my composure. At the end of the number, Que was suppose to grab me by the back of my neck and slowly pretend to kiss me as the lights turned down.

When that part came, Que grabbed my neck so hard, I gasped for air loud enough for everyone to hear me in is microphone. He had a tight grip on my neck and yanked my head back. I never moved and kept my eyes locked on his.

He gave the band a gesture with his hand that told them to make the music softer. So the band broke it down to an almost nonexistent sound. I was getting so uncomfortable but I stayed in character and never took my eyes off of him.

Que looked at me and I couldn't understand his expression. This moment was not suppose to last this long, but I went with the flow. He quickly yanked my body close to his and went in for a kiss.

I started pulling my head back and he squeezed my neck tighter. We were not supposed to kiss for real and it felt like he was really trying to. I knew not to embarrass him by not kissing him, so I prepared myself to give him the fake closed mouth television kiss. The lights went down slowly and that was our signal to let go of each other. Que never let me go and continue to hold me close, looking at me like he was contemplating on actually kissing me.

As long as he was still holding me, the band had to keep playing softly. He was making me nervous but I knew he enjoyed trying to break people down and I was not about to let him. I stood my ground.

He needed to conquer everything around him and I was the only one left untouched by him and he seemed to have a problem with that. Soon he let go of me and I exited the stage as planned. Que told everyone to stop in the microphone.

"Damn, I hope I don't have to do that again," I mumbled to myself.

"That's was perfect. I'm not going to hold Music that long during the tour, I just wanted to test you guys to make sure you are on point because you don't suppose to stop the song until I let go of her, no matter how long I hold her. That was great. I love it when you guys pay attention. Good job Music for not breaking character," Que said in the microphone.

I was happy to hear that he was testing us because I thought he had snapped on stage. Raven seemed to be relieved also because she couldn't accept him kissing me. As Raven prepared for her solo performance, I looked at the other dancers who was showing jealousy on their faces. Que took the solo dances from them because they wasn't giving him what he wanted and that made them continue to hate us.

Raven waited for her cue and went on stage to perform. At the end of their performance Que actually tongued kissed Raven on stage, which was not part of the act. He hit her butt while she was being whisked off the stage on an overly size red chaise chair.

We completed the entire show and we were all exhausted and Que wanted to run through the show again. Everyone cringed at the thought of repeating the show, but sucked it up and got it done. Que was excited and felt impressed by our performance. He told everyone how happy he was and how he couldn't wait until the tour started.

We rehearsed at the new facilities for the next four days and felt comfortable the show was going to be a hit. Finally, Que announced to everyone that we were going to be leaving the house to start the tour.

Our first place we were going to was Dallas. We had a long tour ahead of us and I was ready for it to begin and end, so I could be with Johnny.

CHAPTER 16

It was finally time for us to show all of our hard work to the world. It was one o'clock in the morning, and we were getting ready to head to Dallas, the first stop on the tour. The show was already sold out and another show had been added.

The promoters wanted to add more shows, but our schedule wouldn't permit it. Our schedule consisted of tour dates and televised award show performances, which made it impossible to do anything else.

I was mentally drained and physically strong. With all the rehearsals, my energy level was through the roof and my dance skills were enhanced. Raven and I had never rehearsed so much in our life, but it made a difference in our performance.

We packed our clothes and double checked to make sure we were not leaving anything in our nicely posh prison. After setting our luggage outside our bedroom door as instructed, we headed to the tour bus.

Once we got outside and saw all the buses, we immediately stopped, not knowing which bus to get on. We didn't want to go through the same thing we went through when we first started, so we waited outside for Macy.

"Why aren't you guys on the bus?" Macy asked, while approaching us.

"We don't know which bus to get on," I said.

"Get on the black bus," she instructed.

A large smile appeared on our faces when she told us to get on Que's tour bus. Although I didn't want to ride with him, he had the best bus and I wasn't giving up my spot to anyone. Raven and I boarded the luxury bus and was happy to smell the vanilla-scented candles burning.

"Road trip," Que screamed as he walked on the bus. When he saw me and Raven, he smiled. We had passed our initiation and were able to finally ride in style.

He seemed to be in a great mood and was excited to start the tour, but I just wanted to relax. It seemed like everyone had the same feeling as I did because we got in our beds and went straight to sleep.

The bus was quiet for the ride to Dallas. Four hours later, Que woke up the entire bus with loud music coming from the recording studio he had built on the tour bus, which took up the entire back room. I didn't understand where he got all his energy from, but I was just happy he was the one working and not us.

However, Que made sure everyone was awake by opening up the door and letting the music flow throughout the bus. Within seconds, everyone was up and peeking out of their beds. Que danced down the aisle, grabbing everyone and pulling us out of our beds to join him.

He was hyped and ready to show the world his new and improved show. After thirty minutes of the spontaneous dancing, everyone returned to their beds and rushed to get some much-needed sleep as Que continued to work.

~~~~~~~

We pulled up in front of the arena in Dallas ready to do the sound check. For this show, we didn't have time to check into a hotel. So, we had to shower and dress in the arena dressing room. I always hated using the shower area of different venues because they were usually dirty and disgusting.

Before walking into the arena, which was gigantic and overwhelming, we were instructed not to talk to anyone that wasn't part of our tour. Once inside, we were ordered to go directly to the stage. It was always a thrill to see the arenas empty and imagine all the people that would fill the seats. It made your adrenaline flow and pumped you up for the show.

When Que entered the building, his staff told people to look in the opposite direction until he had entered his dressing room. He wanted the hallways clear when he walked down them.

It was hard for the promoters to book acts for the tour because Que didn't like anyone they recommended, especially if it was a male artist or group because he would start to feel intimidated. He would complain the whole time which made the artist so uncomfortable they eventually left in the middle of the tour.

His insecurities were truly showing and the media was soaking it all up. On one show, he complained that the male artist stage looked better than his. He demanded that the artist didn't have a band or back drop. He wanted to make sure his show was going to be the hottest thing on his tour.

Que didn't have that many problems with female artists on the show. However, they had issues with him always trying to have sex with them. If the female artist didn't want to have sex with him, he would insist that they leave the tour. He didn't have a problem kicking people off his tour because he knew they could be replaced.

It was very hard for entertainers to work with Que. His reputation of being a controlling, sex-crazed, insecure, crackhead artist had gotten around the entertainment grapevine. The industry respected his music because he consistently created number one songs, but they didn't respect him. Most of the artists only dealt with his attitude because they needed him for their next hit record.

Que was acting like a male diva. He was being so ridiculous and controlling, but because he was the headliner of the tour, the promoters and staff jump at his every demand. Que was very rough on us at sound check and made us perform like it was the real show. He complained about every little detail and worked us like dogs.

Once we finished sound check, we noticed two men wearing suits walk into the arena and up on the stage. We thought it was strange because Que always had a closed sound check and no one was invited in. When the two men walked right on stage, we all stopped and looked on in shock because we knew Que was about to go off on them.

"We're looking for Que, Music, and Raven," one of the men said.

"Can I help you?" Security asked, trying to stop them.

"We can talk in my dressing room," Que told them, stepping forward, knowing their visit had something to do with Slyy's murder since they were asking to speak with me and Raven, also. Que then told us to follow him and the men to the dressing room to talk.

"What's going on?" Que asked in a deep voice as soon as he closed the door of his dressing room.

"We need to talk to you guys about the night Slyy was murder. Can you tell me what you saw?" One of the men asked.

Que started telling them that he only noticed Akira running out of the room with blood on her hands and that he didn't see or hear anything else. He said he was as shocked as everybody else. Raven and I followed his lead and gave the exact same story with a little extra wording on how scared we were that a murderer had been amongst us.

The two men, who were both writing in their notepads while each of us gave our recollection of that night, appeared to be satisfied with our answers. When we asked if they had any leads on the killer, they said they were working on it and that we were the last people they needed to talk with to conclude their investigation.

"What's going to happen next?" I inquired.

"Now that we have spoken with everyone, we will be going to court," the man said.

"Are we done, because I have a show to do?" Que asked.

"Yes, sir, and thanks for your time. We didn't want you to relive that night, but we need to do our job," the man said.

"No problem. Feel free to stay for my show. I can arrange two front row tickets for you, if you like," Que offered.

"That would be wonderful. Thank you," the men said, looking excited.

"Sure. My people will take care of you. Nice meeting you," he said, as we all walked out of the room.

Once we got back to the stage and away from the two men, we felt relieved. I was happy it was over and that they were satisfied with our answers. Their visit was unexpected and completely threw us for a loop, even though I figured they would catch up with us sooner or later. At least now, we didn't have to worry about their visit any longer.

"You guys did a good job. Raven, you really acted your butt off with those fake tears in your eyes," Que said.

"Those were not fake tears. I was scared to death and couldn't stop shaking. I guess they thought I was reliving the situation," she said.

"Well, at least it's over with. Now let's get ready for the show tonight," he told us as we went to our dressing room.

I started to think that was the reason why my mother had been calling me so much. Maybe those men went to visit her looking for me and scared her. I'm just glad it was over, and hopefully we wouldn't have to deal with it anymore.

Exhausted, I wanted to lie down and get some rest on the couch in our dressing room, but I didn't have time. The other dancers were just as tired as we were and immediately started popping pills.

"What is that?" Raven asked them.

"This is just something to keep our energy up," Heat responded.

"What is it?" I asked.

"It's our energy pill," Swagg said.

"Where can I get some? I'm tired as hell," Raven said.

"You can get them from Que," Swagg replied.

"Can't you just give us one of yours?" I asked.

"We were told not to share. Talk to Que. He'll hook you up," Swagg told us.

"Why do we have to talk to Que? These stupid bitches are making me sick," Raven whispered to me.

Everyone took their showers and headed to craft services to eat. Once the other dancers left the room, Raven quickly started going through Swagg's bag.

"What are you doing?" I asked, while laughing.

"I'm getting me some energy pills. If she won't give them to me, then I have to take them. I'm tired as hell," Raven said, searching her bag.

As soon as Raven found what she was looking for, she opened the container and started pouring some in her hand.

"What the fuck is this?" Raven asked, shocked.

I walked over to her. "What's wrong?"

"These ain't no damn energy pills. These are drugs!" Raven said.

"Drugs!"

"Uppers! These bitches are crack heads," Raven told me.

"If we have to get them from Que, that means he's using them, too," I replied.

"Damn, Que is an undercover crack head!" Raven said, disappointed.

"Uppers are not crack," I responded.

"Uppers, heroin, marijuana are all drugs. People crave them just like crack, so they're crack heads to me."

"I've seen Que popping pills, but he told me that they were for his tooth. He takes them a lot. He's probably addicted to prescription drugs too," I said.

"Do you want one?" Raven asked.

"I don't do drugs!" I yelled.

"I know. I was just checking. That's the one thing I will never do," Raven said, putting the pills back into the container.

"How did you know they were uppers if you don't do drugs?" I asked.

"I've been around a lot of people that do drugs, and I know what they look like," Raven told me.

"Maybe this explains Que's crazy attitude," I said, thinking.

"His ass is just crazy. He's probably doing some other drugs, too," Raven responded.

After Raven put the container back in Swagg's bag, we left the room to go fill our bellies and then return to the tour bus so we could try to rest before the show.

Three hours later, Macy walked on the tour bus and announced we had one hour before show time. We woke up from our short nap, grabbed our bags, and went to our dressing room to prepare.

Although I didn't do drugs, I could see how some people started using them on the road, because I really needed something to give me a burst of energy. Instead, I did my usual and grabbed some candy for a sugar rush. Raven stuffed candy in her mouth, as well, and we started getting ready to take the stage.

"It's show time!" Macy yelled, as she opened our dressing room door.

Raven and I were ready and eager to experience Que's fabulous show. All the media and press were there to cover also. The entire front row was filled with entertainers and music moguls.

The only difference from Slyy's first show was the backstage area was completely empty. Que didn't like anyone back stage before the show. This was actually relaxing because you didn't feel the eyes gawking at you as soon as you opened the dressing room door. Sometimes you just needed time to yourself before you walked on stage.

We headed to the side of the stage and waited for Que. Everyone looked casual, which was a totally different vibe from what we were accustomed to. We were always dressed to impress on Slyy's tour, but Que's tour was much more laidback.

Raven and I stood out because our faces were done, which made us look stunning, and our hair was done to perfection. The band members quickly complimented us and stared the entire time we waited on the side of the stage. When Que arrived and looked around to make sure everyone was there, he took an extra long look at Raven and me. Instantly, we looked away.

"You guys look like you're about to walk on a runway in a fashion show. You look beautiful, but all that make-up is not needed," Que told me and Raven.

We just looked at him embarrassed that he had announced this in front of everyone, but we knew not to respond. The other dancers looked at us like they were happy Que had said something, and they were excited that we would have to look as drab as they did for the remaining shows.

"You guys don't have time to wash your face now, but just make sure you don't have all that make-up on from now on," Que said, looking directly at us.

"Okay," we replied in unison, totally embarrassed.

The band got into position and the crew hooked all the dancers and Que up to cords so we could be lifted in the air for our grand entrance. Que looked at us and nodded his head, giving us the stamp of approval to have a good show. Butterflies started forming in my stomach. I hadn't felt nervous before a show in a long time.

I looked over at Raven, winked, and whispered, "Have a good show."

Raven winked back and whispered, "You, too."

The lights were lowered, the band started playing, and the stage lights flickered. Suddenly, all the lights on the stage were cut off, creating total darkness. You could hear the concern of the crowd as they started talking, thinking something was wrong.

As soon as it seemed like the audience got louder, eight bright spotlights shined on us as we entered hanging upside down from above the stage. The spotlights changed colors, and as each color changed, we switched into acrobatic positions. Que never moved and came down on stage in a standing position.

Our last position as we hit the stage was a perfect Chinese split that we held until the crew unhooked us. Then Que gave the band a signal and the music started. The crowd continued yelling in amazement. We knew the significance of the opening number because it's one of the most important elements in the show that draws the audience in.

The show went great with and the audience loved the concert. My solo number went great, and when Raven did her solo number, Que did exactly what he had done during rehearsal; he kissed her deeply. The more the crowd screamed, the longer the kiss lasted. Every woman in the audience was jealous of Raven, wanting to be in her spot.

The closing performance was a magic number, and everyone except the band disappeared on stage. Que had hired the best magicians to pull this off, and it was worth every dollar he spent. The crowd jumped to their feet and a loud roar erupted in the arena. When it seemed like they couldn't take it anymore, Que reappeared and said his goodbyes.

"Great show," Que screamed, as he exited the stage.

We went back to our dressing room smiling and in good spirits. A good show always puts performers in a good mood, and the atmosphere in our dressing room was all love. With no time to waste, we showered, dressed, and boarded the tour bus to head to the next city.

The reviews Que received from the show were incredible, and people were talking about it everywhere. More shows were definitely going to be added, so the tour would get longer. A longer tour was wonderful words to our ears because it meant more money.

CHAPTER 17

We were already three months into the tour and had two more months to go before we went overseas. The shows were wonderful and running on schedule. Raven and I conformed to the plain look of the show and still gave an amazing performance.

Every show was sold out and was always given excellent reviews. Surprisingly, Que's tour was strictly professional with no issues, and we kept the same schedule. We performed, boarded the bus, and then headed to the next city. My only complaint was the horrible hotels he had us stay in while he stayed in five-star hotels.

Que had even let up a little with the control issue. He seemed to not care where we were while on the tour, just as long as we were ready to perform when it was showtime. We were happy not to be kept as prisoners anymore.

The only time he wanted constant control over us was when we got on the tour bus and entered the arena. However, after being told what to do twenty-four hours a day, we were able to deal with these terms.

I talked to Johnny on the phone more than I expected, and we seemed to really be getting closer. I couldn't wait to visit Los Angeles and hang out with him. He wanted to fly out to some of the shows, but he knew if he ran into Que, things would get bad for me. Still, we were going to find a way to see each other.

When the bus made a stop at a truck stop, everyone raided the store to buy chips, candy, and soda. While the bus driver filled the gas tank, we turned the television on hoping to get some reception since we were now stationary. We were only able to get the news channel, which we immediately started watching when we saw a picture of Slyy on the screen.

We sat front and center waiting to hear some news about Slyy. The reporter said they had found Slyy's daughter, but they were not releasing her name to the press until they spoke with her. They were also waiting on Akira's trial for the murder of Slyy and mentioned that Janice's family had checked her into a mental hospital. Janice really loved him and was still taking his death hard.

"Damn, Janice is messed up," Raven said.

"I want to know who his daughter is so I can marry her," Que said, not caring about Janice.

"Marry her?" I said.

"She's going to be rich and I want some of that money," Que replied, smirking.

"You're greedy," Raven said.

"I just want to stay rich," Que said laughing.

"That's ridiculous," I said shaking my head.

Once the bus driver drove away, we started losing the reception and the television became fuzzy. We tried to fix it, but had no luck. So, we did what we usually did and put a movie in the DVD player.

While on the road, Que's record company informed him that his album went double platinum and that he had won another Grammy. So, this put him in a good mood all week. It was cool seeing him so excited.

He even let us stay at the same hotel he did one night, but quickly reminded us the stay was only for that night. He didn't want us to get used to the good life. Que believed there was only one superstar on the tour and it was him and he was going to be the only one given the star treatment.

"I have something for you guys," Que announced with a big smile on his face.

"What?" Raven asked, smiling back.

He grabbed a bag from the back room and started handing out boxes with bows on them.

"I want to thank you guys for working so hard and making my shows hot. I know you put up with a lot, but it was all worth it. I know you heard my album went double platinum, so you know I'm floating on cloud nine. I just wanted to say thank you by giving you a little something."

When we opened the box, my eyes bucked and Raven's mouth dropped open. Que had purchased all the dancers diamond bracelets and earrings.

"Those are real diamonds!" Que informed us.

"Thank you!" We cheered.

He didn't have to tell us the diamonds were real because you could tell by just looking at them. They gave a sparkle that fake diamonds couldn't give. I was impressed by his generosity and quickly put my earrings and bracelet on.

I saw Que wink at Raven and give her a secretive look. That's when I quickly peeked into her box before she closed it. He had given her diamond earrings, bracelet, necklace, and a ring. She closed the box before anyone else could see. He definitely didn't want the other dancers to know he gave her more than them.

Being inspired, Que headed to the back room to start a new song, leaving us to admire our new jewelry. Curious to know what he was working on, Raven and I followed behind him.

"You should put Music on your song," Raven told Que.

"That's right. You can sing a little," he said, laughing as he led us into the studio.

Que created a hot song in no time, and we now understood why he produced for everyone and made number-one hits constantly. Raven and I chilled and listened to the music while watching him work.

"Come on, Music. Lace this track for me," he said.

"I'm cool," I said.

"Come on. Just for fun. Sing this hook for me."

"Okay, I'll sing it," I said, giving in.

Que gave me the lyrics for the hook, and after reading them, I tried to sing them for him. By the look on his face, he was impressed by my skills.

"Wow! I didn't know you had it like that," Que said, amazed.

"Thanks," I responded bashfully.

"After you sing this hook for me, I'm going to do a track for you. It will just be for fun," Que said, more inspired to create.

"Are you serious?"

"We're going to make a lot of money off of your voice."

I did the hook for him with no problems and only in two takes. Que was so impressed and hyped that he quickly gave me lyrics to a track he had been working on for his next album and asked me to sing the lead parts.

We recorded at least two songs and I was singing the lead on both. I even did a duet with Que on one song. He told me that he wanted to work with me and produce my album. He said people would love me because I was a great dancer and singer.

He quickly made some calls to set up a meeting with his record company. Although I was hesitant about working on a singing career, it felt good behind the microphone. It gave me a feeling I never felt before. I felt comfortable, relaxed, and confident.

"Bitch, I want twenty percent," Raven said.

"Twenty percent of what?" I asked.

"The manager's fee is twenty percent of all that money you're about to make once Que produces your album and get you a record deal. I've always told you to do something with your voice. There's a lot of money to get," Raven replied, excited.

"I guess I will see what happens with this singing thing," I said, smiling on the inside.

"We're rich, bitch!" Raven yelled, imitating Rick James.

I listened to the song as Que played it back, and I have to admit that I was impressed with my singing skills. With my voice and Que's hot tracks, we definitely had a number one song on our hands. I was ready. It would be my new career. The great thing about this new career was I could run my tour the way I wanted to.

CHAPTER 18

Several weeks had passed, and we had one week left on the tour. Que had started receiving some negative comments about his show, saying it was becoming too sexual. The media didn't like the scene he did with Raven and complained that it was too graphic.

With each show, Que got raunchier with his performance with Raven. First, it started out with a long kiss, then it moved to him fondling her, and then it was a fully clothed love session on stage. The media thought it was a bit too much.

Que's record company was concerned about the repeated bad reviews and suggested he change the x-rated part of the show to something a little more PG. Que didn't like people telling him what to do and how to run his show. He was upset and didn't want to change a thing, but he had no choice.

The last week of the tour was pushed back one week so he could make some changes to the show. He knew he wasn't going to make the changes they wanted; he only intended on adding more of the things the media didn't like. He did what he wanted when he wanted, and that had made a monster out of him.

When we returned to the same house in Atlanta, we rehearsed hard in order to make the necessary changes to his show. Que was on a mission and continued to make our life a living hell. He was rough on everyone and mean. He got plea-sure out of knowing he was about to piss off his record company and the media.

He made everyone stop eating food for the entire week we rehearsed, telling us it would help us become more focused and keep our minds right. The only thing fasting did was pissed me off and kept my stomach hungry.

After a couple days of fasting, a few of the band members passed out and a couple of the dancers vomited. There were several times when Raven and I almost fainted. Que then allowed us to drink water, orange juice, and some type of nasty green smoothie that his chef made. I'm not sure what was in the smoothie, but when a person is starving, they will eat anything.

Everyone was getting weak from not having solid food, and we weren't performing a hundred percent. Finally, one of Que's managers suggested he allow everyone to eat because we could die from the strenuous rehearsals, and then he would have tons of lawsuits on his hands.

Que didn't want to ever hear the word lawsuit since he had been sued so many times. This was the only thing that snapped him out of whatever horror scene he was trying to put us through.

We were finally allowed to eat chicken, fish, and vegetables only, which tasted like cheeseburgers, fries, steak and potatoes to me. By now, I knew he had snapped and didn't have all his marbles. Que was a disaster waiting to happen, and I hoped I would not be around when he exploded.

Que gave the other dancers a solo performance that was even more x-rated than Raven's performance. It was obvious to his record company that they couldn't tell him what to do, and he didn't care who didn't like it. His fans loved the improved show, but the media criticized the new changes and started giving him a bad name.

Que deserved every piece of bad press he received. He was creating enemies everywhere he went and had developed an "I-don't-give-a-fuck" attitude that was rubbing people the wrong way. With all his dirty little secrets, I was surprised he continued to treat people so horrible and disrespectful. I knew it would only be a short time before his dirt was revealed because he was doing too much all the time and he had a cocky attitude.

His attitude was even getting on Raven's nerves. He was so unpredictable, and she couldn't stand his new personality. He did take care of her financially, but not without demanding so much from her that she started getting turned off. She spent more time on her knees, and it seemed like the money wasn't coming the way it used to. Raven was quickly becoming old meat to him.

I had started completely ignoring all calls except those from Johnny. I just wanted to finish the last week on the tour, and then I would get back to everyone that called me. I constantly saw my mother's number, along with Sydney's and a few other friend's telephone numbers on the caller ID.

There was another number that constantly appeared. I didn't recognize the name or number, but they left a message wanting me to contact their office immediately. I knew it couldn't have been a bill collector because all my bills were paid on time. I wasn't sure what it was about, but it would have to wait until I got home.

I was shocked to see that Blanca from Slyy's tour had called me twice. I hadn't spoken to her since the tour was over. I didn't know what she wanted either, but she would have to wait like everyone else. No more interruptions.

After a long bus ride, we arrived in sunny Los Angeles, and I was excited to see Johnny. We had managed to talk to each other often, and he had even flown out to a few cities to sneak and see me. I really loved how much he seemed to care for me and wanted to be around me.

We had it all planned out for when I arrived to his city. We were going to see each other before sound check and after the show since we were not leaving until the next morning. As soon as I checked into the hotel, I showered, changed clothes, and left out to go meet Johnny, who was waiting for me in front of the hotel. He picked me up in a beautiful silver two-door Bentley. It seemed like they were giving Bentleys away because everyone seemed to have one in California.

He got out of the car as soon as he saw me and walked over to give me a hug and kiss. We stood outside the hotel door kissing and hugging each other, not caring who saw us at the moment. Then we quickly jumped in the car to enjoy the time we had together.

"I've missed you," I told him, rubbing his leg while he drove away.

"I've really missed you," Johnny said, blushing.

"Where are we going?"

"We're going to my house. Is that okay?"

"Yes, that's perfect."

Thirty minutes later, after almost having sex while driving, we pulled up in front of a large, beautiful house. I looked around and was impressed by what I saw. Johnny didn't lie about how he was living. I knew he told me that he was wealthy and living great, but I had to see it to believe it. Now I believed.

"Welcome to my house," Johnny said proudly.

"Wow, it's beautiful," I said, continuing to look around.

We walked into a nicely decorated house that was beautiful and made me feel at home. It was decorated in neutral colors and it was obvious that he had hired an interior designer to create such a unique warm feeling.

It was a five-bedroom home with a full recording studio and pool. Seeing that he was a bachelor, I was impressed that his home was decorated with such taste and style. You could tell all the furniture was expensive, and he didn't miss out on any detail.

Looking at his house, I wanted to move in immediately and start a family with him. I could see myself in his kitchen making gourmet dishes for him and our kids. The granite countertops and two stainless steel refrigerators made me want to start cooking.

We talked as he allowed me to look around his house freely. When we went outside to see the pool, I removed my shoes and clothes and jumped in the water with my panties and bra still on. Johnny couldn't resist and joined me.

We played in the water for a while and then headed to his bedroom where we made love for hours. My telephone rang interrupting us, and I had to answer. Just like I thought, it was Raven giving me a call to make sure I would be on time for sound check, which was in a few hours. After I hung up, Johnny and I decided to get dressed and go grab lunch.

"Music, I'm falling in love with you," Johnny told me.

"Really? Because I've already fallen in love with you."

"What are we going to do about this?" He asked.

"What do you mean?"

"I want to be with you, and I can't do that if you're in Chicago. We need to work on our living arrangements."

"Don't you think moving in together is too soon?"

"Not if you know you love someone," he replied.

"I don't know what to say."

"Just say yes when I ask to marry you, because I will marry you one day," Johnny said, as he grabbed my hand.

I looked at Johnny hoping his words were true. I felt comfortable with him, and it felt like we belonged together, but only time would tell.

CHAPTER 19

The next day, we arrived at the next city and prepared to repeat the same schedule. Like clockwork, we arrived at the arena for sound check and made sure things were on point. The shows had been going so well with no mistakes that Que was actually not working us that hard.

I had injured my ankle and was praying for a quick recovery. It wasn't that serious, but enough to have me in pain the entire show. Whenever I came off stage, I would immediately put ice on it and prop it up until it was time to return to the stage.

Dancing is hard on your body, and I could feel mine breaking down slowly. I was looking forward to the two-week break that was coming up. I was planning on going home and relaxing in my own bed. Then I would return to the tour to finish up the last two weeks that were left.

We were shocked to see our dressing room decorated nicely because normally we got whatever room was left over and there was not effort put into the décor. Que took up all the dressing rooms and wouldn't give any to the artist on the show and was stingy with his own staff. This time we had a nice room with hot food and drinks.

I double checked my hair and make-up to make sure Raven had hooked me up right. She did my face for the show and I was happy because she did wonders with blush, eye shadow and eyeliner. I told her she was in the wrong profession and should have been a make-up artist. She would always joke and say all drag queens know how to put on make-up.

"It's show time!" Macy yelled.

Raven and I came to the side of the stage a minute late and Que was furious. He told us he was going to fine us fifty dollars. We still had five minutes before it was time to go on stage, so to us we were not late.

Looking at the frown on Que's face, I knew he was definitely going to take that money out of our paychecks and we wouldn't be able to do anything about it. We sucked it up and went on stage to give another fabulous performance.

After the opening number was over, I went to my dressing room to change for the next song. I had ten minutes before I was due back on stage, but it seemed like one hour to me. I had time to chill, ice my ankle, and grab something to eat. Hearing my cell phone continuously ringing, I decided to answer it and was shocked to hear Slyy's assistant's voice.

"Music, have you gotten my messages?" Garrett asked as soon as I answered my phone.

"No," I replied, irritated that he was calling me and more irritated that I had answered.

I hadn't seen Garrett since Slyy's funeral, and I still remembered when he slapped me so hard I flew across the bed. He was a person I never wanted to talk to again, and I wished he was six feet under with Slyy. I couldn't believe he had the nerve to be calling me because he knew I didn't like him. Still, I really wanted to hear what he had to say.

"How are you doing?" He asked seriously.

"I'm good. What do you want?" I asked annoyed.

"I wanted to talk to you."

"I'm in the middle of a show right now and don't have time to talk," I said, trying to rush off the phone.

"Oh, that's right. I forgot you were on tour with Que. Have you spoken to anyone?"

"Spoken to whom? About what?"

"You sound like you don't know what's going on."

"What do you want?" I asked slowly with much attitude in my voice.

"I heard they found out that Slyy's daughter is…" Garrett instantly paused.

"Who is it?" I asked, while dressing for my next routine.

"You," Garrett said.

"What! Is this some type of joke?" I said, laughing to myself.

"No. That's why I'm calling to check on you," he responded.

"I think you have the wrong person," I said nonchalantly.

"I saw it on the news and they even showed your picture," he told me.

"Slyy is not my father. My father died when I was ten years old," I replied casually.

"You need to see what's going on," Garrett said, sounding concern.

"And now, you're concerned about me. Goodbye, Garrett." I hung up and laughed to myself because I knew he had made a mistake. Not thinking anything else about it, I continued getting dressed.

Five minutes later, my telephone rang again. This time, it was Janice. Again, I was totally shocked. I didn't have a friendship with her anymore and never thought I would talk to her again. Hearing her voice brought back good and bad memories.

"Hello," I said, answering the telephone.

"Music, are you okay?" Janice asked.

"I'm fine. Why?"

"I know you just spoke with Garrett. He tried to tell you about Slyy, but you didn't believe him. It's true, Music. Slyy is your father. Haven't you been talking to anyone?"

"Why do you guys keep saying Slyy is my father? My father died a long time ago."

"Music, you need to turn on the television because it's all over the press. I've been trying to contact you, but you never returned my calls. I'm sure people are trying to contact you about this. Maybe you should check your voicemail messages to see what's going on. If it's not true, then you need to let the media know, because they are showing your picture all over the world."

"This must be some type of mistake. They definitely have the wrong person. I will straighten this all out when I get home tomorrow. Right now, I have to be on stage in a few minutes. Thanks for letting me know. I have to go," I said.

"Call me if you need me."

"Okay, thanks." I said hanging up the telephone, knowing I would never call her again.

I don't know why the media thinks I'm Slyy's daughter, but I knew it had to be an error. Although I was starting to question all the calls I was receiving, I needed to find out what they were talking about.

"Hello, Sydney. Look, I don't have much time to talk, but have you been watching the news?" I asked her as soon as she picked up the telephone. I stared at the clock to make sure I wouldn't be late for my next number.

"Music, I've been trying to get in contact with you. I guess you haven't been watching television. Something crazy is going on and you need to come home," she said.

"What's happening? Does it have something to do with Slyy? If so, I've already heard about that crazy situation. You know that has to be a mistake."

"I don't know, because your mother is acting very strange. Just come home so we can figure this out. Oh yeah, the press has been camped out at your house for a week now, so you might not want to go there."

"Are you serious? What is really going on?" I asked, totally confused.

I trusted my cousin Sydney and knew she wouldn't lie. I still felt like it had to be a mistake. I had a weird feeling because I knew who my father was, but something had to be going on if I was getting all these calls. *This has to be a misunderstanding that I will clean up once I got home.*

As soon as I hung the phone up, it rang again. It was Johnny. A smile came across my face, and I quickly forgot about all the drama that was going on. Hearing his voice made me relax.

"Hey baby," I said.

"Your picture is all over the news and they're saying Slyy was your father. Are you okay baby?" He asked with concern.

"I don't know why they're saying that because my father is dead. I'm wondering what is going on, too."

"Why would they think you're his daughter?"

"I don't know, but I will find out once I'm done with this show."

"I just landed in New Orleans and can't wait to see you. We will deal with this together," Johnny said.

"Okay, I will see you soon. I got to go on stage now," I said, then hung up.

Before I could start really stressing about it, Macy was telling me it was time to go. I rushed to the stage, while trying to convince myself it was all a mistake and would be cleared up soon. I knew my father wasn't Slyy, so I let all those crazy thoughts disappear and I continued on with the show unaffected.

CHAPTER 20

Raven and I decided to stay in New Orleans for a few days before going home, and Johnny flew in town to hang out with me. Now that we were on our two-week break, I could see what was going on with this Slyy situation. I decided to call my mom to see why she had been calling me so much.

"Hi, Mom," I said softly, unsure of how I felt.

"Music! I've been waiting for you to call me. Baby, we really need to talk. I know you heard strange things by now, but I want to be the one to tell you everything in detail," my mother said desperately.

Tears rolled down my face like a faucet I couldn't turn off. Hearing her response told me that everything was true. *But how?* I still couldn't grasp the idea that Slyy was my father, but I wanted to hear the details. I still was hoping it was all a big misunderstanding.

"Baby, you still there?" my mother asked nervously.

"I'm here, but I don't understand what you're trying to tell me."

"Music, let's talk in person. Where are you?"

"I'm in New Orleans. Mom, what's going on?"

"Music, I need you to listen and don't interrupt. This is very hard for me, and I'd rather do it in person. But, since things have gotten out of control, I will give you all the details."

"I'm listening."

"Your mother's name was Stacy Jameson."

"Stacy Jameson! Your sister?" I said screaming into the telephone.

"Yes. Please don't interrupt so I can get it all out."

"Okay, go ahead," I said, as I curled my body up in a ball, bracing myself for what I was about to hear.

"Your biological mother was my sister Stacy. She dated Slyy when she was young, and she became pregnant with you. A few months after giving birth to you, she died of a drug overdose. Your mother had a drug problem, but didn't use drugs while she was carrying you. Once she delivered you, she went right back to her old habits. With Slyy not being around, that sent her over the edge and to her grave. Slyy's acting career had taken off, and he was afraid that if the media found out he was with someone with a drug problem, it would ruin his career. So, he stopped coming around."

"I can't believe this!" I said in utter shock.

"I'm so sorry, Music. Please let me finish."

"Go ahead."

"He made sure you were his daughter and got a DNA test done as soon as you were born. I promised my sister I would always take care of you, and Slyy promised he would be involved in your life. But, he got so wrapped up in his career that he forgot all about you. The last time he saw you, you were four months old and we were at your mother's funeral. He said he would be back in town to check on you, but we never saw or talked to him again. He was adamant about keeping all of your personal documents like your social security number and birth certificate with him. I hated Slyy for not being a part of your life and decided to make it easier on you by letting you think me and my husband were your real parents. I never respected Slyy because he didn't financially take care of you, even though he could afford to, and he never tried to have a relationship with you either."

I couldn't absorb all of this information. I wanted to run away somewhere. I felt like my head was about to explode. I felt myself loosing it, and all of a sudden all I could do was holler.

"Why is this happening to me?" I yelled so loudly that Raven came running into the room.

Raven tried to ask me what was wrong, but I couldn't seem to form words to tell her. All I could do was yell and cry like someone was beating me. I scared myself and felt like I was about to go crazy. By the look on Raven's face, she was also scared and didn't know how to help me.

Raven grabbed me, holding me tightly, terrified at the condition she saw me in. When she grabbed the telephone to see who I was talking to, my mother immediately gave her a short version of what was going on. Raven was so shocked that she couldn't do anything but hold me in silence as she listened to me fight through the pain.

There was a knock on the hotel room door, and Raven didn't know if she should get the door or stay and help me. She decided to answer the door because she needed a minute away from the crazy scene going on.

When she opened the door, Johnny walked in, and immediately, she felt relieved to see him. After she gave him a quick update on what was going on, he dropped his bags on the floor and started running toward the sounds of me crying loudly.

Johnny ran in the room, hugged me tightly, and rocked me back and forth without saying a word. I held on to him like he was the last person I would ever see. I held on to him hoping he would tell me it was all a joke. I held on to him praying he could fix the situation.

We lay in bed for hours before I could get one word out, and that was asking for something to drink. Johnny didn't even try to talk to me about the situation. He just sat in silence with me. He knew eventually I would talk, but for now, he just wanted to be with me.

My cell phone never stopped ringing, and the same number I didn't recognize seemed to be calling even more. Johnny insisted that I needed to answer it because I couldn't run from the situation and needed to deal with it. However, I was in no condition to talk or move. I had become a zombie. Johnny grabbed my phone and answered it for me, determined to start getting some answers on what was happening. The look on his face told me the call was important, but I still didn't move.

Johnny hung up the telephone, looked at me, and said, "I know you're stressing out right now, but you have to deal with this because it's not going to go away. I'm not going anywhere. We're going to deal with this together."

Still numb, I couldn't respond, but he knew I agreed with him.

"Music, you know I'll be right here with you, too. We're going to get through this like we have gotten through everything else," Raven said.

"Thanks, guys," I replied softly.

With thoughts of Slyy being my father, my head started pounding. Now both of the men who were supposed to be my father were dead. I couldn't digest the thought of Slyy being my biological father and my mother not really being my mother. I now had to add to the nightmare that my own father abused me.

"That was Slyy's attorney on the phone," Johnny told me. "He has been trying to contact you. He has an office in Chicago and will be flying from California to meet with you in a few days."

"About what?" I mustered up the strength to ask.

"About Slyy's estate," he replied, while hugging me.

"Awww shit! You're about to get paid," Raven said.

I rolled my eyes at her because this was not the time to be thinking about money.

CHAPTER 21

A couple of days had passed and we had just landed at Chicago O'Hare airport. Raven and Johnny were still right by my side taking care of me. The media continued talking about Slyy being my father and constantly showed pictures of me dancing on stage with him.

All I wanted the media to do was give me some time to deal with this, but they insisted on driving me crazy by talking about it on the television, radio, in newspapers and magazines.

"Hey, sweetie, are you okay?" Sydney asked, hugging me as tight as she could.

"No," I replied, truly believing I would never get over this. I was just doing what Raven and Johnny told me to do.

"Thanks for picking us up. Music is not doing well and I'm actually scared," Raven told Sydney.

"You must be Johnny," Sydney said, smiling.

"Nice to meet you," Johnny responded with a smile.

"Thanks for being here with Music. This is really hard for her," Sydney told him.

"I'm here as long as she needs me," Johnny said, while putting the luggage in the car.

"You're a good guy." Sydney told Johnny. "Music, I suggest not going to your house because I'm sure the press is still there," Sydney warned me as we drove off.

"Damn!" I said.

"Don't worry, baby. I'll get a hotel room and put it in my name, because with all this press you don't need people to know where you are. I'll take care of everything," Johnny assured me, then grabbed my hand and squeezed it.

"Thanks, baby," I said, still miserable and wanting to die.

"You guys can stay at my house," Raven offered.

"That's not a good idea because the press has been at your house too. They know you're Music's best friend and they figured she might come there," Sydney said.

"Don't worry, Raven. I'm making hotel reservations right now for all of us," Johnny said, as he whipped out his cell phone to make a call.

"Thanks for being on top of things, Johnny," Raven said, impressed by his actions.

"Sydney just head downtown and take your time," Johnny told her.

"I only stay at the hotels," Raven told him.

"I only stay at five star hotels, so you don't have to worry," Johnny said cocky. "We're all set. I got a suite for us."

"You're a big baller," Raven said.

"I'm just taking care of my baby," Johnny said.

"Before we go to the hotel, I need to go by my house," I said.

"Why?" Sydney asked.

"I guess I need to see things for myself," I said.

"I understand. Let's drive by," Sydney said.

As Sydney drove down my street, before we made it to my building, I could see at least five cameras set up in front. I told her to stop and turn around before she got to my building, so we wouldn't be seen. I couldn't believe my eyes and couldn't stop the tears from running down my face. *Damn, it is true,* I thought, finally accepting it.

As soon as we arrived at the hotel and entered through the back door as instructed by Johnny, two staff members were waiting there and quickly escorted us to our beautiful, posh, two-bedroom suite.

Johnny had a lot of connections and was really laying out the red carpet for us. He said he had been in the business for a long time and worked with too many artists to count, but he never bragged about how much clout he had.

Once inside the suite, I rushed to the television to see if I could find out what was going on. Raven rushed to the computer to do the same. It didn't take long before we saw our pictures plastered all over the television screen. I purposely didn't do this in New Orleans because I was running from the truth.

As soon as I turned the television on, my picture was staring back at me. They talked about me working with Slyy and not knowing he was my father. They showed pictures of me dancing with him and even had interviews of Garrett and some of Slyy's dancers talking about working with me. I just stared at the television because it felt like they were discussing someone else and not me.

Raven confirmed that my pictures were all over the internet. Every gossip website and blog page was talking about it. Everyone wanted to know who I was and if I knew he was my father. They wanted to know who my mother was, but that was something I couldn't explain because I didn't remember her. There were even a few celebrities who wanted to know if I was going to step into my father's footsteps and sing, and if so, they wanted to produce my album.

Everything was coming at me all at once and all too fast. My head was spinning and I wanted to die. I was happy to have Johnny, Raven, and Sydney by my side. They were showing how much they loved me and had my back, and I couldn't get through it without them.

My mother continued to ring my telephone, begging me to call her back because she was worried about me. I didn't know how I felt about my mother not telling me the truth all these years. A part of me wanted to be angry with her, but another part of me felt thankful that she took good care of me. I had a great child-hood. I loved my mom and dad, even if they were not my biological parents.

I didn't want my mother to worry about me, but I just didn't have anything to say to her. So, I asked Raven to call her to let her know I was doing fine and just needed time alone. My mother was understanding and begged Raven to tell me that she wanted to see me. I agreed to see her, but just not now.

I didn't have any strength to take care of myself, so Johnny ran a bath for me, washed me and dressed me every day. He was incredible and showing a side of him I didn't know existed, and I was impressed but couldn't show him.

Johnny tried everything he could to get me out of my funk but nothing was going to lift my mood. We ordered room service and I listened to Johnny, Raven and Sydney talk about what I needed to do. They talked like I wasn't in the room. We prepared for my meeting the next day with Slyy's attorney. I still couldn't function by myself and I needed them now more than ever.

Raven picked out an outfit for me and helped me prepare my mind for the meeting. I wasn't thinking about what I was going to wear because I had bigger things to think about, but Raven wanted to make sure I was well put together with my hair and make-up done and a fierce outfit.

The press found out where we were staying and had been waiting outside of the hotel to get an interview. The hotel was a big help by alerting us about the press and making sure our privacy was kept. They even allowed us to leave out of a private exit, all courtesy of Johnny's status.

Sydney picked us up from the back door of the hotel, and we headed to my meeting with Slyy's attorney. Johnny knew I was in no condition to speak for myself, so he prepared to do all the talking for me at the meeting. I was just a body they were carrying around.

"Are you ready?" Raven asked me, while adjusting my clothing.

"I guess so," I replied, not sure of what to expect from the meeting.

"Don't worry, baby. I will handle it for you," Johnny said, comforting me.

"I don't know what I would do without you guys, I couldn't do this alone," I said, feeling thankful for my friends and family as tears formed in my eyes.

The hotel wasn't far from Slyy's attorney's office; we were there in five minutes. Johnny looked at me, asking me with his eyes if I was ready to go inside. When I looked down at the ground, he knew it was all up to him and that I was just there for the ride.

"I got you, Music. No matter what happens, I'm here for you," Raven said, as she helped me out of the car.

Without saying a word, I put the hood of my jacket over my head and tried to cover my face. I didn't want to be recognized and have my picture blasted all over the television some more. I felt like I needed a drink, or something to help me deal with it.

No one knew I was meeting the attorney, so there were no reporters with cameras outside of the tall office building. We walked into the lobby and quickly got on the elevator. The doors opened to Slyy's attorney's office, which took over the entire fiftieth floor.

"We're here to see Mr. Mergson," Johnny told the receptionist, while Raven, Sydney, and I went to take a seat on the black leather couches.

"Your name is?" The receptionist asked.

Johnny paused for a second because he didn't want to give my name, but he knew we were in a safe place. "Music Jameson has an appointment with Mr. Mergson."

"You can have a seat. I will let him know you are here."

Five minutes later, a lady came out and told us to follow her. Sydney was very quiet because she was still shocked at what was going on. We walked into a conference room that had a long large table that seated at least twenty people. The view from the window was incredible, and the pictures on the walls were exquisite.

"Would you like something to drink?" The lady asked us.

"No, thank you," Johnny answered for all of us.

"My name is Mrs. Lowe, and I need to take a swab of Music's mouth and take some blood before we get started. I'm a nurse, so I know what I'm doing," she informed us after noticing the look of concern on our faces.

"What is this for?" Johnny quickly asked.

"It's a DNA test," Mrs. Lowe said, flashing a sympathetic smile.

Johnny walked over to me with Mrs. Lowe and watched her closely as she gave me the test. With no emotions, I opened my mouth and then stuck my arm out, while Raven and Sydney looked on with the same sympathetic look. It was quick and painless.

"Mr. Mergson will be with you shortly," Mrs. Lowe said, as she gathered her belongings and rushed out of the office.

"Music, are you okay?" Johnny asked, as soon as she left the room.

"Yeah, I'm fine. Thanks for helping me with this."

"I told you I'm here for you," Johnny said, then leaned over and kissed me.

It was so surreal. I felt like I was watching someone else's life on a movie screen. I just wanted my life to be back to normal again. I put my head down and let the tears run down my face. Wanting the hood that was over my head to hide me forever, I pulled it down further over my face and closed my eyes.

A short, old, stubby-looking man walked into the conference room. His presence stated that he was all about business and was in no mood to play around. You could see the power as soon as he entered the room and knew he had won many cases.

"Hello, Music. It's nice to finally meet you," Mr. Mergson said, as he walked right up to me and grabbed my hand.

In a sincere tone, he thanked me for coming to meet with him and said he knew how hard it had to be on me. Really, he had no idea what I was going through.

Looking at me, he knew I was taking it hard, so he didn't force me to talk. He directed everything to Johnny, who was also showing a lot of power. Johnny was very professional and also had a no-nonsense attitude while talking to Mr. Mergson.

"Who are you?" Mr. Mergson asked.

"My name is Johnny and I'm Music's fiancée," Johnny replied seriously.

I blinked my eyes and looked up when I heard him say that. I guess he wanted to let him know he was close to me. That way he wouldn't have a problem sharing information with him.

"I take it that you will be doing all the talking for Music, correct?" Mr.

Mergson asked Johnny.

"Yes. As you can see, she's in no condition to talk. She's having a hard time dealing with this, and we need to know why you wanted to talk to her," Johnny said.

"First, introduce me to your friends," Mr. Mergson said.

"This is my best friend Raven and my cousin Sydney. We can discuss anything in front of them," I said softly.

"Good. So let's begin. We will have the DNA results in a few hours. Then we can discuss in detail what is going on. Someone will be here shortly to meet with Music in private because we need to take a picture of your birthmark. Until then, we have to wait. Someone will come in to take your lunch order, as well. By then, we can discuss business. Is that okay?" Mr. Mergson asked as he stood up and headed for the door.

"That will be fine. We'll wait, but why are you taking a picture of her birthmark?" Johnny asked, as he shook Mr. Mergson's hand.

"We need to take every step to confirm that Slyy is Music's biological father. This is just part of the procedures. We will go over everything after we get the results. I will see you guys in a couple of hours," Mr. Mergson said, as he walked out of the room while staring at me.

They were covering everything to confirm I was Slyy's daughter, and I needed this confirmation more than them. I didn't understand why they needed a picture of my birthmark, but I would soon find out.

We had a great lunch, and I even started talking more and feeling relaxed. Sydney was acting crazy as usual, and I even laughed at her jokes. Raven had to turn her phone off because it kept ringing, and Johnny made a phone call to book us another room at a different hotel.

Four hours had passed and we were still waiting for Mr. Mergson to come in with the results. I started getting nervous and felt like I was on the *Maury Show* waiting to hear who the father of my child was. Mr. Mergson's assistants were very professional and kept coming in the room to ask if we needed anything.

Johnny jokingly told them that he needed a shot of vodka, and five minutes later, he had a glass of vodka in hand. Anything we wanted they supplied for us and was showing us how people get treated when they pay for high-priced attorneys.

Five and a half hours later, Mr. Mergson and three other people walked into the conference room. My heart dropped and I immediately became nervous. Everyone else was apprehensive, and right away they walked over to me and held my hand. Mr. Mergson and his staff sat down as he began speaking.

"Music, thank you for being so brave through all of this, because we know this is difficult. It looks like you have a pretty good support system with you, and that's important. I'm not going to delay this any longer. The DNA test confirmed that Roger "Slyy" Rort was your biological father. I have some documents here for you to review," Mr. Mergson said.

He slid some papers across the table to me and stopped talking long enough for me to look at them. He then continued speaking, saying, "We have confirmed all tests, checking your social security number, birth certificate, legal documents, DNA test, blood test, and birthmark. We also spoke with your mother, who also confirmed details, and we are positive you are Roger Rort's daughter. Your father had detailed information about his daughter, which helped us to positively identify you. I would like to first start by showing you a few items that your father wanted you to see."

"Wait. I need a minute," I said, as I leaned my head back on the high leather chair to take it all in.

After a few moments, I opened the envelope and pulled out the items inside. The first thing I noticed was a picture of Slyy holding a baby, and that baby was me. On the back of the photo, it had "me and my daughter". There were other papers in the envelope but my eyes went straight to the handwritten letter that I quickly started reading.

To my daughter,

I was so excited the day you were born, and I fell in love with you because you were my first and only beautiful baby girl. You've made me make a better person out of myself and strive to make a great life for you. We both have the same unique birthmark, a perfectly shaped heart on the inside of our right thigh that makes me feel connected to you. Even though I feel like I don't know you because I haven't seen you since you were a baby, I will always love you – you're my daughter. I know you will not understand why I left you and haven't been in your life, but I was young and got wrapped up in my career. I put myself first. I'm sorry. I've always thought about you and wanted to see you, but I thought it would make things too complicated if I showed up in your life. I vowed to always take care of you financially and make sure you would be well taken care. If you're reading this, then it means I'm dead. Please don't be sad, but take everything that I have for you and make the best of it. I love you with all my heart and please continue my legacy. You are my beneficiary on my life insurance, bank accounts, my companies, properties and any other legal documents I have. Since you don't know me, I figure you are not after my money, because everyone around me is. So, I feel comfortable in knowing that when I die, you will get everything I own. I love you and never forget that. I know I wasn't a good father, so please forgive me. Take all my money, houses, cars, and businesses and live comfortable. If you have any talent like me, live your dreams, baby girl!

Love your father,

Roger "Slyy" Rort

As I started crying uncontrollably, Johnny immediately started comforting me. I did have a heart-shaped birthmark on my inner right thigh, and I never even thought anything about Slyy having grey eyes like I did. Everything was coming together and confirming he was my father.

"Why is this happening?" I asked, while continuing to cry.

"I'm so sorry, Music. You can look at the other items later," Mr. Mergson said, as he opened up a file.

"Thanks."

"I know this is a lot to take in all in one day. We will go over everything in detail tomorrow. For today, just let it all process, because tomorrow we have much to discuss and I need your full attention. Music, are you listening to me?"

"I heard you," I said through tears.

"Get some rest and we will meet here in the morning. All the paperwork and details will take at least a week to go over, and you will have to fly out to California to tie up some loose ends. You need to meet with Slyy's accountant and business manager next week. I also suggest you don't talk to the press about this because your father wouldn't want that. Let's keep this as private as possible. Per your father's request, I will be working as your attorney, unless you would like to get hire another one. If so, please get a good one, because now that Slyy has passed away, tons of people will be trying to sue you. I'm the best attorney around, and I've been handling your father's business for over fifteen years."

"Thanks Mr. Mergson. I will keep you as my attorney."

"Wonderful. My secretary will have you sign some papers and we will be on our way. As my client, once again, I suggest you not talk to the press or anyone else regarding this situation. Everything must be kept confidential, as well. The people in this room, I will need you to sign a confidential agreement before you leave. Don't make a move unless you consult with me first. I'm here to help you, just like your father would want me to," Mr. Mergson said, as he got up from his chair and walked over to give me a hug and a handshake. He felt like a savior because I needed his help and services badly.

"I need some time to get myself together before I can deal with this. Can we postpone the meeting tomorrow? I'm just not ready."

"How much time do you need?" Mr. Mergson asked.

"I need a few weeks. This is so hard for me to believe. It's all happening too fast."

"The best thing to do right now is to continue doing what you were doing. This will help keep your mind off things."

"I was dancing and have to go back in a couple of weeks to finish the tour."

"That's perfect. Finish up the tour. That will get you focused and ready to deal with this. I know this is much to handle, but I really need you to be strong."

"I will be ready. I will meet with you after the tour ends. Thank you," I said.

I left the office relieved that I had time to get it together emotionally. Although I had no desire to dance, I knew it would be the best thing to get my mind off of things. I also wanted to finish what I'd started. I was just hoping I could make it through the shows.

I knew once I started dancing, I would be fine. One thing I knew how to do was perform, even when dealing with difficult personal issues. The show must go on.

~~~~~~~~

We waited until late in the evening and snuck into my building. It felt great to be back in my house, even though my telephone hadn't stopped ringing since I'd been there. I planned to hide out, relax, think about what was going on, and find a way to deal with it.

Johnny had to leave to start working again, and I was sad to see him go. He had been my backbone, and I couldn't function without him. He didn't want to leave me, but I insisted he return back to his life. Although I still had Raven and Sydney there to help me, I knew I needed to deal with it on my own.

The media was still pestering me about giving them a statement. I was getting offered interviews, photo spreads, and even money to tell detailed information about Slyy. They wanted to know what was going to happen to his businesses, but I couldn't answer those questions yet.

I had gotten several calls from Slyy's industry friends sending their condolences. Most of them wanted money; the rest just wanted to hang around me to get money. Garrett even had the nerve to call me again, but I wasn't showing him any love. There was no way he was going to be a part of my life.

Que called me and was speechless. He felt so bad that he couldn't even form words to make a sentence. I told him I was handling it and not to worry about it, but he sounded traumatized on the telephone.

I heard in the sound of his voice sadness and fear. He didn't know how I was dealing with knowing he killed my father. I knew his fear was about to turn into survival, and he needed to know I wouldn't turn him in to the police. But, I had no intention on talking to the police because he didn't know Slyy was my father at that time. Every day he claimed to be calling to check on me, but I knew it was to see if my motives had changed.

I finally took the time to speak with my mother to get more information about my biological mother, her sister. Although a drug user, my mother was a smart and talented woman. She couldn't deal with Slyy leaving her, so she relapsed and went back to using drugs.

My mother was so apologetic and didn't want me to hate her for withholding the truth about my biological mother, but I didn't. I loved her for taking care of me. Before we hung up, she promised to bring me a box of my mother's belongings that she had been keeping.

I got consumed in reading the blogs, and each time I read something, it made me want to kill someone. The rumors were killing me slowly more than my own issues. Even though my heart ached every time I read articles about myself, I couldn't stop reading them.

The rumors I was hearing were devastating. The headlines read: "*Slyy's daughter sleeps with her father*"; "*Slyy's daughter takes her father from his fiancée*"; "*Slyy's daughter was a whore*". I knew the dancers had to be talking to the press about things they didn't know. I wanted to retaliate, but I knew karma would come back and bite them in their asses.

What would news be if there weren't haters adding their fabricated comments to make the story more colorful? It seemed like no one wanted to know the truth; they just wanted dirt and lies. That's what entertained people.

After a few days alone in my apartment with Raven and Sydney calling me every hour, I felt revived and strong. I had no more tears to cry, but I was still on an emotional roller coaster. Yet, I made a decision to deal with it and go back to being me. I had hid long enough. It was now time to take a stand and go back to my normal life, the life and career I worked so hard to achieve.

CHAPTER 22

Raven and I flew to Minnesota to finish the last two weeks of the tour. Que allowed everyone to stay in the same five-star hotel he was checked into, and treated all the dancers and assistants to a suite. We checked into our hotel and read the itinerary that was left for us at the front desk. We were in a different city every day and were flying instead of being transported on the tour bus.

"Are you ready to dance?" Raven asked, as she grabbed a bottle of water out of the mini bar.

"I'm fine. I actually can't wait to dance," I said, lying down on the couch.

"How are you handling things knowing that Que killed your father?"

"He didn't know he was my father at the time, so I don't have a problem with Que. I'm still traumatized picturing you giving Slyy oral sex, though."

"I feel dirty."

"Don't worry about it. You didn't know he was my father when you were stealing from him," I said, while smiling and trying to cut the tension because it was obvious she felt bad.

"This is odd."

"I wish Johnny was here, but he's in California working."

"Girl, he has been a good man to you."

"Yes, he has. He's going to mess around and make me marry him," I replied.

"You better snatch him up before someone else does."

"I'm happy we have the day off today, but I hate that we had to fly in early for the show. You know how Que likes to make sure everyone is here and ready."

I thought about things we could do on our day off and decided we could go shopping and then get our hair done and a massage. I had the whole day planned out and quickly informed Raven of our schedule.

"Let's not waste any time. Let's go," I said, excited.

"I'm not going to be able to hang out too late because Que invited me to dinner tonight. He got a private suite just for the two of us," Raven said, blushing.

"So you're blowing me off for Que?"

"Don't be mad. You know how I feel about him," Raven said, as she picked out her outfit for her date with Que.

"Why did he get another suite? Why can't you go to his suite to have dinner?" I asked.

"His staff is in his suite having meetings all night, so he got another suite so we could have some privacy. No one knows he has the suite but me," Raven said.

"Enjoy your private suite and dinner."

"I will tell you all about it in the morning," she told me. "Now, let's go so we can get back and I can get beautiful for my man."

"Now he's your man?" I said.

"Once his dick entered my mouth, he became my man," Raven replied, as she closed the door on our way out.

~~~~~~~~

We made it back to the hotel in time for Raven to take a bath and get dressed for her date with Que. She was so excited and I was so hungry. I decided to order room service and enjoy a night of peace and quiet alone.

However, Raven got a call from Que, who told her he wouldn't be able to meet her for dinner because his meetings were running late. Still, he wanted her to wait for him in the suite and he would call her when he was on his way. She was disappointed, but still excited she would see him.

She invited me to go to Que's private suite with her to order room service and have dinner. So, I agreed to eat and leave before Que got there. After she packed a few items, we took the elevator to the 26th floor.

We opened the door to the large, stylish suite and the entrance way was stunning with marble floors and a chandelier. We walked in and went around a corner into an amazing living and dining room area. The suite had two bedrooms and was decked out in a contemporary décor.

We laughed, talked, and raided the mini bar. Raven wasn't expecting Que for hours, so we knew we had time to relax and enjoy. We ordered room service and went into the bathroom so I could give my final stamp of approval for the short, sexy, black dress she was going to wear for Que. We were alarmed when we heard someone opening the door to the suite.

Before Raven could get to the door, Que walked in surprising her by his early arrival. I peeked out of the bathroom but didn't come out to say hello because I wasn't supposed to be in the suite. I wasn't even supposed to know about the suite.

Que walked into the living room and plopped down on the couch. Raven saw me trying to get her attention, but motioned for me to go back into the bathroom. She knew Que would be mad if she told him that I was there. She finally was going to spend some alone time with him, and she didn't want to start it off with him upset.

They sat on the couch, talking and kissing. An hour later, I was still in the bathroom, peeping out the door and waiting for her to take him into the bedroom so I could leave quietly. Raven tried to get Que to go into the bedroom several times, but he wanted to relax in the living room and finish watching the movie we had ordered.

"I feel so connected to you. You know me so well, and you got me thinking about you all the time," Que said, pulling Raven closer to him on the couch.

"I've been thinking about you, too," she replied, while kissing on his neck.

"I'm trying to be a gentleman and not rip your panties off," Que said, laughing.

"Thanks for respecting me. Now let's go in the bedroom," Raven said softly.

"I don't want to go in the bedroom. I'm comfortable right here," Que said.

"Okay," Raven said, nervously trying to think of another plan.

"I can't keep respecting you if you're going to keep kissing me like that."

Raven didn't comment and continued kissing him as she rubbed his chest. Things got so heated I thought I was watching a love scene in a movie. Que appeared to be totally hooked on her.

"Can you get me some water so I can take my medicine? My tooth is killing me," he told Raven.

"Sure," she said.

When Raven walked into the bathroom to get him some water, I hit her on the head.

"Get rid of him," I whispered.

"I'm trying," she whispered back as she grabbed a glass from the counter and filled it with water, while peeking out the door to make sure Que was still sitting on the couch.

"I'm not going to stay in here forever," I said, annoyed.

"Please don't mess this up for me. You know I would do this for you," Raven pleaded.

"Do something so I can sneak out of here," I said, hitting her again.

"Okay. Just be quiet," Raven whispered, and walked out with the glass of water in her hand.

After Raven handed Que the water, he took out two pills from his pants pocket and popped them in his mouth

"I can afford the bottled water in the mini bar," Que said sarcastically.

"Why pay for it when it's free from the faucet?" Raven replied thinking quick on her toes.

Que didn't waste any time getting right back to kissing and hugging her, and they didn't seem like they were going to stop anytime soon.

"Take your dress off," he said softly.

Raven stood up slowly and grabbed the straps to her dress as he nodded his head anxiously, telling her to be quick. She closed her eyes and gave him a slow seductive striptease, while he leaned back on the couch and watched her every move.

She dropped her dress to the floor, revealing her matching lace bra and panties. She continued to move her body slowly as she started breathing heavily. She rubbed her hands across her breasts, but instantly stopped.

"What's wrong?" He asked.

"Nothing," Raven said looking uneasy.

 "I know women wear padded bras, so you don't have to be embarrassed. Now take that bra off," he demanded with a smile.

Raven hesitated. Her problem wasn't a padded bra. Her dilemma was she didn't have breast at all and wore a silicon bra for the illusion of perfectly shaped C-cups. The bra made her breasts look and feel natural, but as soon as she took it off, you realized all she had was a flat chest.

She had a big decision to make and needed to decide if she was going to reveal her secret and tell him that she was a man. She had been in this position many times and felt like she could handle this situation. The only thing that made it difficult for her was that she had feelings for him. Her plan was to take his money and not to involve her feelings, but she wasn't playing by her own rules.

I was eager to see what Raven was going to do. This was better than any movie I have ever seen. I waited, anticipating her decision. I saw Raven give him a look that told me what decision she had made.

"Don't make me beg," Que said, desperate to see her naked.

"Do you care for me?" Raven asked.

"Don't start this shit right now," he said, annoyed.

"No matter what, you promise to always care for me?" She asked.

"I will still care for you even if you have small breast," he replied, laughing.

Raven never responded.

"Stop stalling so I can make love to you," he said anxiously.

Raven turned all the lights off and lit his favorite scented vanilla candles. The candles were the only light in the dark room, which gave her body a soft silhouette glow. Raven turned her back to him, removed her bra, flung it behind the couch, and covered her chest with her hands.

She took his attention off her non-existent breasts and controlled his eyes with booty-shaking movements. He stood up to take his shirt and pants off, as his dick stood at attention ready to burst. He was naked and eagerly ready to feel Raven.

Raven walked behind a large high back chair that was tall enough to conceal her body from the waist down. She turned her back towards him as she continued to dance. She quickly removed her panties and the tape that was holding her dick securely between her legs.

"Come here, baby," he said, putting a condom on.

She moved from behind the chair and walked towards him. As soon as she got close enough for him to see her entire body clearly, she suddenly stopped. He looked at her flat manly chest and then down at her large erect penis. He grabbed his mouth, turned his head to the side, and looked totally puzzled.

Raven looked startled and didn't know what to expect next. She finally found someone she really cared for and hoped he was able to see the person inside, not just the seven-inch dick she had hanging between her legs.

"Baby, say something," Raven said tensely.

Que frightened her when he quickly jumped up from the couch and punched her in the jaw. She hit the floor hard and blood flew out of her mouth, leaving her in a daze. He kept coming after her, repeatedly kicking her in the ribs.

With both of his hands, he grabbed her by the neck, lifted her off the floor, and slung her naked body into the wall. He rushed after her in a rage and lifted her off the floor again with both hands wrapped tightly around her neck. He slammed her into the wall and started choking her.

I rushed out of the bathroom to help Raven. Que never saw me because his back was towards me, but Raven was looking directly at me and frantically motioned with her hand for me to go back. Confused, I slowly walked back to the bathroom while keeping my eyes on them.

I couldn't understand why she didn't want me to help her. It was hard to watch him choke her without doing something. Still, I did what Raven instructed me to do and walked back into the bathroom and continued to peek out the door.

"What the fuck is going on, Raven?" he yelled, while continuing to choke her.

He had a look in his eyes like he was ready to kill. Raven struggled to breathe as she tried to speak. I glanced around the bathroom for some type of weapon to help defend her.

"Please stop," Raven pleaded, while wheezing for air.

He loosened the tight grip around her neck to allow her to explain what he already knew.

"I'm going to kill you!" He yelled, never completely letting go of her neck.

"I'm sorry. Please let me explain," Raven said, panting as tears rolled down her face.

"This is fucked up!" He yelled, while looking around the room.

"I'm not trying to hurt you. I just wanted you to like me," Raven said, crying and struggling to breathe through every word.

He punched her in the side, and she screamed out in pain. He continued to choke her while still looking around the room uneasily. When I opened the bathroom door to step outside, she gestured for me to go back. Again, I returned to the bathroom frustrated and scared.

"I didn't think it mattered." Raven said.

"You think I like men?" He shouted.

"I know who you are," Raven said crying uncontrollably.

He never said a word and continued listening to her as he looked around the room again.

"Your secret is safe with me," Raven said, trying to sound convincing.

"I should kill you," he growled through his teeth.

While he continued choking her, she immediately grabbed his dick and started stroking it vigorously. The more she stroked, the harder he choked her.

"Stop fighting it," Raven said.

"Fuck you!" He yelled.

Using all the strength she had left, she kept stroking his rock-hard dick, and soon, he started to loosen the hold he had on her. It appeared he was slowly losing control as he allowed Raven to fondle his dick that was now pulsating.

He then grudgingly leaned his head back and stopped choking her. She instantly dropped to her knees and started sucking his dick so powerfully that he started moaning and his body started jerking.

Raven knew she was right about him all along. She had him right where she wanted him, with his dick in her mouth. He put both hands on the wall and gave in, allowing her to taste him. She sucked his dick and licked his balls until she knew he was about to cum. Then she stood up and started kissing him fervently.

"I understand you," Raven constantly repeated, as she guided him to the couch.

The more she repeated herself, the more he seemed to relax. By the time they made it to the couch, it seemed like he had totally forgotten she was a man. Still, he was very rough when he threw her on the couch and fucked her in the ass. Raven was enjoying every rough thrust he delivered, until she opened her eyes and saw me watching them.

She put her finger up to her mouth, signaling for me to be quiet. I couldn't believe Que was having sex with her. I finally saw Raven work her magic on a man; she had skills. I was taken aback at Que. When you think you know someone, you really don't. I would have never guessed he would have sex with Raven.

She begged him to slow down, but he kept a strong thrust until he pulled out and came all over her ass. Once he was done, Raven stood up, bent him over, and rammed her dick in his ass, which to my surprise, didn't make him flinch. He moaned with every stroke from Raven, and it was obvious this wasn't the first time he had sex with a man.

Once Raven had the best orgasm of her life, she lay on top of Que as they kissed and cuddled. They both had to catch their breath, so it took a minute for them to say anything to each other. I was still in the bathroom sitting on the floor with my mouth wide open.

"You felt good," Raven said, taking a deep breath.

"Damn!" Que said, exhaling.

"This will be our little secret," Raven assured him.

"I know who I am, and I'm comfortable with myself," Que said sounding embarrassed.

"I knew you liked dick all along," Raven whispered in a sexy tone.

"How did you know?" Que ask curiously.

"My dick told me," Raven said, then kissed his lips softly.

"You really took a chance," Que said, while rubbing her dick.

"You didn't have to beat my ass, though!" Raven snapped.

"I'm sorry."

"You're going to pay big time for this," Raven said, smiling.

"I'll take care of you," he told her as he rubbed her legs.

"I like Gucci, Prada, Louis Vuitton, and anything else that's expensive. My bank account needs a little love, too," Raven said seriously.

"If you tell anyone about this, you know I will kill you," Que said seriously, as he started to rub her butt.

"Don't worry. I won't say a word."

"This will destroy my image. I have a lot to lose if this gets out," Que said.

"I have a lot to lose, too. No one knows I'm a man, and I want to keep it that way."

"Does Music know you're a man?" Que asked.

"No," she lied.

"Then we both have another secret to keep. Don't tell Music what happened tonight."

"I won't say a word. She doesn't even know I'm a man, so you know I can keep a secret," Raven said, continuing to lie.

My head was spinning thinking that Que had fooled me for all these years. He was the biggest dog sleeping around with every woman in town, but I guess being a dog was his cover up since he really liked to sleep with men. Que had done a great job of misleading people.

Que's cell phone started ringing, but he ignored it and continued talking to Raven. Once he realized his phone wasn't going to stop ringing, he answered it. Then he jumped up and put his clothes on fast.

"Where are you going?" Raven asked.

"I forgot I have a meeting, and I'm late."

"But I thought we were spending the night together. Remember our dinner date?"

"I'm sorry, baby. It's business," Que said.

"I understand. I had a good time with you," Raven said, as she put her dress on.

"I'm glad we spent this time together. You were worth every minute. I will give you a call later," he said, then leaned over to kiss Raven on the lips.

"We're still cool, right?" Raven asked to confirm her feelings.

"Yes. Why wouldn't we be?" Que asked, confused.

"I just wanted to make sure because I really like you," Raven said, blushing.

"I like you, too. You're my little secret. You are a beautiful woman with a big-ass dick. Most people wouldn't be able to handle that, but you know I can," Que said.

"I understand. That's why we're so perfect for each other," Raven replied.

"I get to enjoy a beautiful woman with the package of a man. This is too good to be true," Que said.

There was suddenly a knock on the door interrupting their conversation. Que started walking to the door, while Raven stayed on the couch

"Who could that be? No one knows we're here," Raven asked, while stretching out on the couch.

"I'm going to find out. Don't move," Que told her, as he went to answer the door.

From where Raven was sitting, she couldn't see the door or hear anything, but I could see and hear everything. The bathroom was in a good location, giving me a perfect view of the living room and front door. Que opened the door and looked shocked as he tried to stop Johnny from walking in.

"What's up?" Johnny said, smiling.

"Keep your voice down. You can't be here right now," Que whispered to him.

"Why? You're not still mad that you saw me kissing Music, are you?" Johnny whispered, as he walked in and closed the door.

"No, I'm not mad. So much is going on that I just forgot you were coming. I'm in a meeting and can't hang out with you right now." Que said.

"I stuck to the plan just like you said. I had to kiss her to make her think I really liked her. She never mentioned anything about Slyy's murder. Now that she knows he's her father, she's too busy dealing with that. I did exactly what you told me to do, and it worked out," Johnny said, sounding like an obedient servant.

"That's good. It was painful seeing you kiss her," Que said.

"That shouldn't bother you because we both sleep with women, but we know where home is," Johnny said.

"Your home is right here," Que said as he grabbed his dick.

"I want you," Johnny said as he stuck his hands in Que's pants, grabbing his dick.

"I'll call you when I'm done. Go back to your room. I'll meet you there in an hour," Que told him.

"Alright," Johnny said, disappointed.

Que leaned over and tongued kissed him before he quickly got rid of Johnny and shut the door. I fell on the floor when I saw Johnny. *What the hell is going on? There is no way Johnny's gay. He just made love to me like a straight man.*

My heart couldn't take the pain it felt. Johnny had deceived me and had me dreaming of us being married with kids. There was no way that was going to happen since it wasn't me that he wanted. Unable to stop the tears, I covered my mouth so they wouldn't hear me crying hysterically.

"I got to go," Que said as soon as he walked up to her lying on the couch.

"I don't want you to leave," Raven said, rubbing on his leg.

"I will see you later, so keep that dick hard for me." Que said.

Raven walked Que to the door and kissed him goodbye. They seem like they were about to have sex again at the door, but Que's cell phone ranged and took his attention off of her. He quickly answered the phone and gestured to her that he had to leave immediately. As soon as the door closed behind him, I ran out of the bathroom and quickly ran up to Raven, startling her out of her daydreaming.

"What the hell just happened?" I asked.

"Oh my God, I forgot about you!" Raven said, blushing.

"I know you did! You slept with Que!" I screamed.

"Music, you can't say anything!" Raven pleaded.

"I can't believe this!"

"Girl, his asshole is as big as this room! He has definitely been sleeping with men for a long time," Raven said.

"It looked like he was trying to kill you. I was so scared."

"I can take a punch. Most of them like to fight it out first before they give in. He's going to pay big time for hitting me."

"I'm so sick of seeing you get your freak on," I said.

"You have seen me do some of my best work," Raven said laughing.

"You took a big chance on him. What if he didn't sleep with men?" I asked.

"Then you would have been helping me beat his ass."

"You got to stop doing this. You could really get hurt."

"It was well worth it. Now I really got him wrapped around my finger. He will do whatever I tell him. You just promise you won't say anything about what you saw."

"I've been keeping your secret all this time, so you know I won't say anything."

"Music, have you been crying?" Raven asked.

"Yeah."

"What's wrong?"

"The person that knocked at the door was Johnny."

"Johnny! What was he doing here?"

"He was here to see Que."

"About what?"

"Que and Johnny are fucking each other. They were kissing right at the door. I saw the whole thing," I said, crying.

"What!" Raven yelled to the top of her lungs.

"Johnny was only dating me to see if I was going to say something about Que killing Slyy. Que set the whole thing up. Johnny never cared about me."

"I'm so sorry, Music."

"This hurts."

"I can't believe this. I wish I would have known that Que liked men because I could have been had him."

"Forget about Que. I can't believe Johnny likes men. Why didn't I see the signs?"

"You can't always see the signs. I didn't notice it, and I'm just as shocked as you are."

"Words can't explain how I feel right now. I'm going to call him and curse him out."

"Don't do anything stupid. Let's just see how this will play out. Just pretend you didn't see anything. I don't want Que to know you were in the bathroom, and if you call Johnny, you will give it away."

"It's going to be hard not to say anything."

"Women talk too damn much! Now you know he's sleeping with Que, so what is there to say? Leave it alone because you can't make him stop liking dick."

"You're right. I guess there's nothing to say."

"I told you never to involve your feelings with a man because they're either going to cheat on you with a woman, or a man. I'm going to show you how to handle a situation like this," Raven said, looking at me like she had a master plan.

CHAPTER 23

We headed to New York to do two shows and then a live television awards show performance, where Que was nominated for album of the year. Things were going good for me until the other dancers started complaining to Que that they were not happy about the press hanging around trying to talk to me. I knew it was all a front to get rid of me, because most dancers wanted to be in the spotlight and this put them right in front of the cameras.

All the attention from the press started to wear on me, and their line of questioning made me feel very uncomfortable. If it wasn't for Raven telling me not to worry about what people were saying I would have left the tour.

Instead, I put my feelings and pride aside every night and walked on stage to do what I was paid to do. On the inside, I was dying, but on the outside, I tried to keep a smile on my face and pretend like nothing happened.

It was our last week on the tour, and I felt good that I was able to finish it. We were only doing a short version of the show and wouldn't have to work too hard. Que was previously informed to tone his show down for television, and he told them he would, but he had no intention of changing anything. He had been labeled the bad boy of the industry and everyone was waiting to see what he was going to do.

I hadn't spoken to Johnny and refused to answer whenever he called or texted, which was nonstop. I decided to let him suffer by wondering what was wrong with me. I would keep my mouth shut until I felt the time comes for me to say something.

Raven thought things would be different after her and Que slept together, but he continued to treat her how he always did. He stayed distant from her and hardly spoke. This was driving her crazy. Sure, her heart was hurting, but she was fine with the situation because her bank account was loaded and her wardrobe didn't need anything else. She just couldn't handle him ignoring her in front of everyone.

Even I didn't understand Que's action, but knew he only cared about himself and wasn't thinking about her feelings. He was still a dog whether he slept with women or men.

Raven walked to the back of the tour bus and was about to go in the room when she overheard Que talking to his security. He was joking about how he slept with all the women on the tour and how freaky Raven was in bed. He told them he was playing Raven and was going to let her go once the tour was over because she was too clingy.

The security guard sounded shocked that he had slept with Raven and more stunned that he said he had slept with me. Raven was mortified and hurting but it didn't stop her from continuing to listen to their conversation.

Que told his security how Raven was just a whore and had slept around in the business. He told them that she would do anything for him and if he called her in the room right now, she would drop to her knees and suck his dick.

Security laughed and it sounded like they were giving each other high fives. Que made Raven sound like a prostitute who he was going to kick to the curb soon. He didn't have any respect for her, and she had heard enough.

Raven pulled me to the front of the bus in private to tell me what she had heard Que saying. I couldn't believe he had told them that he slept with me. I could barely feel her pain because I was too upset about his lies.

"I'm sorry, Raven."

"I can't believe he would do that," Raven said, as a tear rolled down her face.

"He's only doing that because you slept with him. Now he has to get rid of you because he's too afraid someone might find out his little secret," I said.

"Wow, I just didn't think he would do that to me."

"Oh, you thought since you have a dick, he would treat you differently from how he treats a woman? Your dick isn't any different from any other man's dick. I thought you weren't going to get your feeling involved," I asked.

"I wasn't trying to, but I can't help it."

"Don't worry about it. He's not worth your pain," I told her.

"You know how I feel about men getting over on me. It drives me crazy, literally."

"Raven, don't do anything stupid."

"He's going to suffer," Raven said, while staring into space.

"You're scaring me. Just let it go."

"No!" Raven said loud enough for the other dancers to hear.

"We have a few more shows left, and then you won't have to see him any-more," I said, trying to calm her down.

In the middle of my sentence, Que opened the door and yelled for Raven. She turned her head and rolled her eyes.

"Are you going to go see what he wants?" I asked.

"No, he's just trying to show his security how he has me in check. Well, I have a surprise for him. I'm done with him and his money. It's over!" Raven said, furious.

I had heard that from her before, and when she said she was done with someone, it was truly over. I also knew Raven was very revengeful, and she was not going to let this slide.

"Que is nothing. Just leave it alone."

"I can't do that," Raven said with fire in her eyes.

Que continued to call Raven and then he sent his security to get her. When Raven ignored them, they left her alone. Que opened the door and stood in the doorway looking at Raven, frowning because he didn't know why she wasn't obeying him. When he slammed the door, Raven smiled.

She continued to ignore Que the entire ride, which started to irritate him. He walked up to Raven's bunk bed and pulled her privacy curtain open.

"What!" Raven snapped.

"I need to talk to you. Can you please come to the back room?" Que asked.

"No, thank you."

"Please," he said, pleading but also demanding.

Raven gave in, but regardless of what he said, she was going to make him pay for disrespecting her. Once they got in the room, he tried to explain that he knew she was listening outside his door and that was the reason he said those things about her because he wanted to teach her a lesson about eavesdropping.

Raven knew he was not telling the truth because she knew Swagg had told him earlier that she was standing outside of the door. Still, she played along with his little game since she had no intention of ever sleeping with him again.

Once Que thought his lies were working, he started feeling comfortable again. However, as soon as his back was turned, Raven commenced to paying him back by stealing his expensive custom made diamond bracelet while she sat in the room listening to some of his music.

"Come here baby," Que said, while patting on his leg for her to sit down.

"What do you want?" Raven asked playfully.

"Suck my dick, baby," Que said as he kissed her in the mouth.

This made Raven furious, and it took everything in her to continue to pretend like everything was back to normal. But, with only one day left on the tour, she didn't care anymore.

"I think you should suck my dick first," Raven said, then kissed him.

"What!" Que said, as he pushed her away.

"I said suck my dick," Raven said, trying to sound sexy.

"Have I ever sucked your dick?" Que asked, annoyed.

"No, but that's why I'm asking you to now."

"You're tripping right now. Do what I tell you to," Que ordered, as he tried to push Raven down between his legs.

"If you want me to suck your dick, suck mine first. What's the problem?" She asked, while trying to pull her dick out.

"Put that away. What if someone walks in here?" Que said upset.

"Oh, but it's okay for them to walk in and see me sucking your dick," Raven said, sounding equally annoyed. "I just want to see how your lips feel."

"No! Now get the fuck out!" Que yelled.

Raven was humiliated and felt disrespected. Still, she didn't want to walk out of the room with him being upset with her. So, she played the game, which was something she knew how to do well.

Kneeling between Que's legs, she pulled his dick out and started sucking it. Que was moaning extra loud, and she knew he wanted the entire bus to think he was screwing her. The more Raven sucked his dick, the angrier she became because she knew he was making a fool out of her.

Raven continued sucking him, though, and after he came in her mouth, he immediately told her that he needed to get back to work. Basically, that was his polite way of dismissing her. She was ashamed and embarrassed to walk out of the room because she knew she had put herself into the same category as the other dancers, and she didn't want to be in that boat with them.

"Okay, baby, get back to work," Raven said, trying to sound normal, but on the inside, she was crying.

Que never said a word. Instead, he turned the music up and started working as Raven opened the door slowly and walked out. Security had a smirk on their faces, and as they walked to the back room, they were pulling money out of their pockets. Clearly, Que had bet money that he could screw her, and from the sound of it, they had to pay up.

"Are you okay?" I asked, while walking over to her. It had been a long time since I had seen her broken up over a man, and it saddened me. She looked like she wanted to jump off the moving bus.

"I'm good. I'm just going to go to sleep," Raven said, as she got in her bed and tried to close the privacy curtains.

"Don't let that get to you. You're stronger than this. You need to stop trying to be in a relationship with him. It's over and he's no good," I told her.

Raven never responded, but the look in her eyes told me that she was upset and just needed to sleep it off. Allowing her to have time to herself, I got in my bed and closed my privacy curtains, as well.

CHAPTER 24

It was the final show of the tour and I was ready to get it over with so I could deal with my situation. I desperately needed my life to get back to normal. Raven and I made sure we had all of our personal belongings with us because it was the last time we would see the tour bus again.

Everyone was taking the tour bus home, but we declined. We were ready to get home fast, so we paid for our airline tickets and were scheduled to take a redeye flight right after the show. We were taking our luggage to the show and would have a car waiting to take us to the airport as soon as the show was over.

Raven and I walked into the arena for the last time and it felt bittersweet. We loved dancing for a living, but under these conditions, it made it hard to enjoy the talent we were given.

We knew if we wanted to continue living our dreams and taking it to another level, we needed to make a lot of changes within ourselves. We went to our dressing room to get dressed one last time and we seemed to be more pumped up than before.

"Thirty minutes before show time! Macy yelled as she stuck her head in our dressing room.

"Thanks Macy," we yelled.

"Anything goes for the last show. Que will allow you to do whatever you want to on stage as long as you are able to perform. Enjoy the show and have fun," Macy said as she closed the door.

"Wow, is she serious?" I asked.

"Que allows everyone to have fun on the last show. Just make sure you're able to do the choreography while you're having fun," Swagg warned us.

"I'm not in the mood to play no games," Raven said.

"Me either. I just want to do the show and go home," I said.

Since it was the last show, Raven and I decided to do a full face of make-up especially since we knew Que didn't like it. We spiked our hair up and looked more beautiful than ever. I was surprise the other dancers didn't try to put make-up on and look different for the last show, so we offered to do their faces.

We were shocked when they were eagerly excited to have their faces done. We had thirty minutes to do five faces and we moved quickly. I was amazed at how beautiful they looked and it confirmed to me that every woman needs to wear some type of make-up. It enhances our face and makes us the beautiful creatures we were intended to be. I guess this was the only thing we could think of at the last minute to join in the fun. We did their hair and make-up and watched them become more confident.

For each of our solo performances, we decided to wear our own clothes. Whatever we felt like wearing we were going to put it on. One of the dancers said she was going to wear her pajamas for her sexy solo number and another said she was going to put on a blonde wig we found in the dressing that must have been left behind from another group. We knew Que hated blonde hair, so this was going to be perfect.

"Ten minutes till show time!" Macy said as she opened the door.

Raven seemed to be doing much better then she was last night on the tour bus after Que had humiliated her. I was happy she was able to shake it off and keep moving. Raven was a strong person and I wasn't worried about her getting over this. I knew it had damaged her a little but it wasn't going to stop her. The tables had turned that quickly and I was now taking care of Raven and trying to keep her strong.

Raven didn't have too much to say and was much quieter than normal. I didn't want to bother her by continuing to ask her "what's wrong" so I just walked around like everything was normal.

We put on our outfits for the last time and doubled checked our make-up and hair. We made some final touches to the dancer's make-up and took pictures to capture the moment. They were feeling excited about the last show and since they were looking good, they were feeling good.

"It's show time!" Macy announced for the last time.

We headed to the side of the stage for our last performance and as usual waited for Que. After waiting ten minutes for him we started getting worried. It wasn't like him to be late and miss the cue to start the show.

No one knew where Que was and the show was already fifteen minutes behind schedule. His staff and promoters were getting worried and we started frantically looking back stage for him. We went into each room looking for him when suddenly Macy yelled out to everyone that she had found him.

She opened the door to the bathroom that was right next to the stage and Que was tied to a chair with a sock in his mouth and a sign on him that said 'Let the games begin'. We didn't know what was going on and everyone quickly untied him.

His security was cracking up laughing and falling all over the hallway floors. Once everyone looked at them, we realized this was their prank for the show. Anything goes on this show and no one was off limits. They started the show off with a bang.

Once Que was untied, he didn't even get upset because he knew the rules for the last show of the tour because he made them up, so he had no choice but to go with the flow. He told the security to watch their back as he laughed and told everyone to head to the stage.

We ran to the stage to get the show started. We were now thirty minutes behind schedule and it was costing Que a lot of money being late. The show started and everything was going great and the crowd was hyped and loud.

Towards the middle of the show, we were doing our routine and Que's security ran on stage and sprayed everyone including Que with silly string. It was all in our hair and face and was hard for us to see. I couldn't do anything but laugh and Raven was laughing so hard she started crying. We wasn't trying to join in with the pranks, but looking at the band and how funny they looked with silly string all over them broke the ice.

We changed for our next number and I was waiting on the side of the stage for my cue to go on. Two of the dancers had already entered the stage and Raven was right behind them.

When it was time for me to enter on stage, someone grabbed me from behind and pulled me to the floor. They cover my mouth and started tickling me. Once I was able to get loose and see who it was, I saw Que's face. He was cracking up laughing and rolling on the floor. I got loose and ran on stage trying to catch up with the rest of the dancers who had already started the choreography.

My adrenaline was running and my body was shaking when I got on stage. I had never experience anything like this before and it was actually fun. The pranks continued the entire show and even the band got involved. Everyone played along and it was starting to get out of control because no one wanted to stop. The audience didn't know what was going on and they thought it was part of the show.

When the dancer came on stage with the blonde wig, Que just shook his head, but when the other dancer came on stage with her pajamas and fluffy slippers instead of her sexy gown and heels, Que started laughing right in the middle of his song.

He immediately stopped the show and explained to the audience what was going on and that normally his show is not this wacky. The audience laughed along with him and enjoyed the show being entertained.

When it was time to do my solo number, I had forgotten that I was upset with Que and was too wrapped up in the pranks. I couldn't think of anything to do for my performance, so I didn't do anything which totally scared him because he was constantly waiting for me to pull a prank the entire time I was performing.

The show was going great, and towards the end, Raven entered the stage on an enormous red chair to start her number. She danced around Que and did her performance effortless. Right on cue, he grabbed her and started kissing her. This time, it was extra long. They got into it, and afterwards, he sat on the chair as she took her long, flowing red dress off to reveal her sexy red underwear that was cover in diamonds. This was the new addition to the show that Que was getting the most reviews about.

Raven straddled him on the chair and they began to pretend they were having wild, passionate sex. The crowd went crazy, and the fans wished they were in Raven's spot. Cameras were flashing, and the press couldn't get enough of this semi porn show. Que grabbed her ass and breast, squeezing and rubbing on them. He was so into it that his dick got hard. Raven looked like she was equally enjoying herself.

When I heard all the loud noise coming from the audience, the rest of the dancers and I ran to the side of the stage to see what was going on. Raven and Que were going off script and giving the audience more than they were supposed to.

"This is my baby right here. She's every man's fantasy," Que said into the microphone, as he kissed Raven. "Who wants to take her place?" He asked, teasing the women in the audience.

The audience grew louder and out of control. The women in the audience were asking to come on stage to get their freak on with him. Enjoying the moment, Que was dragging the number out too long and was going completely overboard with it.

Getting cocky, Que told Raven to get on her knees, and the audience started screaming. Furious, Raven straddled him instead and hoped the number would end soon. Que grinded on her harder and pretended they were having sex right on the stage. The press was looking for a cleaner revised show, but they got something they didn't expect.

Que bounced Raven on his lap so hard it looked like she was riding a horse. He continued fondling her and gyrating until he pretended he had an orgasm. The sound of the audience was loud enough to shake the building.

Women loved bad boys, and Que was going to live up to that name. As a true performer, Raven never broke her character and played along with Que's spontaneous sex scene. She was so angry at him, and all she kept thinking about was when it was going to end.

"How many women like it doggie style?" Que asked into the microphone, as the women went crazy and tried to rush on stage. "Turn around, baby and let me show them how I give it to you every night," Que told Raven.

She was furious because of how he was embarrassing her on stage, but she tried to keep it together and finish the number. When she stood up to turn around and face the audience so she could bend over, loud sounds filled the arena. I grabbed my mouth as the audience looked at Raven in shocked.

Raven looked down between her legs and realized her dick was now bulging out of her sexy lace panties. I guess the duct tape didn't hold her in good enough or it could have been from the rough fake sex Que was having with her.

For a quick second, she had a peaceful look on her face and didn't seem to care. I didn't know what she was thinking, but I was embarrassed for her. She just stood in her sexy pose looking around at the audience like it was part of the show.

The flashes from the cameras never stopped and the audience continued screaming out of amazement. Que didn't have a clue what was going on because he was still sitting in the chair staring at Raven's back. He smiled and thought the audience was screaming because of what he was about to do to her.

Raven grabbed the microphone from him and said "Baby, stand up and dance with me."

Que quickly jumped up, not caring that wasn't part of the routine because they had been off the script since the scene first started. He grabbed her from behind and started grinding on her butt. Raven appeared to be enjoying it as she continued talking into the microphone.

"This is how we get down every night. Ain't that right, baby?" Raven asked Que, as she put the microphone up to his mouth so the audience could hear his response.

Que was rubbing her breasts and stomach as he danced with her from behind. He continued rubbing her body, moving towards her dick that was filling out her panties. When he rubbed between her legs, the audience went completely ballistic. The press took numerous pictures of him hugging her from behind while holding her dick in his hands.

When he realized he was grabbing Raven's dick, he jumped back and almost fell. The audience never stopped yelling and screaming with mixed emotions. Some people were stunned and others were happy he was bi-sexual. This was Raven's moment to get him back, and she didn't hesitate doing so. She never planned it, but she just went with the flow, which is something you learn to always do while performing on stage.

"What's wrong, baby? You weren't scared of this dick last night. Don't be shy. Tell the audience how much you enjoy a dick up your ass," Raven said, as she grabbed her dick.

The audience looked confused and didn't know whether to take them seriously or if it was all a joke. Que sat down on the chair and didn't move while trying to think of a way to get out of the situation. Raven wasn't going to let him get away that easy. She saw the uncomfortable look on his face but felt no mercy for him

"Bend over, baby. You know this is how you like it. Or would you rather be on your knees," Raven said before Que snatched the microphone from her.

"We got you!" He said in the microphone.

He started laughing and trying to play it off. Some of the audience sounded relieved, while the other half was still confused. Even though he tried to act like the whole scene was an act, the audience knew they had seen Raven's semi-erect dick.

Que kept talking, trying to convince them that it had only been a joke. When he gave the band the cue to end the song, Raven left the stage as usual. Que still had another two songs to do before he left the stage, so he kept going like nothing ever happened.

I ran back to the dressing room to get our luggage, which was packed and waiting at the door, because I knew it was time to go to the airport - fast. I didn't know what Que would do about her trying to embarrass him and reveal his secret in front of his fans, but I didn't want to stick around to find out.

The other dancers were laughing hysterically when I entered the dressing room, and they thought Raven had just pulled off the biggest practical joke in the camp by wearing a strap-on dick.

I grabbed my cell phone and called our car that was waiting for us at the backstage door. Then I rushed to get our bags and some outfits for us to change into. When Raven came into the dressing room, I was already on my way out.

"Here's something to put on. Now let's get out of here," I told her.

She knew it was time to leave and didn't argue with me. We rushed out of the building like someone was after us. By the time we made it outside, we were happy to see our car waiting for us with the doors open. We threw our bags inside, jumped in, and told the driver we had to leave immediately.

We rode to the airport without saying a word to each other as we changed our clothes. I also called the airline to get us on an earlier flight. Once we pulled up to the airport, we started laughing while grabbing our bags and heading to our gate. We had a lot to talk about, and we were going to do it on the plane ride home.

We made it just before they were closing the gate. After finding our seats on the fairly empty flight, we sat down and tried to catch our breath. We didn't start talking until the plane took off.

"Are you okay?" I asked.

"Yeah, it just feels strange. My dick was on display."

"You should have saw Que's face. He didn't know what to do."

"I didn't know what to do either. I decided at that moment I wasn't going to let him disrespect me. It was time to tell the world Que's little secret."

"You revealed your secret, too," I told her.

"I don't care anymore! It's time I stop hiding who I am. I'm going to be me all day, every day, and whoever doesn't like it can kiss my ass."

"It sounds like you're not going to have a sex change."

"No, I think I like my seven-inch dick."

"That was major what you just did. I'm proud of you for standing up."

"I know Que is going to kill me," Raven said with fear in her voice.

"Don't worry about him. He's going to be spending his time trying to deny the rumors."

Raven took a deep breath and exhaled. She knew she had put herself in a weird position, and she needed to figure out what her next move would be. So, we started thinking of ways to beat Que to the punch. We knew he wasn't going to tell her secret because he had a lot to lose, but Raven didn't want that spotlight on her. She knew the press would be trying to figure out if she really was a man. I told her that we would deal with it when it happened.

We sat in silence the remainder of the plane ride. Everything was sinking in and we both started to feel nervous. When I looked over at Raven, she had a fearful look on her face. We grabbed each other's hand, closed our eyes, and forced ourselves to go to sleep. We knew we were about to face a storm as soon as the plane landed.

We checked into a hotel just in case Que had somehow managed to get to her place after the show ended. It would be farfetched to think that, but we weren't going to take any chances.

Once in the room, I turned on the television to see if they were talking about the show. Que's record company had already started doing damage control for the incident, and his publicist had a statement circulating the news saying it was nothing but a practical joke and that Raven was really a woman. Of course, Raven was happy to hear they were saving her reputation.

The media was eating the story up, and I know Que didn't like them questioning his sexuality and probing into his life. He had treated so many people wrong that it wasn't hard for the press to find people who had something negative to say about him.

After we spent our time feeling sorry for ourselves, we snapped into action to take back control of our lives. We started making plans, and the first order of business was figuring out what Raven was going to do about Que. The easiest solution for the present time was for her to disappear until we knew what the next move would be.

Raven's cell phone continued to ring with calls from Que, and he left her several threatening messages.

"I don't know what type of game you're playing but you fucked with the wrong person," Que said right before Raven hung up.

"How did I become involved in this? This type of stuff doesn't happen to people making honest money in the entertainment business. I'm too cute to running scared from somebody," Raven said.

"This wasn't the life I signed up for. I just wanted to dance, get paid, travel the world and be happy. This is turning into a nightmare," I said motionless.

Chills ran down my spine because I knew Que was capable of killing someone, especially if it meant protecting his career, money, and reputation. He wasn't going to allow anyone to ruin his life. Not only was I scared for Raven, I was also scared for myself because I knew if he killed Raven, he would definitely kill me next.

CHAPTER 25

Raven had been so preoccupied with my situation that she couldn't focus on Que and the 'Homosexual' headlines that were floating around the media. She wanted to be there for me, but needed to start dealing with her own life drama.

Although she really cared for Que, he had crossed the line and hurt her feelings, and she didn't quite know how to handle that. She was in a place she hadn't been in, and it was slowly depressing her.

Que was being stalked by the paparazzi, and after thinking about all the things he put us through while on his tour, we didn't feel sorry for him at all. Although I didn't want to see anyone suffer, I knew he couldn't keep treating people horrible and not have karma come back and stomp him.

Raven's friends, who were watching her place, informed her that a car was sitting in front of her house almost every day. She knew it had to be Que's people waiting for her to come home. Her telephone never stopped ringing. Que was determined to get in contact with her. It seemed like everyone on his staff called her and wasn't giving up until they spoke with her. The phone calls were starting to stress her out and make her even more upset. She wasn't used to someone threatening her and she didn't like being bullied.

Raven's cell phone rung so much, I was starting to get annoyed, but I knew she didn't need to talk to him right now. Starting to get fed up, she was ready to deal with the situation head on. She couldn't pick up her telephone quick enough to curse him out.

"What!" Raven yelled into the phone.

"Finally, you answer. Where the hell have you been?" Que shouted.

"I've been around. Why are you calling me so much?"

"We need to talk."

"Talk about what?"

"You need to get with my publicist so he can talk to you about doing a press conference to clear this shit up. Things are crazy right now and I don't need this. I need you to fix it."

"You want me to tell them that I'm a man and you like to get fucked in your ass?" Raven asked sarcastically, liking that the tables had turned on him.

"Don't fuck with me, Raven. My life, career, and money are on the line, and I'm not about to lose it all."

"My career is on the line, too."

"You don't have nearly as much to lose as I do. Fix this shit now!" Que yelled.

"Why should I help you? You don't give a fuck about me. I tried to be nice to you, and all you did was treat me like the rest of your bitches," Raven snapped. "You hurt me."

"I'm sorry. I didn't mean to hurt you," Que said, trying to make her feel better.

"You just like doing things and not being accountable for it. You get away with murder, literally."

"Oh, you're bringing that shit up again? Your ass can go to jail, too. Just remember that," Que said, raising his voice.

"You need to stop threatening people. I'm not the one that killed Slyy."

"Don't talk about that shit on the phone. Your ass was right there, so you're just as guilty."

"No, you're guilty."

"People are not going to believe I killed Slyy, a multi-platinum selling artist. But, they will believe a gold-digging desperate dancer did."

"So you're trying to frame me?"

"I will if I have to," Que replied.

"What happened to trust?"

"I'm not going to jail for anyone."

"You're unbelievable."

"It's business, nothing personal." Que said.

"This is personal."

"Are you going to do this for me?" Que asked.

"Yeah, I'll do it," Raven said, giving in.

"Thanks. I will call you tomorrow and give you all the details about the press conference. All you need to do is tell the press you're a woman and it was all a joke. We even have a fake penis for you to show and tell them you were wearing. It's that simple."

"Simple, huh?"

"This will keep my secret and yours, if you do this press conference," he reminded her.

"You're right."

"Can you do that for me?"

"I'll take care of it for you," Raven assured him.

"Good. I will call you tomorrow with the details. Don't go missing again."

"I won't. When will I see you again?"

"I'll hook up with you after the press conference. Thanks for taking care of this for me. You know I'm going to hook your pockets up," Que said, sounding totally relieved.

"You better. Talk to you tomorrow."

I sat there upset because I couldn't believe she gave in to Que that easily. I really thought she had lost her mind. This wasn't the Raven that I knew.

"Don't ask," Raven told me, as she got up and walked away.

"Are you really going to do the press conference?" I asked.

"If I do the press conference, my secret would be kept along with Que's."

"Doing that press conference is only going to make the media dig deeper into your past."

Raven knew by the look on my face that I didn't agree with what she was doing, but it was her life. I wondered if she was making the right decision. I couldn't worry too much about her, because after the press conference, her life would be back to normal and mine would still be chaotic.

Sydney sat on the couch feeling the same way I was, but she wasn't going to tell Raven she was making a big mistake. She felt like Que was winning again if she did the press conference.

It had been eating me up inside not telling anyone and holding all my secrets in. I knew I needed to reveal the nightmare to someone. We ordered room service and I told Sydney all the secrets about Slyy, the tour and the abuse.

Raven even told her about her secret, which is something she had never done before. We also told her about Que's secret of killing Slyy. It felt good to release all that I was holding in.

Sydney leaned back on the couch in disbelief. She was shocked but didn't show it and knew it was difficult for me to tell her the story. She hugged me and told me she was sorry for everything I went through. She even held Raven because she knew this was a big secret and she wanted her to know that it was safe with her.

"This is so far-fetched," Sydney said shaken.

"Welcome to my world," I said exhaling.

"Are you going to be okay? This is a lot to deal with."

"As long as you are by my side, I will be great."

"I love you Music and I'm here for you." Sydney said with compassion.

"Thank you. I really need you here because I can't do this alone."

"This is part of being in the entertainment business. If it wasn't crazy, it wouldn't be right. I've been through crazy things with artist and I know how it goes. Just know I'm here for you too," Raven told me.

"Let's just enjoy tonight because tomorrow I have a meeting with Slyy's attorney," I said.

The next day, I walked into the attorney's office ready to start my new life, and this time, I wasn't hiding my face. I was back to my fashionable self and stepped in the office looking fresh like a million bucks. The way Raven, Sydney, and I were dressed, we made everyone take a double look. We looked important and were dressed to impress.

Raven had given me a new outlook, and I was ready to accept who I was and what my life had become. It's a journey that would take me a long time to recover from, but I was ready and willing to go through the storm. I had a long path ahead of me and didn't know how I was going to handle it. Still, I knew I had to deal with it some kind of way.

I felt sad for not having my mother with me to deal with this. Although I forgave her for not telling me, I didn't want her around me. I felt like I had been deceived. It certainly explained why my mother hated him and didn't want me to work with him. I loved my mother, but I needed to do this alone.

"Good morning, Music. How are you?" Mr. Mergson's assistant asked, while escorting me, Raven, and Sydney to the conference room.

"I'm good. Thank you," I said.

"Mr. Mergson will be with you shortly. Would you like something to drink?"

"No, thank you."

Ten minutes later, Mr. Mergson walked into the office with the same no-nonsense attitude as before. He sat down and quickly got down to business. He began telling me that handling Slyy's business was going to take some time. He wanted me to be prepared and know what I was getting into.

It seemed like we had talked for two hours before taking a break. I was tired and my ears had gone deaf. There was so much to do that I just wanted to walk away from everything. When I informed him that Johnny was no longer in my life, Mr. Mergson quickly said he would take care of it. I didn't know what he had planned to do, but I trusted he was going to handle it.

"I'm happy to see you doing better. I was afraid if you walked in here the way you did two weeks ago, I was going to have to postpone this meeting. There is a lot of business to handle, so I need you to be alert and able to handle things."

"I'm trying to deal with this the best way I know how."

"Per your father's request, you will inherit his entire estate," Mr. Mergson said.

Unable to speak, I looked at him with a weird expression, not quite sure I heard him right. I know I read that in the letter that he written to me, but I didn't believe it. My father had never been a part of my life, and I didn't understand why he would want to leave his entire fortune to me. *What about Janice?*

"Music, did you hear me?"

"Yes," I said, shaking my head in disbelief and swallowing deeply over the huge lump in my throat.

"Your father was worth five hundred and fifty million dollars. He owns three mansions, five cars, one yacht, clothing and perfume line, and a recording studio. You will also own all of his masters for his albums, and you will receive all of his residual checks from his movies."

"Oh my God!" Raven and Sydney said, as they grabbed their mouths.

"Are you okay?" Mr. Mergson asked me.

"I'm fine, just trying to take it all in."

"Are you going to accept his estate?"

"Yes. Definitely yes!"

"That's wise. So we can move on with the paperwork then."

My father had helped me become more comfortable living my dreams touring the world as a dancer and not letting the drama that comes along with touring affect me. He taught me how to handle money and business while on the road. I would gladly take my inheritance from the dirt bag they called my father.

"We have tons of paperwork to fill out and a lot of things to go over. We will meet with Slyy's business manager so you can decide if you want to keep him as a part of your staff. I also suggest you get a financial planner or keep the one your father already has. You will be taking over everything as soon as you sign these papers," Mr. Mergson said, as he handed me a pen.

"How do I handle all of this? I don't know where to start," I said, while reading over the papers and preparing to sign them.

"Don't worry. Your father has a staff of seven that now works for you. I suggest you use them to help you get situated. You don't have to keep them on board, but they will help you to figure things out and assist you. You will have a business manager, accountant, publicist, manager, two bodyguards, and a personal assistant," Mr. Mergson said, as he gathered the papers I had just signed.

"This is all happening too fast."

"You will get used to it. The bodyguards and personal assistant are here in Chicago to start working with you today. You need the bodyguards because now that the media has broadcasted your picture all over the world, you need to be protected. Once we're done with our meeting, I will introduce you to them."

"It really feels strange that I need bodyguards and an assistant. Can they start tomorrow? I need a minute to let this sink in."

"No problem, but you really do need them. I'll introduce you to them tomorrow."

"Thanks."

"I've booked a flight for us to fly first class to Los Angeles to take care of more business, to meet your staff, and to take ownership of Slyy's property. I got first-class tickets for Raven and Sydney, as well, because I knew you would be taking them with you. We leave next week. Are you ready for this?"

"I have no choice. This is my new life and I'm going to accept it. I'm ready."

"You definitely will have a different life. One thing is for certain, you will not have to worry about money."

I'm a millionaire now. How do I handle this? What do I do next? Will money erase the abuse from my father and pain I have in my heart? I strived to live my dreams and become successful. I should be happy now that I'm rich, but with all the drama that is coming along with it, I'm miserable.

CHAPTER 26

Raven and I met Que at the hotel where he was staying to be closer to the press conference that was being held in Chicago. Que suggested that he and Raven show up together to show there was no problems between them.

We were planning on taking Que's tour bus to the press conference because that's the only vehicle large enough for me and Raven, Que, his two bodyguards, his assistant, his manager and publicist, two record executives and an entourage of five.

Since Raven had agreed to do the press conference and get on with her life, she brought me along for support. Dealing with her problems helped me not think about my drama. I didn't think she should have agreed to do the press conference, because Que had treated her so badly and now he was continuing to get his way. But, I understood that if she made the announcement, the media would stop hounding her and they would not discover the secret that she had hidden all of her life.

We headed to the penthouse suite of the hotel and knocked on the door hoping this would all be over soon.

"Thanks for coming," Que's publicist said when he opened the door. "Do you guys want something to eat or drink?"

"No, we're good," Raven said.

"Que is waiting for you in the office. We'll be leaving in about an hour," he said as we followed him.

When we walked into the office, we instantly noticed the enormous balcony and beautiful cherry wood floors. The overly-sized leather furniture was unique and decorative. The spacious sitting area had a sixty-inch flat screen television that came down from the ceiling. The fireplace was burning and the scent of vanilla filled the room. The desk was creatively shaped with four computer screens that were hooked up especially for Que.

I removed my four-inch stilettos and ran my toes through the shaggy brown and white rug. Raven sat on the couch and didn't say much, while Que tried to avoid looking at her. The tension in the room between them was thick, and they were making me uncomfortable. I picked up a magazine and flipped through the pages while waiting for Que to speak.

"I'm happy you showed up," Que finally said, as he reached to give us a hug.

"Hey, Que," Raven said unconcerned.

"It's nice to see you, Raven," he said, and gave her a hug and kiss on the cheek.

"Good to see you, too," she replied, forcing a smile.

"What's up, bro," I said, as he hugged me tightly

"I've been worried about you. How are you holding up, Music?" Que asked.

"I'm dealing with it the best way I can."

"I don't know what to say to even help you."

"It's okay," I replied.

"I feel so bad that I killed your father. Damn! That sounds crazy to say," Que whispered, while continuing to hug me tightly.

"Stop stressing out over it," I said,

"This is turning into something strange," Que said, while I pulled away from his tight grip.

"Yes, it is strange, but we will get past it."

"I hope you're not going to start feeling like you need to do the right thing."

"What do you mean by that?" I asked.

"Sending me up the river."

"So you're worried about me snitching?"

"It's a thought."

"Que, I thought you trusted me?"

"I do, but now that the situation has changed, I don't know what's on your mind."

"I have the same feelings, so I don't care."

"That's a relief," he said, then exhaled.

"So you're scared," Raven said with a smirk.

"I'm not scared. I just don't want to go to prison," Que snapped back.

"I thought you never wanted to mention this?" Raven asked, surprised that we were talking about it.

"I needed to know what your plans were and what I needed to do."

"What were you planning on doing? Killing us, too?" Raven asked, staring at him.

"Sometimes you have to do what you have to do," Que replied softly.

"Trust is all we have. Don't you remember that, Que? I haven't told anyone. Have you?" I asked, knowing he had told Johnny and I had told Sydney.

"You know I haven't said anything to anybody," he lied.

"You don't have to worry about anything. I love you like a brother, and even though you have put me through some shit, I don't want to see you locked up," I said seriously.

"Thanks, Music. I knew I could trust you. I love you."

"I love you, too, but you're still an asshole."

"So much love in the room," Raven commented, sounding annoyed.

"I think you guys need to talk. This tension is killing me right now," I told them.

"You're right. Can I talk to you, Raven?" Que asked, while reaching his hand out to grab hers.

"About what?" Raven asked, irritated.

"Can we just talk, in private?" Que said, pulling her up from the chair and towards the door.

Raven gave in and followed him. Her heart still cared for him, but her mind told her to run far away.

"Music, we'll be right back. Make yourself comfortable." Que said, as they left out of the room.

Thirty minutes passed, and they had not returned. Growing restless, I started walking around to stretch my legs. While I looked out of the window, there was a knock at the door. I didn't respond, thinking if I didn't answer they would go away. The knock got louder, and I continued ignoring it. Suddenly, the door slowly opened and someone called out Que's name.

"Que, are you in here?" Johnny said, as he stuck his head in the door.

Recognizing his voice, I quickly turned around and almost lost my balance. Our eyes met, and it felt like time stood still. I hadn't seen Johnny since I found out he was sleeping with Que. I didn't know what I would say if I ever saw him, and my plan was to avoid him forever.

"What are you doing here?" I asked, shocked and angry at the same time.

"I...I... I," Johnny stuttered, trying to find an explanation. He was shocked to see me.

"Why are you stuttering? Why are you here?"

"Que rehired me. Why haven't you returned my calls?" Johnny asked, walking into the room.

"Why are you fucking Que? You faggot!" I yelled, completely catching him off guard.

"What the hell are you talking about?" He asked.

"Why didn't you tell me you were gay?"

"I don't know what you're talking about."

"I would have never thought you slept with men until I saw it with my own eyes. You fooled me and hurt me deeply. I cared about you and you lied to me.

How could you?" I said, fighting back tears.

"I didn't lie to you. I don't sleep with men. I don't know where you got that from."

"I saw you that day you came to Que's hotel room. He was talking to you at the door and you grabbed his dick and kissed him. I guess you have amnesia now."

"What are you talking about?"

"You can play dumb all you want, but I know what I saw. I also heard everything you said to Que that night. So you dated me for him, huh?"

"Music, let me explain," Johnny said, knowing he was busted.

"There's nothing you can say. I hate you!" I shouted.

"You got it all wrong. I care about you. Let me talk to you." Johnny said as he started walking towards me.

"Get away from me!"

Raven and Que walked into the room, and the tension became so thick I couldn't breathe. Raven looked shocked to see Johnny in the room, but then a smirk appeared on her face because she knew things were about to hit the fan. Que had a stunned but irritated look because he knew Johnny was not supposed to be in the room.

"What's going on in here?" Que asked.

"Tell your boyfriend to get away from me," I said.

"What?" Que asked, shocked.

"I said tell your boyfriend, the man you're fucking, to get away from me. I don't have anything to say to him."

"You're fucking Johnny?" Raven asked, ready to instigate.

"No! Where are you guys getting this from?" Que asked, as he quickly closed the door.

"What is Johnny doing here? I thought you fired him?" I asked.

"I rehired him," Que said with power.

"Que, we know you guys are sleeping together, so you don't have to play the role with us," Raven said.

The room was instantly filled with silence, while we continued looking at each other, not knowing what to say next. I didn't want an explanation, but I could tell Raven wanted to hear what they had to say. She enjoyed watching Que squirm.

"So you're cheating on me, Que?" Raven asked, as she laughed inside.

I looked at her and rolled my eyes. I knew she wanted the situation to escalate; she was enjoying it.

"I don't sleep with men!" Que shouted.

"Music knows you and Johnny are sleeping together," Raven divulged.

"What kind of twisted shit is this?" I said.

"Obviously, you are mistaken," Que asked.

"You sleep with men, and you were sleeping with my boyfriend. You not only broke our trust, but you set this whole thing up," I said.

Que couldn't say a word. He looked puzzled as he searched for some type of explanation. Johnny never said a word and kept his eyes glued on me. Raven was fighting back the smile on her face and enjoyed seeing Que struggle. I let my guard down falling in love with Johnny, and he broke my heart into pieces.

"Do you have anything to say?" I asked Johnny, who put his head down in shame. "You really hurt me. I was in love with you and I can't believe you played me. You're a great actor," I said as tears rolled down my face.

"You screwed me; I screwed you. Hell, we all screwed each other," Raven said.

Tear escaped my eyes, and Que finally was defeated. I closed my eyes trying to figure out what to do next, while Raven continued to make a joke out of the situation.

"We need to leave in twenty minutes," Que's publicist said, as soon as he opened the door.

"Next time, knock on the door before you open it. We'll be out in a minute,"

Que told his publicist, clearly upset.

"I'm sorry," his publicist replied, then closed the door quickly.

"Let's get out of here," Raven told me, as she proceeded to the door.

"Raven, I really need you to do this press conference. Don't leave," Que said, sounding desperate.

"I'll stay and keep my promise," Raven said.

"Good. Let's go take care of this," Que said.

"So no one is going to say anything about what just happened?" I asked.

"I don't have time for this right now. We will deal with it later," Que said.

There was a knock on the door and it was Que's publicist telling us we needed to leave. We left the room without saying a word to each other. We got on the tour bus, which was full of people, and proceeded to the press conference.

I continued to stare at Johnny because I knew it was making him uncomfortable, and he continued to look embarrassed. Raven was ready to do what she said she would, by covering for Que.

"Raven, can I speak with you?" The publicist asked.

"Sure," Raven said, walking towards the back of the bus for privacy. When Raven waved for me to come with her, the publicist didn't look happy.

The publicist told Raven everything he wanted her to do by giving her a handwritten statement to review. He wanted her to be quick and short. Raven read the short statement, which basically said that it was all a prank and she was really a woman.

"Girl, that was a good prank," the publicist said, laughing.

"Yeah," Raven said, shaking her head at the fact that even Que's publicist didn't know the truth, at least he pretended he didn't.

We walked back to the front of the bus ready to get the press conference over with. Que looked frustrated and continued to look around the bus at everyone laughing and talking loudly. He was still bothered that his secret was now out in the open and I could tell he was doing some serious thinking.

"Before we pull off, I want everyone off the bus except, Raven, Music, Johnny and my publicist. The rest of you ride on the other bus. We need to discuss things before the conference and you guys are too damn loud," Que said annoyed.

Raven and Que continued going over everything detail by detail, while the rest of Que's entourage followed behind us on the other bus. Raven received instructions on how to look, when to smile, and what to say. This was so intense I started realizing this was how it's done when most celebrities got in trouble. It's all fake and a well-written script.

"Are you ready to do this?" Que asked Raven.

"As ready as I'm going to be," she said, while putting on lip gloss.

"Thanks, Raven," he said, sounding sincere.

"You're welcome," Raven responded, as they looked at each other.

"This really means a lot to me," Que said sincerely.

"I know. You always get your way."

"What do you mean by that?" He asked.

"You wanted me, so you screwed me. You wanted Johnny, and you screwed him, too," Raven said, as she started getting upset.

"I'm not about to get into this conversation right now," Que said.

"Anything negative dealing with you, you don't want to talk about it," she responded.

"You need to let this go," Que said.

"You need to tell the truth about fucking Johnny. It's not like I don't know that you sleep with men!" Raven shouted.

"Lower your voice!" Que said, grabbing her arm tightly.

"What are you going to do? Beat me up again?" Raven asked sarcastically.

Furious, Que looked at Raven. He was fuming inside, but had to keep his cool. Raven was fed up with him and was happy it was all out on the table. She really wanted him to come clean and be honest about his sexuality. However, it seemed like he wanted to keep hiding.

"Let's deal with this love triangle later. You guys have a press conference to do," I said, interrupting them.

"Let's get this over with," Que said, frustrated.

"Okay, Rupaul," I said, walking away.

"You need to stop. You're fucking with the wrong person," Que said, approaching me.

"What are you going to do? Kill me, too?" I said.

"I will if I have to," Que replied seriously.

"So it's like that?"

"It's business, nothing personal," Que said calmly.

"So you're just a stone-cold killer. You go around killing people that won't do what you want them to do. Maybe I'll kill you before you kill me," I said, trying to sound tough.

"Music, please stop talking," Que said.

Johnny stayed at the front of the bus and tried to make conversation with the driver as he stood up watching the road from the window. I didn't care about him anymore because I knew I couldn't compete with a penis. I could tell he was so uncomfortable and wanted to say something but he knew Que would be furious.

Que's publicist sat on the couch and never got off the telephone, as he took care of business. Que went to the back room and started blasting music, as Raven and I sat at the table and talked about Que and Johnny's love life.

Raven and I laughed at the look on Que's face when he saw Johnny in the office. We couldn't stop laughing knowing that this was killing him inside. We wanted to keep talking to him about it just to get on his nerves and stress him out more. He had put us through so much on his tour and it was now payback time.

I opened the refrigerator to get a bottle of water, and suddenly I was thrown against the window, hitting it hard, and then was thrown back against the refrigerator. I landed on my side and curled up in pain as the food fell out of the cabinets onto my head. I continued to get tossed around, but grabbed the bottom of the table legs and held on tightly. It all happened so fast, and after a couple of minutes of feeling like an earthquake hit our bus, it stopped.

I lay on the floor dazed, confused, and in pain wondering what just happened. When I opened my eyes to see where Raven was, I couldn't see anything. Then she yelled my name and I felt relieved. However, I couldn't move because my leg was stuck under the refrigerator that had fallen on top of me. Raven was thrown to the front of the bus and was lying on the floor next to the publicist.

The publicist rushed over to help move the refrigerator off me. Still shaken up and in pain, I had a large lump on my head and my leg appeared to be broken. My arm was cut from the items in the cabinets falling on me. As for Raven, her head was bleeding and her arm had a large deep cut on it from the broken window.

While holding her arm, Raven limped over to the window to see what happened. The bus was lying on its side, and it was obvious we had been in a bad accident. All I could do was lie on the floor praying that help would come soon. Raven came to lie next to me, as we tried to endure the pain. The publicist didn't seem to be hurt that badly, only suffering a few cuts and bruises on his face and body.

As we lay on the floor, we watched Que's entourage enter the bus frantically, even though it was still on its side. Some went immediately to the back room to check on Que, while the others stayed in the front to see how bad our injuries were.

I looked toward the front of the bus and noticed I didn't see Johnny or the bus driver. When I asked one of the crew member's kneeling beside me and holding my hand where was Johnny, he said that him and the bus driver had been thrown through the windshield and were lying outside in front of the bus. They continued telling Raven and I not to move and to stop talking. Seeing the look on their faces let me know that our injuries were worse than we thought.

I heard the others telling the publicist that a speeding eighteen-wheeler ran into us as it merged onto the expressway, causing our bus to go out of control and flip over a couple of times. While listening to the details of the accident, I held Raven's hand as she lay in pain trembling like she was going into shock. The pain shot through my body while I continued going in and out of consciousness.

It seemed like hours had passed before the paramedics arrived on the scene. I felt like I couldn't hold on any longer and was happy to see their faces as they helped us onto stretchers and took us off the bus. Once I was outside, I looked over and saw Johnny and the bus driver's bodies being covered with white sheets. I couldn't believe they were both dead.

I looked at Que on a stretcher, and he was motionless, bleeding from the head, and looked like he wasn't breathing. There were at least three paramedics working on him, giving him CPR while his publicist covered his mouth hoping for the best. Before I could start worrying about him, I blacked out.

I woke up from a two-hour surgery of leg reconstruction feeling groggy and still in pain. It took me a moment to grasp what was going on. I looked around the sterile-looking room with absolutely no décor and realized I was in the hospital. I couldn't move my leg and my head had a bandage wrapped around it. When I turned my head to the side, I saw my mother staring back at me. For once, I was happy to see her.

"How are you doing?" She asked, concerned.

"I'm fine, Mom," I said weakly.

"I was so worried about you. The accident was all over the television. Thank God you're alright," my mother said, sounding relieved.

"How is Raven?" I asked, afraid to hear the outcome.

"She broke her arm and a couple ribs, but she's out of surgery and doing fine."

"What about Que?"

"The last time I checked, he was still in surgery. I'm not sure what his injuries are."

"I want to get out of here," I told her.

"You need to relax. The press is going crazy outside of the hospital, so this is the safest place for you to be. Your attorney sent your bodyguards to watch your door to make sure no reporters got in."

"I never thought I would need bodyguards, but I'm happy I have them. Can you tell one of them to watch Raven's room, also?"

"I've already taken care of that."

"Thanks, Mom."

"Get some rest, and I will be back to check on you."

"Okay," I said, still feeling sleepy from the anesthesia.

I slept for hours and woke up still feeling the same way I did before. With tears rolling down my face from the unbearable pain, I pressed the nurse button to beg for medication. My nurse quickly answered and came right in to assist me.

"How long do I have to stay here?" I asked her.

"Depending how things go, you might be able to leave next week," the nurse replied.

"Next week! How bad is my leg?"

"Well," the nurse said, stalling.

"Tell me the truth. How bad is it?" I asked.

"Your leg was crushed. The surgery went well, but it will take some time for you to fully recover."

"Will I be able to dance?"

"You will be able to dance one day, but until then, you will need to go to therapy to strengthen your leg. Now get some rest and I will be back in to check on you," she said, as she left room.

I couldn't stop crying. Dancing was all I knew, and if I couldn't dance, I didn't know what I would do. So, I vowed to keep the faith that one day I would dance again. I would work hard at getting better and strengthening my leg. I had been through too much to let this stop me.

CHAPTER 27

A week had passed, and I was still in the hospital slowly moving around and learning to use my crutches. Johnny's death was still on my mind and I had nightmares every night about the accident. Since I had only spoken to Raven on the telephone, I went to her room to check on her.

"Hey," I said, as the nurse rolled me into Raven's hospital room.

"Nice ride you got," Raven said, referring to my wheelchair.

"How are you doing?" I asked.

"I'm good. The doctor said my ribs are healing fast, and my arm feels good with the help of pain medication," she replied, smiling.

"I'm happy we're doing well so we can get out of this hospital. You know Que is still in a coma."

"I'm so scared for him. I can't believe this is happening," Raven said sadly.

"I know."

"Guess who I heard came to see him?"

"Don't keep me guessing. Who?"

"Janice," Raven said, giving the gossip like the five o'clock news.

"Are you talking about Slyy's fiancé?" I asked.

"Yes. My nurse told me that she's been visiting him every day."

"Why would she be visiting Que? I didn't think they really knew each other that well."

"Pussy always finds good dick."

"What?" I said, cracking up at her comment that somehow made perfect sense.

"Why else would she be here if they weren't fucking? She wouldn't fly to Chicago from Los Angeles just to visit him in the hospital."

"I can't even see them together. So was she cheating on Slyy?" I asked, puzzled.

"Obviously, she was cheating. She didn't even come to visit us. We were in the accident, too," Raven said dramatically with a smile.

"You know she doesn't like us. I see she has a secret of her own."

"She knows you're Slyy's daughter, so I would think she would want to talk to you, especially since she's been trying to get his money and estate."

"That's exactly why she doesn't want to talk to me. She ain't getting shit!" I said.

"I can't believe Que is sleeping with her knowing he killed her fiancée. Que is so dirty," Raven expressed. She was a little stunned, but mostly her feelings were hurt.

"He's a dirty dog and his entire entourage is filthy."

"Can you believe his publicist had the nerve to stop by my room to see if I was still going to do the press conference?"

"A press conference! Are you serious?" I asked, shocked.

"Can you believe him? He's thinking about a press conference at a time like this. He wants to still fix things and said he was just doing his job, even if Que is in a coma."

"Are you going to do it?"

"I said I would, so I won't break my promise, but they will have to do it my way," Raven said, sounding confident.

"Make sure it's on your terms."

"Since I've been in this hospital, it has given me time to think. I'm not helping people who don't give a damn about me. It's not like Que will be at the conference," Raven said, laughing.

"Girl, you're crazy," I replied, laughing with her. "So you're being released tomorrow. I'm jealous."

"When will you be out of here?" Raven asked.

"I have to stay another week because of the condition of my leg," I responded sadly.

"Stay here and heal so when you get out you will be strong," she told me.

"Are you going to be alright?"

"I'm great! I've never felt better," Raven said.

"That's good. When I get out of here, you're going to Los Angeles with me so I can meet with Slyy's people and see his property."

"You mean your property. You're rich!" Raven said with excitement.

"Oh yeah, right, my property. It still seems strange," I replied. "Please make sure you bring me a change of clothes because I can't leave out of here with those bloody clothes I came in with."

"We can't have you looking crazy when you leave, because the media is parked at the front door of the hospital." Raven said.

My nurse entered Raven's room and told me it was time for me to go back to my room. So, I gave Raven a hug and allowed myself to be rolled away.

It's funny how an accident can restructure your thoughts and make everything clearer. I was happy to be alive, ready to live my life to the fullest, and never take anything for granted. I wasn't going to allow people to walk all over me anymore. I was going to take a stand and start letting people know how I felt.

My nurse rolled me to the elevator in my wheelchair and we waited for the doors to open. She was no different from Raven's nurse as she gave me the latest gossip of the entertainment business. She knew exactly who I was, and acted like my protector. I felt comfortable around her because she had a warm personality. We laughed as we waited for the elevator doors to open.

"Oh Lord," I mumbled under my breath, as Janice and I looked at each other.

"Excuse me," my nurse said, as she rolled me in the elevator.

I didn't say a word to Janice and hated that I was in such a small space with her. She had a strange look on her face and appeared to be uncomfortable. I looked straight forward at the door without even acknowledging her. The man standing next to her hit her on the hand to let her know it was me sitting in the wheelchair.

"Hello, Music," Janice said rudely.

"Hey," I replied, not looking at her.

"Can we talk?" she asked.

"About what?" I said, still facing forward.

"I think you know what we need to talk about," Janice snapped, as she tried to control her anger.

The elevator doors opened, and my nurse rolled me out without either one of us saying another word. Once in my room, I sat up in my bed, turned the television on, and tried to find something good to watch.

I was extremely bored sitting in the hospital but knew it would only last for a short while before my friends and family came to visit me. Sometime I would have my security come in the room to watch television and play spades with me until I got sleepy.

I heard the familiar voice of Janice outside of my room telling my security she needed to talk to me. However, my security knew who she was and also knew I had no desire to speak with her, so he told her that I wasn't in the room. Janice was very persistent, though. She told my security that she saw me go in the room and demanded to talk to me, saying it was important.

After he told her to wait, he informed me what was going on. Although hesitant, I told him to let her in the room, but for him to wait right outside the door. Looking around the room for a weapon just in case I needed one, I couldn't find nothing more than a pen and the television remote control, which I placed closely by my side.

"Thanks, Music," Janice said, slowly walking into the room after security patted her down, searching for weapons or video equipment.

"What's up, Janice?" I replied, getting a little irritated.

She sat down in a chair next to my bed. "Since the opportunity has come, I think we should talk."

"Okay, talk," I said, annoyed.

"Music, this is really a bizarre situation with Slyy being your father and..." Janice hesitated.

"And what? You're still accusing me of sleeping with your husband?" I said with anger.

"Well..."

"Well what?" I said, interrupting her. "You constantly harassed me about sleeping with Slyy. I thought we were friends, but you turned on me and believed everything that everyone told you." I said, feeling relieved to get my feelings all out.

"I did think you were sleeping with Slyy because of what everyone was saying. I still don't really know what was going on, but hearing that he is your father now puts me in a bad position. I thought we were friends, too, but in this business it's hard to be friends with women when they want your husband," Janice said.

"Still, you're accusing me of sneaking around with Slyy."

"Yes. I believe what they were saying about you, and you should feel fucked up that you were sleeping with my fiancée, who was also your father," she replied with a smirk.

"Look here, bitch! Your so-called husband..." I stopped myself before telling my secret.

"What? Don't stop now. Que told me all about you and Slyy. He confirmed what I suspected. That you were sleeping with him."

"Slyy raped and beat me while I was on tour with him. I didn't willingly sleep with him. I struggled during the entire tour with the abuse and rumors, and you made it a living hell for me. Slyy didn't care about you or anyone else. He only cared about himself. Your fiancée and my father was a dirty pig, and I hate him," I said, while looking directly at Janice, not caring that I had told the secret I had planned on taking to my grave.

"So that's the lie you're going to tell to make yourself look good in this situation," Janice said, smiling.

"Fuck you! I don't have to explain anything. If you weren't so busy accusing Slyy of cheating on you all the time, maybe he wouldn't have been raping me. You got on everyone's nerves acting like such a diva. People couldn't stand you, so if those are the ones you listened to and believed, then shame on you. You're the stupid one. Now look at you. You're sleeping with Que. So, I guess you were cheating, too. Yes bitch, I know you're sleeping with Que," I shot back. As a tear quickly rolled down my face, I wiped it away fast because I didn't want her to think she had gotten to me.

"Bitch!" Janice snarled.

"You old dried-up bitch, you're just like any other woman. You're so insecure and too busy hating the next woman that you can't live your life. You were so busy trying to check me that you should have been checking Slyy. Now you're sleeping with Que, who doesn't give a damn about you because he's sleeping with everyone else," I said.

"If you weren't so green, we wouldn't be going through this right now," Janice replied.

"What are you talking about?" I asked.

"I wanted you, but you appeared to be wrapped up into Slyy and not thinking about me. Slyy and I thought you would make a good piece of ass for a threesome," Janice said, leaning closer to me.

Shocked, I said, "What?"

"Slyy was just trying to break you in for me, and that's when we found out you were a square. I knew you needed work, but I was willing to stick in there just to taste you. It's too bad I didn't get that chance."

"I don't sleep with women, so you would have never gotten a chance to taste me. You nasty bitch," I responded with disgust.

"Don't knock it until you try it," Janice said grinning, as she sucked on her finger.

"Slyy didn't want to sleep with you, so why in the hell would I? Is that why you guys wanted to do threesomes? Because neither one of you wanted to sleep with each other?" I said, appalled.

"Slyy and I love men and women. That's why we got along so well. Our relationship was a publicity stunt; it kept our sexual appetite undercover. I loved him, but didn't want to sleep with him. Still, I wasn't willing to give him up to anyone because our relationship worked. So, I wasn't going to let you take him away from me. Slyy knew I wanted to sleep with you, but I guess he wanted you for himself, and you know he didn't take 'no' for an answer. So, if he raped you, it's only because you wouldn't give him what he wanted."

"Wow! I am not into carpet munching or beaver bumping, so you will never get a chance to be with me." I said, not believing what I was hearing. "You can just continue sleeping with Que and leave me the alone."

"Now you know I can't do that. I have been with Slyy for years and we were about to get married. So, I deserve some of that money and his properties," Janice demanded.

"Are you serious? You cheated on my father and now you want his money? If he was alive and knew you were cheating on him, he wouldn't give you a dime. Take your stupid ass back to Que and see if he will give you some money. Oh, he won't because he's cheap as hell and only fucking you with no intention on being with you. Why do you think Slyy didn't marry you right away? Because you're a low-class, low-life, nasty bitch," I replied, while laughing inside because I really didn't know if what I was saying had any truth to it. Still, it felt good now that I knew exactly who she was.

"You don't know what you're talking about," Janice said.

"I know exactly what I'm talking about. If you think I'm going to give you one dime of Slyy's money, you're crazy. You're not getting anything! Not even the toilet paper out of the bathroom. You disgust me and deserve what you get, which is nothing!" I said, laughing out loud and pissing Janice off.

"The fact still remains that you fucked your father, and the media would love that juicy piece of gossip."

"I didn't fuck my father!" I yelled.

"Whatever happened between you and Slyy, I don't care, but the media will love it," Janice threatened, smiling.

"I don't give a damn what you tell the media. You can tell them what you want, but you better be prepared when the storm comes." I said, fuming.

"No one will believe your story. You're just a dancer. No one gives a fuck about you or has any respect for you. The press will definitely believe that a dancer slept with the artist because it happens all the time. You're nothing but a groupie to them."

"Dancers have had a bad name, but I guess it's time to tell the truth about what dancers really go through. It's time to clear our names and get the respect we deserve. So, say what you want," I replied, knowing she was right about dancers making a bad name for themselves. However, I also knew there were professional, respectable dancers in the music industry because I was one of them.

"No one will want to hear that bullshit from you, especially after I tell them you were a whore," Janice said.

"You're the one who will look like a whore, sleeping with your fiancée's friend, trying to sleep with me, and now you're upset that I don't want you and won't give you any of Slyy's money. You will not come out looking good in this situation. I just might have more juicy stories for the press than you," I responded, rolling my eyes at her.

"I just thought we could talk woman to woman about this situation," Janice said.

"If you wanted to talk woman to woman, you should have come in here as a woman."

"I do believe we can work this out," Janice said, sounding like she was on the verge of begging.

"I looked up to you, but you turned your back on me and treated me like dirt. You were the only one on the tour that I trusted, and you fell into the same trap everyone else did. So, don't look to me to help you get anything from Slyy."

"I helped you get comfortable on tour and showed you the way. You knew how the game was played, and Garrett told you the rules of touring. So, don't act like you're so innocent and pure, because you're not. If I have to fight you for Slyy's estate, I will," Janice said, as she stood up.

"I'm definitely not a perfect person, but you're not going to be in my room talking to me like I'm some lowdown dirty bitch. Obviously, you're the whore in the room. Go ahead and fight for something you will never get. Now get the hell out of my room and go back to Que's cheating, lying, whorish, dirty-dick ass." I said.

Not having another word to say, Janice walked out of my room with her head hanging low. She knew I was telling the truth about Que, but I didn't know if she was going to try to fight for Slyy's money. I was prepared and knew I needed to inform my attorney about my secrets with Slyy, just in case she did go to the press.

~~~~~~~~~

I was finally able to leave the hospital a few weeks later, and as promised, Raven brought me a nice outfit to put on and helped me with my hair and make-up. She had healed and was moving around freely. If she didn't have the bandage around her arm, you wouldn't have known she had been in an accident. She wore a band around her waist to support her ribs, but it wasn't visible underneath her clothes. She looked good as new and even covered the bruises on her face with make-up to disguise them. My mother, Sydney, my bodyguards, and assistant was there to take me home.

When we left out the back door of the hospital, the press was there flashing their cameras and bombarding us with questions. I put my dark sunglasses on and headed for the car without saying a word. My bodyguards were blocking the paparazzi, while my assistant shouted out, "No comment!" I didn't know whose life I was living. I now was living like a rock star and needed time to adjust, but it felt good to have them there with me.

On the way home, my assistant updated me on what had been going on with Slyy's estate and my itinerary for the next month. She told me that my bank account officially showed I was a multi-millionaire. His estate and properties were being transferred into my name, and she handed me a black credit card for all my purchases. She also informed me that several music producers have been trying to contact me because they're interested in producing my album.

There were several magazines, newspapers, and talk shows that wanted an interview with me, and my assistant was waiting on me to the give the okay. I told my assistant that I would eventually make a statement, but not now.

When we arrived at my house, the entrance was flooded with paparazzi ready to get a picture of me. So, we went through the private underground parking. It felt good to be home, but also felt crowded with my mother, Sydney, Raven, two bodyguards, and my assistant there with me.

Although I knew my living arrangements were about to change, I was going to miss my home because I had worked hard to get it and keep it. Still, I was ready to live the good life, thanks to my father.

Raven didn't stay long because she wanted to get back home so she could get some rest. After she left, I got in my bed and felt so relaxed. I felt at ease knowing that I had people to watch after me. My assistant checked on me to see if I needed anything, and my mother said she was not going to leave my side. Feeling safe, I closed my eyes and focused on starting therapy so I could get my leg healed and return to dancing.

When I woke up, a turkey sandwich and a bottle of water was sitting on my nightstand. *I could get use to all this pampering,* I thought. After eating, I turned the television on, but then quickly changed the channel because they were still talking about the bus accident.

My assistant knocked on my bedroom door and entered slowly. She asked if I wanted to speak with anyone because my phone was ringing non-stop, but I told her that I wasn't ready to talk just yet.

I scheduled a physical therapist to come to my house for my therapy sessions because it would be too hectic for me to leave. I was happy I wouldn't have to leave my house until I was doing better.

I told my assistant to set up a meeting with one of the music producers that had been continuously calling me about recording an album. He was well known in the industry, and since he lived in Los Angeles, I wanted to meet with him when I got there.

I didn't know what my plans were for the future concerning my career, but I was smart enough not to ignore people that could potentially help me. My assistant appeared happy to hear that I was going to meet with the producer and she couldn't wait to contact him.

I also told my assistant to make an appointment with a psychiatrist for me to meet with soon. One thing I needed to do immediately was talk to someone about my problems. I didn't want to start my new life with negative baggage following me. My assistant looked at me with a funny expression, wondering what I needed to talk to a doctor for, but she knew not to ask any questions and just do what she was told. I almost felt excited about being healed mentally.

My mom and Sydney came in my bedroom, and we watched a movie without discussing any of the drama. This was the best time because I felt normal and stress free. Even though I knew money brought problems, I also knew money would help me achieve my dreams.

CHAPTER 28

I hadn't seen Raven in two weeks and I missed her. She called me several times a day to check on me, but she needed time alone to focus on her life. My therapist visited me daily, and my leg was now strong enough for me to stand up and walk without falling down. I knew I still had a lot of hard work ahead of me to get my leg back to normal.

Raven's press conference was scheduled for today, and she felt eager to get it over. I was excited to be able to attend it with her and wanted to support her. She seemed nervous, but was happy she was calling the shots. They were doing it on her terms; she told them the location, time, and date for the press conference, which would take place on the theater stage after her photo shoot.

Que's publicist had been calling Raven everyday to make sure she knew exactly what to do and say. He wanted everything to go as planned. The media had been talking about the press conference and counting down the minutes. Cameras were already set up outside of the theater waiting to get a glimpse of Raven entering. Que's publicist invited every high-profile reporter, newspaper, magazine and talk shows. They wanted to make sure everyone was covering this story.

The more I heard about the conference, the more nervous I became. This was big, and even though Que's publicist stated how simple it would be, it felt scary to me, and I wasn't even the one giving the speech. Raven seemed to be handling it well and was more anxious for her photo shoot than the press conference.

I arrived at the theater with my mother, Sydney, two bodyguards, and my assistant to hear Raven's announcement in person. We were ushered onto the side of the stage where we were told to wait. I hadn't seen Raven, but was told she was getting ready. So, we sat in the chairs that were provided for us and waited.

A microphone and podium was set up at the front of the stage as they pre-pared for the press conference to start. There were so many people in the theater, it felt like it was about to be a concert. I didn't know this many people were coming, but realized the media loved gossip. So, of course, they wanted to be the first to air Raven's speech.

Finally, Que's publicist and manager walked up to the microphone and thanked everyone for coming, then tried to crack some jokes to loosen up the press who were very stiff. His manager gave a brief update on Que's condition, stating nothing had changed and that he was still in a coma. They asked for everyone to pray for a speedy recovery.

Que's publicist made a few comments about being happy that this would soon be over, and he even joked about people thinking Que was gay, because he was known as the "ladies man". He then announced that Raven would be coming to the stage to clear up all rumors and set the record straight. When he said this, the media quickly adjusted their cameras to make sure they captured every mo-ment. This press conference would be airing live all across the world.

A few minutes later, Raven's entourage walked on stage. I watched from the side searching for Raven. I saw her friends, her mother, and one of my security guards walk on stage, but I didn't see her. I started to think maybe she had changed her mind and decided not to do it.

Then, a man walked up to the microphone. He was dressed in a tan suit, white shirt with no tie, brown Italian-looking shoes, and had a well-groomed thin beard and a low haircut. The man looked stylish yet familiar. I saw the man talk-ing into the microphone, but I heard Raven's voice. Sydney and I looked at each other confused.

"Thank you for coming to the press conference," the well-dressed man said. "Today is a good day for me because secrets will be revealed. My name is Raven, and I was born a man. I have been living my life as a woman, and have worked in the music industry as a successful dancer. This is the first time I have ever re-vealed myself to anyone, and I'm finally comfortable with who I am. I'm here to set the record straight. I was a dancer on Que's tour, and my secret was revealed on stage at his last show. The media has been stalking me so much that it made me go into hiding, and during my time alone, I realized I wanted to be free. Free of the secrets. So, today I'm here to tell you that I am proud to be a man, and when I get dressed, I become a gorgeous, fabulous woman. Que and I have been sexually active. He knew I was a man and accepted me for who I am. We didn't mean for my secret to be revealed on his last show, but things happen and here I am. I'm asking Que to step forward, be free, and let the world know who he is. I pray for a speedy recovery for him and will keep him in my prayers. Now, I would like to show you how I become fierce," Raven said proudly.

By now, my mouth was hanging to the floor, as a vanity table with a chair, mirror, and make-up was brought out for Raven. I had never seen her as a man and was in total shock. The cameras didn't stop flashing, and the theater was in an uproar. Que's publicist and manager tried to stop Raven, but they were pushed aside by her entourage.

Raven sat down and began applying her make-up. Rupaul's song "Cover Girl" blasted loudly through the speakers, and she sang along with the words. Someone pushed a rack on stage with a white dress and white stiletto shoes hanging on it. After putting on make-up, she placed a wig on her head that was styled similar to the short haircut she had. Then, she stood up and took her suit off right in front of everyone. She stood for a second with just her panties on to make sure they got a good picture, and then she put her dress and stilettos on. She took her time, making sure everything was perfect and she was looking beautiful.

She walked back up to the microphone. "Hello, my name is Raven, and I was born a man. I live my life as a woman and this is who I am. So there, my secret is out. I have traveled the world on tour disguising myself as a woman. I will no longer hide who I am. I'm fabulous as a man and a woman. You can either accept me or not." She walked off the stage smiling from ear to ear.

I didn't know she had planned to do this at the press conference, but I guess that's why she wanted to be alone so she could give herself time to grow her beard. I thought she wanted things to be over with so she could go back to her normal life, but she realized she needed to live her *real* life first. Once she walked off the stage, I walked over and gave her a big hug. I couldn't believe her strength and was so proud of her.

"Are you okay?" I quickly asked, concerned.

"Yes, I'm finally happy," Raven said.

"Oh my God! You're handsome as a man."

"I look good as a man and a woman. So who can fuck with me now?"

"You shocked me to death. What made you want to reveal your secret?"

"While I was at home, I had time to think about how much time and energy it takes for me to keep my secret. I work hard every day and it's very tiring. I decided to be free and come out of the closet, as they say."

"That's great! I got your back one hundred percent. Be you," I said, giving her another hug.

"Thanks, Music. I'm happy you were here to share this moment with me. I didn't want to tell you because I didn't want anything to stop me from doing this. I can't express how happy I am right now. No more hiding."

"You can be the next Rupaul," I said, laughing.

"I love Rupaul, but I'm going to be the original Raven. Watch out, bitches."

"Let's get out of here and go celebrate because the reporters are waiting for an interview."

"I'm not in the mood to make any more statements. If they want an exclusive interview, they will have to pay me."

"You haven't changed."

"I never will," Raven replied, as we walked out of the building.

We rushed to the limousine, jumped in, and waited for our entourage. We couldn't stop talking about what had just happened, and we talked fast and openly before our guests got in the limo. Her cell phone continued to ring, and we knew it was Que's publicist, who looked like he was going to faint when he heard Raven's announcement. Raven decided to answer her phone and talk to him so he could stop calling.

"Hello," Raven answered in an upbeat tone.

"What the hell are you doing?" Que said.

"Que! I thought you were in a coma," Raven said, shocked.

"I've been out of the coma for a week now, but didn't want to tell anyone until I was completely healed. What kind of shit was that at the press conference? You just fucked yourself!" Que said angrily.

"I didn't fuck myself. I fucked you. Don't you remember?" Raven replied, giggling. She felt very confident and free after revealing her secret to the world.

"I'm glad you think this is funny. I'm going to fuck you up!" Que yelled, and then started coughing into the phone.

"If you think about doing anything to me, I will tell the cops and the press so fast that you were the one that killed Slyy. Now I know you don't want to go to jail. Well, maybe you do since you like getting fucked in the ass," Raven said sarcastically.

"Are you threatening me? Who's going to believe that?"

"I might have proof that you're a murderer."

"What proof? No one is going to believe a word you say after I get through destroying your name. I'm the one with millions of fans that love me. They are always going to take my side before they take some dancer's side. You are nothing in this business. I run this shit, so you think about that!" Que said as loud as he could.

"I will let you worry to death about the proof I have. You're probably right about no one believing me. But, guess what? I don't give a fuck! I'm going to keep living and being who I am. You, on the other hand, have to live with yourself everyday scared as hell about going to jail and losing everything you worked so hard for. I hope your conscious eats you alive."

"You need to watch your mouth!"

"Since you're fucking Janice, you think you don't have to worry about going to jail?"

"What are you talking about?" Que asked, shocked that she knew this information.

"Everyone knows you're sleeping with Janice. That's messed up, Que. How could you stoop so low and sleep with the woman after you killed her fiancé?"

"Don't worry about who I'm fucking."

"I finally understand. You thought you were going to get some of Slyy's money. I'm sure you were fucking her on the tour. You thought you hit the jackpot. Guess what? Music is getting everything Slyy owns, so you've wasted your time fucking Janice's old pussy!" Raven shouted, feeling happy that Que was not winning for a change.

"I'm coming for you!" He said in a low, serious tone.

"You fuck with me and your ass is going to the penitentiary. So, try me! You just remember I'm not a scared little girl. I'm a man. So, man to man, you better watch your back because I'm coming for you. I will get you before you get me," Raven said and then hung up.

I was scared thinking about what Que would do to Raven, and I knew if he thought about killing her, I was next on his list. Now that I had money and an attorney, it was time for me to talk to them to see what we could do. I wasn't trying to send him to jail, but I wasn't about to live the rest of my life watching my back.

"This is getting out of control," I told Raven.

"I'm not going to live my life running from Que," she said.

"What type of proof do you have?" I asked.

"Girl, I don't have any proof. I just told him that so he could be scared. He doesn't know what I got, so I want him to worry himself to death wondering. If he's going to threaten me, I'm going to threaten him. He's really messing with the wrong person," Raven said.

"If Que has hooked up with Janice, I need to talk to my attorney about this. I don't know what they have up their sleeves."

"They're probably going to try to take Slyy's money from you."

"Or pin his murder on us."

"They need proof to do that. Who's going to believe you killed your father? We got a better alibi than Que, especially since he's fucking Janice."

"Checkmate," I said, as we gave each other high fives.

I woke up feeling like yesterday was all a dream. Once I turned the television on, I realized it was reality and I was still in the midst of it. The media was having a field day with Raven telling everyone that she was really a man living as a woman while dancing in the music business. Of course, they loved this juicy piece of gossip. The entertainment business always had some type of strange things going on, and this fit the bill.

Raven seemed to be feeling free and more relaxed than ever. Revealing her secret lifted a huge load off her shoulders, and now she felt like she could live her life without disguising herself. I was happy for her and knew she needed to release this demon so she could be the person she was meant to be. Still, we didn't know what repercussions her announcement would create, and we were waiting to find out.

We were going to lunch today and to meet with my attorney. It was ten in the morning, and I was wondering what I was going to wear for the day.

"Hey girl," Raven said, sounding refreshed.

"I was wondering when you were going to call me. You better be on time today," I told her.

"Have you been watching television?"

"Yes and your pictures are on every channel."

"Girl, my phone has been ringing off the hook with people wanting to do an interview with me. This is crazy," Raven said.

"It looks like you need some help."

"I do. I can't handle all this by myself."

"You know I got your back. I will have my assistant help. You're going to also need an agent. I will have my assistant get right on it, as well."

"Thanks. I like that you're a millionaire. This could work out."

"It's nice to have money," I admitted. "Now I can do everything I've always wanted to do."

"I need to decide which interview I'm going to do."

"Don't do anything right now until we have a solid plan and a staff. Girl, I think you're about to become rich and famous, too, and without stealing other people's money," I said, laughing hard.

"Yep, I won't have to steal anymore because I'll be making my own money the right way. Hell, I can see a reality show and movie in my future."

"Girl, hurry up and get dressed so we can go eat and then meet with my attorney."

"I'm already dressed and ready. See, I'm already a changed person."

"Okay, I'll see you in an hour."

When I picked Raven up, she was dressed like a man. I really needed time to get used to the new look and who she was going to be from day to day. It actually was fun and exciting. I had two friends, a male and a female who were the same person.

We made it to my attorney's office and were treated like royalty as usual. I waited for my attorney to help me finalize more paperwork and discuss the plans for my trip to California that was scheduled for the next month. Also, I was going to tell him what steps I would be taking with my career.

"Hello, Music. It's good to see you," Mr. Mergson said with a grin.

"Hello, Mr. Mergson. I'm ready," I replied, eager to get started with my new life.

"The first hour we will sign tons of paperwork, and then we will discuss our trip to Los Angeles and anything else you need to discuss," he told me, getting right down to business.

Two hours later, my hand was hurting from signing so many documents. I didn't realize how serious everything was until now. Besides starting my new life, I still had to maintain Slyy's businesses. It was all overwhelming, and I was so happy I had an assistant and staff to help me through everything.

After several hours of discussing my future, I informed Mr. Mergson about my career choice of becoming a singer. He seemed thrilled that I was going to be walking in my father's footsteps. He scheduled some meetings with a record executive of Slyy's record company so I could meet them and discuss my new career.

There was no doubt I would get a record deal, the best promotion team and the hottest producers to work on my project. Even if I couldn't sing, they were going to work with me just because I was Slyy's daughter. However, I wasn't worried about my singing, because according to everyone, I had an amazing voice.

I slowly began telling my attorney about my nightmare on tour with Slyy and everything he did to me. I started crying, while Raven held my hand and tried to comfort me. I felt like I was reliving it all over again. I cried uncontrollably as I went through every little detail, while Mr. Mergson's face saddened. Once I was done, silence filled the room and nothing was said until we were all able to regroup.

Mr. Mergson then spoke softly by saying he was sorry. I didn't know if he believed me or not, but due to my condition at the moment, his face showed he believed every word I said. I never wanted to tell my secret, but felt like I had too since Janice had threatened to tell the press. Mr. Mergson promised to take care of everything and told me not to worry about it. He said we would only address the issue if it ever came up in the press. I felt like a load had been lifted off my shoulders, and I didn't ever want to talk about it again.

I also informed my attorney about Janice possibly trying to get Slyy's money. He laughed at the sound of her name because he had been dealing with her ever since Slyy's death. He told me that I didn't have anything to worry about. She didn't have any rights to his money because I was listed as his beneficiary on everything. He also stated that he had an investigator follow Janice and she had not been faithful when she was dating Slyy. They even had proof that she had been stealing his money, and he was looking at filing charges against her.

I wanted to tell Mr. Mergson about Que killing Slyy, but I just couldn't bring myself to snitch on him. I also knew that Mr. Mergson looked at Slyy like his own son and really respected him. So, hearing that he was not the person he thought he was hurt him deeply. Now that I knew Que had told Janice about my secrets, who knew what else he had shared with her. I needed to cover my butt and Raven's just in case Que tried to pin Slyy's murder on us.

"Janice is definitely sleeping with Que, and I don't know what they got up their sleeves," I told Mr. Mergson.

"Yes, we know that's one of the men she has been fooling around with," he said.

"Seems strange she would be dating Que, one of Slyy's best friends. Sounds like they probably killed Slyy to take his money," Raven said, trying to set up a motive.

"We're looking into all of those scenarios. Don't worry, Music. If it's the last thing I do, I will find Slyy's killer so he can rest in peace," Mr. Mergson seriously said, as he grabbed my hand to assure me.

"Thank you. I appreciate it. It's very scary knowing the killer is still out there," I replied, trying to act sad.

"Don't worry. We will catch the person that killed Slyy, and they will pay with their life," Mr. Mergson said, while looking at me. "You don't know who killed him, do you?" He asked.

"No," I quickly said, then looked at him slowly.

He looked at me with an expression that made me feel like he knew I was lying. We stared at each other as sorrow filled my eyes, and then he looked away.

I was almost ready to tell him just to cleanse my soul, but I couldn't shake the feeling of snitching on someone, even though I knew Que was telling my secrets to people.

"I didn't kill Slyy," I stated softly.

"I didn't think you did. But, if you ever want to talk or tell me anything, I'm here to listen. I can help you," Mr. Mergson said, as if he knew the truth.

"If it comes up, we will address it then. You will handle it, right?"

"Yes, I will handle it. If you know something you need to tell me. I will give you time to think about it, but we need to take care of this. Remember, I'm not here to hurt you. I'm here to help you. I promised your father that no matter what, I will always take care of you and make sure you're okay," Mr. Mergson said seriously.

"I was wondering if you could do me a favor," I told him.

"What can I assist you with?" He asked.

"Akira, one of Slyy's dancers, is in jail waiting on her trial for the murder of Slyy. I know she didn't kill him, and I don't want her to do time for a crime she didn't commit. I would like to hire the best attorney to get her off at my expense."

"That's really nice of you. I can definitely take care of that. I will make sure she doesn't do any time," Mr. Mergson said, as he reached over and grabbed my hand. He leaned his head to side, knowing there was so much more to the story.

"I would really appreciate you taking care of that. Let's get her out of jail now."

"No problem. I will let you know when it's taken care of. You won't have anything to worry about because they didn't have a strong case against her. Janice was the one stating that she killed Slyy, but they didn't have any real proof. She will be out by next week," Mr. Mergson said with confidence.

"Thank you so much. She should be living her dreams instead of taking the fall for someone else," I responded, sounding relieved.

"Music, I need you to take time and think about everything, and come back and talk to me. Don't continue to live with secrets," Mr. Mergson said.

I frowned, pretending I didn't know what he was talking about. But, I knew exactly what he was saying.

Raven and I left out of the room feeling good that we had planted the seed. We weren't going to let Que set us up for the murder. Even though I knew we didn't actually kill Slyy, I still felt guilty knowing who did. I felt even better knowing that Akira would be out of jail and not charged with his murder. However, I was scared because Mr. Mergson's mission seemed to be catching Slyy's killer, and if he knew I had anything to do with it, I don't know what would happen.

CHAPTER 29

Four months had passed and I was starting to get settled into my new life. My trip to California was stressful, but Raven kept me laughing the entire time. There was so much to deal with. Thankfully, Slyy kept his business in order, so that eliminated unnecessary chaos.

I visited my new home and almost fainted when I saw just how big it was, with a staff of six to take care of the home maintenance. I couldn't believe I owned such a beautiful mansion in Calabasas, California. Slyy didn't like the stereotype of all entertainers living in Beverly Hills, so he moved to where rich people lived and most entertainers were starting to flock.

Raven had already claimed her room, and it was obvious what room I would be sleeping in, the master bedroom. However, I wasn't going to lay my head down until it was remodeled. I didn't want any reminders of Slyy. So, I hired the best interior designer in town. Then, Raven and I decided to go shopping to personalize the house.

I checked out the four-car garage and couldn't believe I had my choice of driving a Bentley, Mercedes Benz, Range Rover, or the Porsche. I felt like I had hit the jackpot and was afraid I would wake up to discover it had only been a dream. I almost couldn't enjoy it because I wanted it so badly.

It took me almost a month to get settled into the house and familiarize the staff with my likes and dislikes. I definitely was not running things the way Slyy did, and I surely wasn't as hard on them as he was. Understanding what it felt like to work for an entertainer, I wanted to make sure I respected my staff because they were the ones that ran my household and I needed them. They seemed thrilled that I wasn't some controlling diva. Instead, I was a respectable employer.

The second month, I met with Lobo, the hottest producer in town, regarding my album. He was so excited when he heard me sing that he made a few calls in the middle of our meeting, and thirty minutes later, I was singing for a group of five people. By the end of our meeting, I was offered a record deal.

I continued to employ Slyy's old manager to help me. He had done an awesome job building Slyy's career, and I knew he could work magic for me, as well. He was thrilled and had already scheduled three of the hottest producers to work on my album, along with six different singers and rappers to make guest appearances.

Everything was happening so fast, I couldn't stop to think. So many people were contacting me about doing movies, reality shows, interviews and magazine spreads. It was strange how one moment no one really knew me, and now, I was the hottest thing in town.

My first recording session went well, and I was surprised at how good I sounded. Raven was always right by my side, and I even got her to sing a couple of lines on my song. I officially signed with Slyy's record company and was preparing to do a music video.

The record company wanted to rush the video and song because they were so excited about my project that they wanted it available immediately. Of course, Raven and I were ready to do a video and knew we were going to do some hot dance moves. I let Raven handle all the details, and we hired the best choreographer and dancers from Chicago. Wanting to help my hometown, I insisted we shoot the video in Chicago.

When my manager started setting up shows for me, I began to get nervous. I felt guilty and deserving at the same time. My manager also started representing Raven, who was also getting tons of offers for a reality show, movies, modeling, and her own line of make-up. I decided to financially back her since I had the money to do it.

The first thing we started was her reality television show called "*A Day with Raven*". With her own show, everyone would see how Raven lived day to day and how she became fierce. It would also touch on how there were so many men who dressed like women and were hiding just like she had been before revealing her secret. She was going to reach back and help those people that were afraid to come out. Her show would not only be entertaining; it would be educational, as well.

We didn't want to move to California. We wanted to keep our places in Chicago that we had worked so hard to get. So, we decided to be bi-coastal and live between cities. This would also remind us of where we came from and keep us grounded.

I hadn't spoken to my mother in awhile because I was too busy trying to take care of things. She felt a little sad because of my distance, but she understood I needed the time alone. She was more than happy to pack her house up and move to California to live with me. I never wanted her to work a job again and wanted her to immediately start living the good life.

At first, she was a little hesitant, but she knew I wasn't taking 'no' for an answer. I also invited Sydney, her mother, and Raven's mother to come and live with me. They packed their bags so fast and were ready for this chance of a lifetime. I wanted the people that I loved and trusted the most around me.

I hired Sydney to be my personal assistant because I definitely needed two with everything I was involved in. Raven hired one of her friends to be her assistant, and he moved in with us, as well. We were all one happy family and loving every minute of it.

Now that everything and everyone was in place, I was ready to pursue my new career and life. I knew if my singing career didn't work out, I still had the clothing line, recording studio, Slyy's royalties, and the investment in Raven to help generate money. I planned out everything carefully and tried not to miss any details in order to have a fool-proof guarantee of a successful life.

Que occasionally threatened Raven to make sure she didn't open her mouth up. He was like a thorn in our side that wouldn't go away. We didn't know when he was going to explode or what he planned on doing. Raven and I didn't trust him, and we knew we needed to do something. We just didn't know what.

CHAPTER 30

"Do you have time to talk?" I asked Que when he answered the phone.

I wanted to call him and talk to him about all the threatening calls Raven was still receiving from him. I felt like things were really out of control and needed to stop before someone got hurt. I was hoping I could talk to the person who had once been my friend to straighten out things.

"Hey, Music?" Que said with a scratchy, low voice.

"Are you okay? You sound different," I asked with concern.

"My vocal cords have been fucked up ever since they took the endotracheal tube out of my throat," Que said.

"Wow, you sound like a different person. Will your voice ever be the same?" I asked.

"I'm not sure. That's another thing I have to be worried about," Que said, sounding totally infuriated.

"How is your body healing? Are you going to be okay?"

"Damn, Music. You're asking a million questions," he said as he coughed. "My leg and shoulder were broken and are healing well, but I still have a huge gash on my head and always have bad headaches. I'm in therapy and learning how to use my leg again. My memory is fucked up, but I'm doing well. I'm a fighter, and I'm not going to let this stop me. This is just a minor bump in the road. I'm at home recovering. Just happy to be out of that hospital," Que replied out of breath.

"I never knew the extent of your injuries, but I'm happy you're getting better. I want things back the way they were," I said, hoping for peace.

"Things are the same with me. What are you talking about?"

"You continue to call and threaten Raven. This needs to stop."

"Raven tried to put me on blast. She didn't have to do that press conference. She's fucking up my career and my fans are tripping. What is she trying to prove?" He asked, upset.

"She did what she thought was right. Now she doesn't have to continue living a lie. Maybe you should be honest and stop hiding. Who cares if you sleep with men?"

"I'm not going to have this conversation with you," Que said, with irritation in his voice.

"Why? I don't care if you like hairy balls or a hairy cat. That shouldn't change the way people feel about you as a performer," I told him.

"You don't get it, Music. My career is based off of me being a bad boy, and bad boys don't sleep with other boys. This shit wasn't supposed to get out, and the fact that you saw me and Johnny, damn! I'm fucked up right now. I'm still dealing with his death. I couldn't even go to his funeral because of all the media covering the story," Que said sadly.

"I didn't go to his funeral either. I had to deal with Johnny lying to me and you setting up the entire thing. I couldn't believe you would do something like that. You hurt me, and I will never look at you the same. I guess I really never knew who you were. You have burnt a lot of bridges, and I don't know where we should go from here."

"I will always bounce back. I'm not going to let anyone take my life away from me. I've worked too hard to be broke and unknown again," he said.

"That's your problem. You've let the fame and fortunes go to your head."

"Whatever. Raven has fucked with my life and money. She broke the trust," Que replied.

"You also broke the trust by telling Johnny about Slyy and telling Janice about my situation, although you didn't tell her the truth. I can't believe you," I said, annoyed.

"I didn't tell Janice anything. What are you talking about?" Que asked, confused.

"I don't care what you told her. The fact remains that we were all friends and had made an agreement. So, let's stick to that agreement."

"What agreement?" Que asked.

"Not talking about Slyy's death. I thought I could talk to you because we were family, but I see we're so far from ever being family again. So, I hope you have fun with Janice and enjoy your life," I replied, frustrated at his casual attitude.

"Music, wait!"

"What?" I said now ready to officially write him out of my life.

"Okay, this is going too far," he said.

"Yes, but you're way too deep with Janice and have started running your mouth."

"Janice has nothing to do with this," Que responded.

"She has everything to do with this. Remember, trust? You broke that trust a long time ago," I said sadly.

"So what are you saying?" He asked softly.

"I'm saying you need to stop all the threatening calls to Raven and leave us alone. It's over. What happened in the past should stay in the past."

"Now you're telling me what to do?" Que asked sarcastically.

"I'm just trying to make peace with the situation so we can all move on with our lives."

"You don't make decisions for me. My life is fucked up right now because of Raven big ass mouth, and now I have to worry about if you will run yours. You need to slow your roll and know your position because you're way out of line."

"I know my position," I said.

"Well, stay in your place," Que snapped.

"I don't want to do this with you. I simply called to try to make peace, but you're making this difficult."

"Since you have money now, you think you're running things. Well, you ain't running shit and you definitely don't run me. I run this motherfucking town!" Que said, raising his voice.

"Why are you yelling?" I asked, knowing I had struck a nerve.

"I don't like that you're threatening me and trying to flaunt around your money and so-called power."

"I'm not flaunting anything around, but you're not the only one that has money and power now," I said, feeling good inside that I was annoying him. I knew he didn't like the fact that I had more money than he did.

"You need to really fall back," Que said.

"Or what?" I replied cockily.

"Music, don't do this," Que warned me.

"Do what?"

"Don't start getting cocky. Don't get killed," he said slowly.

"You're going to kill me?" I asked.

"Like I told you before, it's business, not personal. My life is more important than yours, and now that Raven has fucked it up, I have to do damage control to try to fix this. I don't need other shit coming out and ruining my life, too," Que replied, irritated.

"Wow, I never thought it would ever come to this," I said, knowing Que meant what he said. He would kill me without blinking an eye.

"Is there anything else you need to discuss with me?" He asked with a frustrated tone.

"No," I said, and then quickly hung up.

My telephone immediately rang, and the caller ID showed it was Que. I contemplated on answering because I felt there was nothing else to discuss. My best friend had just told me that he would kill me in so many words, and I didn't have anything to say behind that. My curiosity got the best of me and I picked up the phone.

"Music, what the fuck is really going on? Is this how it's going to be?" Que asked, concerned.

"I just want everyone to be happy. I don't know who you are anymore," I said, while the tears quickly surfaced in my eyes.

"It's me, baby. Your brother," Que replied, trying to control the situation.

"You're not my brother."

"We shouldn't go out like this."

"You've already set the foundation and broken my trust," I said, sounding depressed.

"Damn, this is messed up," Que said softly. He knew things were really crazy, and it seemed like there was no turning back. It was all or nothing.

"I'm sorry it has to be this way," I told him.

"You're still my girl and I love you. Do you trust me?" He asked.

"No," I said, while wiping the tears from my face. I knew I could never trust him again. He had shown me who he really was and I didn't want to be around him.

"Wow," Que said, trying to think of what to say next.

"I'm sorry," I responded calmly.

"What are we going to do, because it seems like this isn't going to go away?" Que asked.

"I don't know."

"I can't allow my life to stay fucked up," he said.

"So what are you going to do?" I asked.

"Whatever I need to do to get back on top of the game," Que said seriously.

"Would you kill?" I asked.

"If I have to," he responded quickly.

"Would you kill me?"

"If you try to fuck up my life, I will not hesitate," he said without giving it a second thought.

"You have fucked up so many people's lives. Maybe this is karma coming back and biting you in the ass," I replied with confidence.

"So what are you going to do?" Que asked, looking for answers.

"Live," I said softly, as I hung up the telephone crying.

My best friend was gone and never coming back. I knew he was capable of killing and would kill me without a thought. So, I knew I needed to do what I had to do. I wasn't a killer and didn't have a clue as to what I would do next, but I knew I needed to protect myself. He never called back because he knew our friendship was at the end of the road. It was business and nothing personal.

CHAPTER 31

I was in my home and couldn't believe six months had passed already. My family was with me, and everything was going great. We were all trying to settle into our new lifestyle, which wasn't very hard. I spent more time in California and was deciding on moving there permanently. I had started recording my album with a well-known producer, and I had many entertainers stopping by and gracing my album with their voices.

The press was hounding me daily about getting a sample of the song. They wanted to know if I sounded like my father and if I could hold my own. I decided not to do any interviews and let things settle down first. When I talked to the press, it would be about my new career as a singer.

Que had been quiet and hadn't called Raven or me to harass us. The press was still talking about him sleeping with Raven, and he had a newfound gay fan base. He was having a hard time trying to get his voice to sound like it used to, and even though he was recovering from his injuries, his voice would never be the same.

Que became depressed and didn't want to talk or see anyone, and his camp allowed the press to continue gossiping about him. People that he had done wrong came out and started telling the truth about him and his secrets. Que tried to get a hold on things, but too many people were talking about him. He was no longer in control and couldn't handle it.

In an act of desperation, Que tried to do a publicity stunt and leak out that he was dying in order to get sympathy from his fans and hope to win them back. When his fans found out the rumors were started by Que, they started turning on him. The more he lied, the more he continued to lose his fans.

After hearing through the media and gossip blogs that Que was doing well but wasn't talking to anyone, I swallowed my pride and tried to call him, but he didn't answer the telephone. Que's ego was bruised, and he could not accept that he was not on top anymore. Although he had loyal fans, they just wanted him to stop all the games and stunts and continue to make great music, but he couldn't. Instead, he kept coming up with different publicity stunts that were not working.

He really didn't want to do tours anymore because he was too embarrassed. He made a lot of money on the road, and without him doing shows, his money flow was dwindling down. He became detached from everyone and just couldn't seem to move on. He was angry, humiliated, and broken down.

My attorney did what he said he would and got Akira cleared of all charges of murdering Slyy. I even hired her to work for me so she could get her life back on track. I felt like I owed her that much. She started working with Raven and I on our stage shows, and she was incredible.

Since she had been in jail, her friends had turned against her and she felt alone. The day she got out of jail, I was waiting for her with a limo and took her home with me. I was no fool, and was not going to allow her to live with me because I didn't know her like that, but I did buy her a condo and a Mercedes Benz. She was so happy and couldn't believe I was helping her. Since I couldn't tell her the truth, I had to take care of her to clear my conscience.

CHAPTER 32

Raven was doing an interview with a popular morning show in New York about her new reality show, and I was there to support her. She was also going to discuss her relationship with Que. Everyone was anticipating this interview and it was the most talked about. Raven was on every magazine cover and people wanted to know what she was about.

People seemed intrigued by Raven and couldn't get enough of her. She was likeable and a money-making machine to many people. I was happy to see her so relaxed with her life and more comfortable with herself.

"You look so beautiful," I told her.

"Thanks sweetie. I can't wait to talk with the guy doing the interview because he's so cute," Raven said, while touching up her make-up.

"Girl, you will never change. Don't start with that man. Is he gay?" I asked.

"I don't know yet, but you know I will find out soon," Raven replied, laughing.

"You're still crazy. That's why I love you," I said, laughing with her.

"I heard Que is really struggling. I don't understand him. We could be fucking everyday but he wants to act like a little bitch."

"Girl, I don't know what's going on with him. He didn't answer my call."

"I'm not thinking about Que," Raven told me. "If he was going to do anything, he would have done it by now. I'm not going to live my life being scared of him."

Our conversation was interrupted by someone telling Raven she was needed on the set. I looked her over one last time to make sure she was perfect, and then we walked to the set with our entourage. The staff was extremely nice and made us feel very welcomed. Raven walked on set, while I waited on the sideline cheering her on. Five minutes later, the red light went on, and it was time for the live interview.

"Hello, Raven, and welcome," the host said, greeting her.

"Thank you for having me," Raven said, smiling.

"You are gorgeous, and we're so happy you're here giving us the first exclusive interview. So let's get right into what everyone wants to know. How long were you dating Que?"

"Wow, I see you didn't waste time getting to the gossip. Well, I guess you would call it dating, but we just fucked."

We saw a panicked look on everyone's faces along with a long beep sound.

"Okay, tell it like it is, but can you try to keep it clean. We're live," the host reminded her, while smiling.

"Sorry. Let me say this. I'm happy I revealed my lifelong secret to the world. Everyone knows I slept with Que and have seen me kissing him every night on his tour. So, there shouldn't be a question as to whether or not we were together. I really cared for him, and I'm sorry everything went down this way. He's just not ready to let the world know his true sexuality," Raven said.

"How do you think Que feels about you talking to us today?" The host asked.

"I don't know, but I guess he wouldn't like it. I have to live for me and no one else. I'm telling my story. It's not my intention to reveal his secret, but he happened to get caught up in it. It's a long story."

"Tell us about your life. You were a dancer, right?"

Raven talked about her life as a dancer and how it was to travel the world. She was very candid about things that happened on the road to dancers. She tried to uplift dancers, but still gave it to them straight and didn't sugarcoat a thing.

She mentioned that dancers get raped, beaten, disrespected, and have to keep many secrets in order to have a life on the road. The host was very interested in her story and wanted her to keep talking. I smiled like a proud mother the whole time.

I was feeling good about our new life and felt we deserved the best. We had been through so much that it was time for something good to start happening. Raven mentioned how I was her best friend and how she couldn't have done it without me. Of course, the host started asking her questions about Slyy being my father, but Raven stopped the questions immediately and told the host that she was not there to talk about my situation. The host knew not to continue and allowed her to keep talking about her life and upcoming show.

Once the host had asked Raven questions about me, I started to feel like everyone was looking at me. Maybe it was just me being self-conscious. Still, I felt uncomfortable. So, I walked back into Raven's dressing room to wait for her to finish the interview. I grabbed a bottle of water and sat down on the couch in her dressing room to watch Raven's interview as it was being broadcasted live.

As she was talking, some words ran across the bottom of the screen. I moved to the edge of the couch and tried to comprehend what I had just read. I didn't say a word and waited until they re-ran the words again. GRAMMY AWARD-WINNING SINGER QUE HAS DIED OF AN OVERDOSE. IT APPEARS TO HAVE BEEN A SUICIDE.

My heart dropped to the floor and tears started running down my face. I covered my eyes and tried to figure out what was going on. As horrible as he was to me, I still felt pain in my heart.

Once Raven returned to the dressing room, I had to break the news to her that Que had killed himself. Raven was distraught, but had already heard the news from the staff on the way to the room. We hugged each other and wondered why this was all happening. We thought he would continue on with his life and keep pushing like he always said he would.

"Are you okay?" I asked Raven.

"I'm good. How are you?"

"I'm okay. I'm just hurting. Although he was horrible, he was the brother I never had, and I loved him. I'm just sorry things turned out the way it did," I said, as tears rolled down both of our faces.

We left quickly and headed to the airport as planned. We knew the media would be trying to talk to us, and we were happy to be leaving town. We were on our way to Chicago for another interview Raven had scheduled.

Raven wanted to cancel the interviews, but she knew she needed to continue on with her life. She had no intentions on breaking down. She really cared for Que and didn't want things to turn out this way, but her life mattered more to her and she loved where she was right now.

On the airplane ride to Chicago, we talked about Que's tour and the crazy things that went on. He was a strange individual, but he was talented in his own way. No one would have ever guessed how crazy singers are and the things they put their staff through. Some things are left untold, while others are remembered and laugh about.

CHAPTER 33

We checked into the hotel where we would be staying for the next week. After being greeted by the staff, we were escorted to our room like royalty. We got comfortable in our suite that was on the 32nd floor.

As usual, the two-bedroom suite was amazing, and the large terrace that wrapped around the entire room made it even more incredible. We rushed to the terrace that had a table set for four and lounge chairs. We couldn't believe how beautiful everything looked so high up. When we turned on the television, every station was constantly talking about Que committing suicide. It was something we just couldn't escape.

Three days later, Raven had already done three interviews and still had many more to do. We awakened refreshed and ready to have the breakfast fit for a Queen that room service would deliver soon.

When my cell phone rang, I noticed it was my attorney's number. As soon as I answered, he told me that he was in Chicago and we needed to talk. He wanted me to come to his office immediately. Not knowing what to expect, I was scared to death, but was glad Raven didn't have an interview scheduled that day and was able to go with me. Nervous, Raven and I headed to his office.

Less than two hours later, we arrived at his office and entered the conference room that was filled with five additional people who were not familiar to me. We didn't know what was going on, but we knew it had to be something very serious from the look on everyone's faces. My hands were sweating as Raven and I sat down slowly with our poker faces on.

"Thanks for coming so quickly," one of the men said.

"How are you, Music?" Mr. Mergson asked me. He could tell I was nervous and he wanted to calm me down.

"I'm good, Mr. Mergson. What's going on?"

"This is Mr. Dunwat and his staff. He was Que's attorney. He wanted to talk to you about Que's death," Mr. Mergson said.

"Okay," I replied, trying to sound calm. Raven held on to my hand as we listened.

"It's nice to meet you, Music. I know you have heard about Que's death, and I wanted to talk to you about something we found. Que killed himself and left a suicide note behind," Mr. Dunwat said.

"Oh my God." I covered my mouth as my heart started beating fast. Raven squeezed my hand tightly. We knew we were going to jail.

"I would like to read the note to you, if that's okay," Mr. Dunwat said.

"Yes, read it," I said anxiously.

Mr. Dunwat opened the envelope, pulled out a white piece of paper, and started to read.

"Let the truth be told, I am who I am. What I set out to accomplish, I did. I became famous, rich, a Grammy winner, a platinum-selling singer, and have produced number-one hits for just about everyone in the music industry. My life is complete. My love for women grew for the love of men. I was ashamed and hid the truth all my life. I slept with so many women because I was trying to hide the fact that I was gay and loved men. I used women to cover up my secret life. Raven revealed my secret to the world and it crushed me. I guess I knew one day my secret would get out. So, at least it happened when I was at the top of my game. I'm not as strong as I appear to be, so I'm writing this letter because my life has come to an end and there are no more reasons for living. I loved Raven and enjoyed every sexual moment we had together. I killed Slyy and was happy that he was dead because I was able to take his spot and remain number one on the charts for months. Without him in the picture, my record sells increased and my bank account overflowed. I also want to say that I loved Music like a sister and would do anything for her. I'm sorry for everything I've put her through. I want her to be free of her secrets and disclose to the world that Slyy raped and beat her the entire time she was dancing for him on tour. People need to know what type of person he was. I can't continue to live on with my conscious and reputation because it's killing me. I would never be the same vocally," Mr. Dunwat stopped in the middle of the sentence.

Raven and I held each other and cried like babies.

"He didn't have to kill himself," I said, distraught.

"I'm so sorry, Music. Que left instructions for me to read this letter to you. This is a great loss," Mr. Dunwat said, sounding choked up.

"Why did you stop reading? What else did he say?" Raven asked.

"I read the parts that he specified to read to the both of you. The remaining parts are to be read to other people, and I want to keep that confidential. No one will read the section I read to you. This is a difficult matter, and I'm struggling to read Que's suicide letter to you," Mr. Dunwat said sadly. He had been Que's attorney from the very beginning of his career, and Que looked at him like a father.

"Music, we would like to talk to you about the death of your father, Slyy. Que stated in his suicide letter that he killed your father. Do you know why he killed Slyy?" The man in the corner asked in a deep, serious voice.

"No. I don't know why he would say that," I said, knowing very well that he was telling the truth and clearing his conscious before he killed himself.

"Do you believe Que killed Slyy? We would need to investigate this," the man said.

"I don't know what's going on, but I want my father to rest in peace. Leave all this investigation stuff alone," I said through tears.

"Did Slyy rape and beat you?" The man asked.

"I'm in no condition to discuss anything right now. My friend just killed himself," I quickly replied, while looking at Mr. Mergson and then at Raven. At that moment, I knew Mr. Mergson knew I was lying.

"That's enough questions for today. Music is traumatized right now and we need a moment. If you want to discuss anything else with her, please schedule an appointment for next week," Mr. Mergson said firmly.

"I think that's all for now. We will contact you if we need anything else. Thank you for your time," Mr. Dunwat said, as he and the others left the conference room.

"Are you guys okay?" Mr. Mergson asked us.

"Yes," I said, although totally humiliated from my secrets being completely exposed.

"Que loved me. Why did he have to kill himself? We could have been together and lived happily ever after," Raven said, crying.

"I'm sorry for your loss," Mr. Mergson expressed sympathetically.

"We're going to get through this, just like we do everything else," I responded, trying to convince myself.

"Music, we need to talk about what was discussed today," Mr. Mergson said, going straight to business.

"What do we need to discuss?" I asked.

"We need to discuss you knowing about Que killing Slyy."

"I never said I did," I said.

"You didn't have to say it. Your face revealed the truth to me," Mr. Mergson replied, then grabbed my hands and squeezed them tightly.

"Stop protecting him. He's dead. The world should know the truth," Raven said.

"Shut up," I whispered to her.

Mr. Mergson looked at me, grabbed his forehead and massaged it slowly.

"I need some time. Can we talk tomorrow?" I asked softly, looking at Mr. Mergson with weak eyes.

"Sure, but it's time to tell me the truth. Are you ready to do that?" Mr. Mergson asked, staring at me with piercing eyes like he was reading my soul.

"Yes," I responded hesitantly.

"I will see you tomorrow at nine in the morning. Make sure you're here," Mr.

Mergson demanded.

He wanted to know the truth and appeared angry that I didn't expose this to him before.

"Okay," I said.

"We need to address this immediately, because it won't be long before this gets out to the press and they have a field day with this information. This is serious, and I'm going to need you to be honest with me. I need to know what the hell is going on," he said.

"I will see you tomorrow," I said.

"I need you to be the first to make a statement about the abuse you received from Slyy, before the media gets a hold of this, which won't be long. I will set it up tomorrow. Are you ready to discuss this with the world?" Mr. Mergson asked.

"I guess so."

"Good. I will send a car to pick you up. Be ready," Mr. Mergson said firmly, as he immediately got up and walked out of the conference room.

Raven and I sat there for at least twenty minutes trying to digest everything. Raven was hurt that she would never see Que again and have the opportunity to love him. I couldn't believe my friend was gone. I never would have guessed he would commit suicide. I felt sad but also angry with him for revealing my secret. I guess it was time for me to face reality and deal with my nightmares.

We rode in the car in silence, both of us looking out of the window and daydreaming into space. As tears continued to flow down our faces, we wiped them away and tried not to show our feelings. After everything that happened to me, I thought I was able to live a stress-free life and leave the past behind me. However, the infamous Que had left his mark on the world by exposing everything. Even though he was dead, he was continuing to mess up my life.

We walked into the suite and plopped down on the couch. Raven had opened the doors to the terrace to let the warm air enter our room. We ordered room service and then sat talking about everything that had taken place. I became more depressed and couldn't shake the feeling. I didn't want to announce my skeletons to the world.

I felt like I had dealt with so many things while on tour that I couldn't go through it all again. I didn't want the attention on me because it was not a good feeling. When the attention is good, you love it, but when it's not, you hate it.

After sitting around for a couple of hours feeling like we were hiding out, I became bored and wanted something to take my mind off of things. While Raven was on her laptop reading the blogs and gossip sites, I went on the terrace to relax. I sat at the table, put my foot up on the railing, and looked out at the stunning view from the 32nd floor. I instantly became more depressed and upset that I would have to deal with the truth when I thought it was buried away. Not wanting to deal with my own problems, I cried like a baby.

I got up and walked around the terrace trying to shake off the horrible feelings, but that wasn't working. So, I went into the living room, opened the mini bar, and took out a bottle of wine. After popping the cork, I poured myself a large glass, drunk it down fast and refilled my glass.

Raven asked me to fix her a drink, so I poured her a glass and we both tried to drink our sadness away. Raven went back to playing around on her laptop, and we discussed the things she was reading on the internet.

"Girl, these gossip sites are ridiculous. They don't even know what they're talking about. They are the main people spreading these rumors," Raven said.

"Yeah, they can be brutal. They really ruin people's lives," I said, taking another sip of my wine as I started feeling a buzz.

"Are you read to make that big announcement tomorrow?" Raven asked.

"It seems like I have no choice."

"You know we're going to get through this, right?" Raven said, still surfing the web.

"Yeah, I know. We're troopers," I replied, even though I didn't know how I would get through it.

"Do you remember when we started dancing and how free we felt?" She asked.

"I remember. Dancing made us feel free. We didn't think of any problems or worry about anything," I said, wishing we had those days back.

"Those were the good ole days. Now our lives are filled with drama and chaos. This is what we wanted, but we didn't know how messy life on the road would be," Raven said, still pre-occupied browsing the internet.

"That's why you shouldn't wish or pray for things you know nothing about. We didn't have a clue that we would be wrapped up in all so much bullshit."

"Girl, it's been a rollercoaster ride. I just wish the ride would stop. I'm going to be okay, though, because I'm not going to let anyone stop me from my growth. I'm now comfortable with whom I am, and that's a wonderful feeling. Maybe you should just let those secrets out so you can feel the same way I do. Free," Raven said.

"Girl, I wish I could feel free. I don't like what's going on. Every time I think things have settled down and I can live a normal life, something pops up again and shakes my world."

"That's why you need to address to the media everything that happened so you can move on with your life. You never wanted to snitch on Que, but he snitched on himself. You never told anyone what Slyy did to you, but for some reason, you're still protecting him. Why do you allow people to misuse you and then you continue to be loyal to them? They don't give a fuck about you. If Que gave a fuck, he wouldn't have told your secrets in a letter. Now you know that shit is going to be all over the press. He checked out of this world still trying to make you suffer. I hope he rots in hell," Raven said, getting upset.

"Trust is a big thing for me. I'm not trying to protect them. I just didn't want to put my business and their business out in the public. Now they both are dead, and I don't think it's necessary to tell their secrets. That's not going to help how I feel. I'm still going to be fucked up in the head," I said, then started crying again.

"I told the world my secret, which is something I never thought I would do, but I'm glad I did because now I can live my life the way I should - without hiding. You need to do the same. Fuck them. Get on with your life. They're dead and don't have a life to live, but you do."

"I just want my life back. I want to be happy," I said.

"Girl, you should be excited with all that money you got. Why the hell aren't you happy? Don't let this knock you off your square. Get over this shit, because it will pass," Raven told me.

"I don't think I can." I said as I continued to drink and cry.

"You're just worried about what people are going to think about you. Let them talk, because they will always have something negative to say. They will never know the truth and will make up their own stories so they can continue to gossip. The people that are your friends and family know exactly who you are, and that's all that matters. Fuck everyone else! Girl, now you're making me mad," Raven said, giggling.

When Raven didn't get a response, she said, "Music, did you hear me?" Still no response from me, she yelled. "Music!" Still silence. Raven got up off the couch and walked towards the terrace while mumbling to herself, "Girl, I know you hear me talking to you."

"Bitch, I know you're not about to jump off the terrace?" Raven yelled to the top of her lungs, while rushing out to me.

The more I sat at the table on the terrace and drank, the more depressed I became. There was no way I could handle what was about to happen. I knew the media would love this juicy piece of information about my life on tour with Slyy, and the rumors and gossipers would twist it into something that would be negative on my end.

I felt like I would come out looking like a whore, which is what every woman tends to become in the media, once they're involved in some type of scandal. I knew Slyy had millions of fans who would not accept the truth about him, and would probably degrade me. I couldn't handle that and felt no desire to live.

I climbed on the table that was close to the railing of the terrace, stood up, put one foot on the ledge, and was proceeding to put the other foot on the ledge, when Raven came yelling and screaming, scaring me half to death. I wanted to know how it felt to be free. Since Que and Slyy were dead, they had to be free of problems, humiliation and drama.

"Music, get off of that damn ledge," Raven said slowly.

"No," I replied, determined to feel free.

"Don't do this. Please don't kill yourself."

"I'm not strong like you," I said, looking down.

"I love you. Please get down now," she pleaded.

"This will never go away. I can't go through any more drama. I'm tired and only can take so much. My life will never be the same," I rambled.

"Who cares what people think? You can get through this," Raven said nervously.

"All I've ever wanted to do was just dance. I didn't know all this other stuff came along with it. This was supposed to be a dream job, not a nightmare."

"You accomplished your dreams and danced your ass off. Now you're rich and about to start a new career. Bitch, if you don't get your ass off that ledge, I'm going to kill you. You're about to be a superstar. Please get down, Music!" Raven pleaded, as she slowly walked closer to the ledge.

"Get back Raven, or I will jump," I said, noticing her getting closer.

"Okay, but just get down. Don't do this."

"It's funny how we allow people to destroy our lives. How their words affect us. How much people gossip about things they know nothing about and not caring that it is destroying people's lives. Money and power doesn't make you happy. I'm so tired," I said.

"This will pass and we will laugh about this while we're sitting in your mansion sipping on Champagne," Raven said trying to remind me what I had. "I'm going to call someone so they can talk some sense into you." Raven said feeling extremely on edge.

"Don't call anyone," I told her. "I'll be fine. I just need a moment to get my mind together."

"You don't have to do this. Please. I love you," Raven desperately pleaded with me.

"I love you too, that's why you and my mother are the beneficiary of my entire estate."

"I don't want your money. I want you here with me. Why are you saying this?"

"I just want you to know that you will be taken care of. I've always had your back and I love you, Raven."

When Raven realized I was not getting off the ledge, she continued begging me not to jump. She quickly glanced in the living room area of the suite to see if her cell phone was nearby, but when she looked back at me, I was gone.

"No this bitch didn't jump!" Raven said, while standing there stunned with her mouth open, and afraid to look over the terrace thirty-two floors down.

Be careful what you wish for because you might not be able to handle it.

MORE NOVELS BY
W I N K K

www.ingramcontent.com/pod-product-compliance
Lightning Source LLC
Chambersburg PA
CBHW070309260626
47160CB00003B/784